RED DEUCE

RED DEUCE

THOMAS ROEHLK

MERIDIAN EDITIONS

Published by Meridian Editions
Westport, Connecticut

Hardcover ISBN: 978-1-959170-10-5
Paperback ISBN: 978-1-959170-08-2
eBook ISBN: 978-1-959170-09-9

Cover and book design by John Lotte

First edition

For Elizabeth

RED DEUCE

PROLOGUE

October 2006

MANDY DOUCETTE was in the informational part of her interview for the post of vice president and chief compliance officer, a new C-suite office with LaSalle Enterprises in Chicago. Her recruitment away from the Department of Justice was intended by LaSalle to gain her solid compliance experience. As she went through the informational session, she was assessing it through the lens of the compliance lawyer that she was. To do this, she had to understand all of the company's vulnerabilities. LaSalle had a lot of business segments to think about, and that could make the job interesting, if an onerous prospect for her.

One easy clue to help in the assessment was determining if there were any security clearances needed in order to work in the unit. She sensed right up front that this company had a significant compliance profile.

There was no subtlety to it in this case. The giveaway was the large-type, bold-faced statement on the application form saying, APPLICANT MUST HAVE OR BE ABLE TO QUALIFY FOR, TOP SECRET SECURITY CLASSIFICATION.

Mandy asked the interviewer, "Why does LaSalle need a top-secret security clearance?"

The interviewer responded, "LaSalle's business is, in large part, supplying and equipping the U.S. Defense Department, making for a very good reason for the security protection. LaSalle's business has morphed over time from the industrial and transportation focus it excelled in for many decades, to high-tech defense sector products and systems accounting for the dominant percentage of its business currently. For instance, LaSalle is now a leading manufacturer of electronic countermeasures, those little gizmos that would scare away missiles aimed at fighter aircraft. If you walked through a manufacturing facility for these items, you'd see people huddled over tiny mechanisms in 'clean room' settings. A stealth product that repelled or avoided radar would be a completely different process, but equally important and confidential. That's just a sample; there are many more justifying the top-secret security clearance."

Mandy asked, "What about acquisitions? Is LaSalle active in buying defense businesses?"

"Sure, it's quite active these days. Each time it's bought one, compliance personnel have assessed it for its protections. A bad security risk in an acquired business could threaten the entire company, not to mention national security."

CHAPTER 1

March 2009

MANDY was on her way to a meeting that had just been called by LaSalle's general counsel, and in the hallway joined Greg Carlucci, the law department's government contracts lawyer, who was headed to the same meeting. He handled negotiating and bidding on defense department contracts for the Defense Systems Division. His work seemed like a rabbit warren Mandy never wanted to go into; but then again, she supposed lots of people thought the same about her job. After all, who would like everybody being unhappy just to see you show up? That's what working in code-of-conduct-land generated. Anyway, Greg had loads of experience in defense work and was well-respected in the department.

Mandy asked him, “Do you know what this is about?”

Greg replied, “Think it’s probably the big Emily Jenkins-acquisition they’ve been working on. Arthur Ross has been distracted for a while about this, and I don’t think he’s very happy about it.”

“Why not? Wouldn’t that expand his empire? He’s the president of the Defense Systems Division, isn’t he?”

“He is. I don’t know if it’s because he has enough on his plate with the businesses he already has, or because this new one doesn’t suit him, but I can tell you one constant that you’ll hear from him in every defense acquisition. *Once these guys get in here, they have access sooner or later to our secrets, and you can kiss them goodbye if there are any spooks among them.*”

Mandy said, “So it’s like buying wood that already has termites deep inside? Does that really seem like a good point to get fixated on? Does he really fear embedded spies?”

Greg said, “Yeah, that’s what he fears. He fears plenty of other things too, but that one’s his top obsession.”

Mandy understood that anything threatening the defense sector was suspect in Arthur Ross’ eyes, and a new acquisition fit that bill. Most people in Mandy’s orbit knew that acquisitions were high-risk gambles, for lots of reasons, but Greg had told her in no uncertain terms that anything affecting the goose that laid the golden egg had a higher profile risk. Since joining the company three years before, Mandy had been frequently involved in the due diligence process for new defense acquisitions.

Ross had a good thing going, and was doing very well with what he had. She'd seen him strut around in his uniform-like suits, and conduct himself as if he expected salutes from his subordinates.

Mandy concurred that those were highly sensitive golden eggs, and if there were a threat to them, it also threatened national security. She thought that whether it was the electronic countermeasures, the stealth technology, the early work on artificial intelligence, or any of a dozen more high-security classification systems under his management, she'd been told when she first joined the company that a problem with any of them could spell disaster for the company and for the country.

Mandy had heard Ross say, in front of anybody who was within earshot, *"Can you imagine what would happen if some enemy got their hands on this stuff?"* Mandy found herself liking Arthur Ross as a kindred spirit. Both of them wondered why there were constant pushes for defense industry acquisitions. There were two individuals who pushed for this common goal. Emily, the senior vice president, strategy, and Harold Menzies, a board member, together pushed for new defense sector acquisitions. *Why do they care so much about defense businesses?*

General Counsel Ed Rosen began the meeting promptly at 9:00 a.m., with Mandy watching him as he announced what was going on.

"Today we're releasing news of a big acquisition of a German company, Allzient. The release goes into the details on Allzient. Please read through it. This business will be an add-on to our defense and transportation segments. I've got to leave for the CEO's call with analysts, so I'm asking Mandy to be in charge if there are any questions or concerns."

Ed left and Mandy said to the rest of the people gathered there, "Well, that was nice of Ed to leave me in charge in case there's anything needing answers, except that I don't know what's going on. I can't answer any questions. Let's listen in on the call together and we can all learn."

Which is what they did. The call was headed by CEO Jim Kerwin, who efficiently described the lines of business which would be folded under the LaSalle umbrella. As a new member of its defense and transportation sector, most of its business lines supplemented or complemented the portfolio. The LaSalle CEO commented on the highlights of the new pro forma combined financial statements. Emily Jenkins discussed each of the Allzient product lines and how they would be additive to LaSalle's holdings. Any casual listener could pick up on her obvious enthusiasm for the acquisition. After the meeting everyone retreated to their offices to figure out what the news meant.

Mandy decided a call to her twin sister Reggie was in order. Reggie was a forensic pathologist with the FBI in Quantico, Virginia. When she answered, Mandy said, "Well, it's happened again. Another surprise acquisition to suck all the oxygen out of normal life for the foreseeable future."

Reggie said, "What is it this time?"

"I'll have to give you the story tonight when I have more details. How's your day starting?"

"Better than yours with a surprise acquisition. I know how those go for you, Miss Queen of Due Diligence. My day has started pretty well, actually. I've got two bodies buried in a cornfield in northeastern Pennsylvania that may be the missing brothers from a Mafia hit a couple years ago. Or maybe not. Don't know cause of death or identification. I've got to hop on a Bureau plane up to the site right now and manage the crime scene."

Mandy said, "Only you would describe two buried bodies as a day *starting off pretty well.*"

Rick Crawford poked his head into Mandy's office, giving her the time-out sign to interrupt her call.

Mandy said, "Reggie, let me call you back."

Rick Crawford was Rosen's assistant general counsel and his right-hand man on acquisitions and merger work. Mandy listened to his news: Allzient had just reported that they got hit with a whistleblower complaint this morning shortly after the announcement about the acquisition.

Rick said, "Allzient's counsel was just contacted by the attorney representing one of their employees, who claimed to have submitted a whistleblower letter to management some time ago."

Mandy said, "Why the hell couldn't this have come up before we made a public announcement? Do you have the letter or know what it claims?"

He handed over a page of bullet points from his call notes and told her the letter was being sent over.

She read the notes to herself. They'd had claims that their government sales units were bribing foreign customers. They claimed to be blindsided by this and knew nothing about the allegations.

"Please get the letter over to me when it comes in."

Rick said, "You know that this is going to make you the primary person on this deal until the issues are cleared up, don't you? It's got a big compliance problem and bribery problem that need sorting out, and those are your two specialties."

Mandy said, "I know. Who wants it? This is just something waiting to blow up in my face. I can feel it."

And with that Rick shrugged his shoulders, just as his assistant came in to hand him some paperwork. Mandy took the occasion while he reviewed what he'd just received to space out and say to herself, *Shit, now I've got an acquisition with a bribery problem with a whole lot of people looking over my shoulder. Ten minutes ago, I was in control of my life. So, this day was starting with bribes and dead guys, and now I'm in it up to my neck.* Mandy came out of her fog and looked at Rick, who was staring at her with a handful of papers.

Mandy said, "Rick, what is it? Is something wrong?"

Rick said nothing and handed her the papers he was holding. The first one was the whistleblower letter from James Whitney that had started all the fuss that day. Then she shuffled it with the other item. It was a copy of that morning's *Baltimore Sun,* which Mandy chose to read aloud.

> "Baltimore, March 3, 2009:
>
> "A body was found on an Amtrak Acela train passing though Baltimore this evening. The Baltimore police department issued a release stating that the death of a James Whitney, of New York, NY, was declared at nearby Johns Hopkins Hospital. No cause of death has been determined, but the FBI is treating the death as the possible victim of a crime. Due to its resources, the FBI

> forensic pathology unit will be called in to help with the analysis. The victim was a financial officer of Allzient Corporation. The investigation by the Baltimore Police Department and the FBI continues."

She jumped up with all of the papers in her hand and said, in shock, "The whistleblower is dead? Somebody killed him! Who does that? I've worked these whistleblower cases for years and never seen one end up with the whistleblower's murder. And for that matter, I rarely see one of these whistleblower letters get ignored or even delayed by management. If they have a compliance officer, it would be pushed right to the front of the line for handling. I think we're seeing unusual stuff happening here, and it makes me really suspicious."

Rick said, "So if you were in your old prosecutor role at Justice, what would you be doing right now?"

Mandy said, "I'd be investigating hard and fast. I guess that question assumes I would have been in the picture already as a prosecutor, but that would only happen by receiving the whistleblower letter. But as far as we know, this Whitney letter has come from Allzient, and not from DOJ. I'm wondering whether DOJ is in the picture already. If they're not in yet, I think they'll be in soon, or I'll need to pull them in — be proactive about this. It will be to our advantage. Let me call Stewart Simons, my old boss at Justice. If he's still there and will discuss it with me, we may know better what to do. But even without that, I think we need to get in Allzient's face right now and get some satisfaction."

Rick said, "Do you think that's our role here, to bring

in the government? Without management approval? Or without demanding that Allzient do it? Are you maybe getting a little too far out over your skis?"

She sighed and ran her fingers through her red hair, then said, "I have a history with this kind of stuff. Let's just leave it at that. But you should realize that this murder and the related whistleblowing is going to bring the Feds in here without me having to lift a finger. We better be prepared to deal with that. Any protocol we thought would govern before, when it was just the other party's bribery problem, is now out the window if whistleblowers are being killed."

After another second of thought, she said, "And I think we have to shoot up to New York for a face-to-face with Allzient tomorrow morning."

Rick flashed her the thumbs up.

Allzient's head of compliance was the main person conducting the discussion from the seller side, supported by internal audit staff and by the corporate security director. Corporate security director Erik Spenser made it clear that he was only there to observe whether there were any security breaches. They were seated in a conference room in Allzient's midtown New York headquarters building. They discussed the bribery in great detail and Whitney's death, but needed to come back for more the next day. They broke for the day and had dinner at a nearby steakhouse, discussing what had been said so far.

"There don't seem to be any obvious faults in the Allzient system," Rick said.

"I don't feel too righteous myself after the engine theft ring hit right under our noses, and only five years after the first one," Mandy said.

"It seemed a little odd that their corporate security director hardly said a word. I even wondered why he was there at all," Rick said.

"I'll ask Allzient to get us personnel files for the people involved in the payments to these government purchasers, as well as Erik Spenser's file."

"I'm also anxious to see James Whitney's supervisor tomorrow. I want to find out whether he knew or suspected anything, so he's a critical player to me," Mandy said.

Spenser had spent the first afternoon of the LaSalle visit with an uneasy feeling. He could not shake off the sense that the redheaded lawyer was scrutinizing him. She kept glancing at him as if she knew something about him. He was now convinced she was someone he had to deal with, unlike the others. He still had yet to make a plan and ask for authority, but his controller hadn't responded to his message. He wasn't eager to do anything that would incur his controller's wrath. Maybe it was a mistake to ask to participate in the meeting with the LaSalle people. Was he exposing himself unnecessarily? He had decided not to show up the second day, and not even go into the office. Instead, he sent another message to his controller asking for a meeting, this time getting a response instructing him to meet that night.

As the meeting time approached, he stepped out of his apartment to the meeting place with his controller, at a nearby New York City library branch. As usual he went to the stacks and was in his spot when he heard his controller's voice start the discussion from the abutting aisle, in Russian.

"What have you got for me?" the controller had asked.

"After our last meeting, I'd dug into the stuff from Whitney's files. I knew from all the hacked email traffic that the most dangerous person was at LaSalle. A woman lawyer named Doucette, with whom I had a meeting today." He'd intentionally been very quiet in the meeting, telling them he was only there to monitor whether corporate security was at risk. Other than that, he'd said nothing. In his position he needed to deal with problems with as light a touch as was possible. He was in a very key position, but that placement also carried a special vulnerability. He had to be extremely careful. No gunplay or drama unless it became absolutely necessary. These days you could perform some pretty fancy footwork without all of the fireworks.

The controller said, "Don't expose yourself any further. Is the meeting still going on?

"Yes," Erik said. "It's continuing."

"Don't show up again. I'll think about what you should do next. Don't do anything for the moment. I'll get back to you. That's all for now."

The controller's last thought, left unsaid, was that it was all over *forever* for Erik Spenser. Spenser had failed spectacularly by letting this bribery mess blossom and threaten the acquisition, and his murder of Whitney was setting the whole house ablaze. That done, Spenser now had to go.

He'd left and walked the five blocks back to his apartment, picking something up to eat on the way. While juggling his bag of food as he let himself into his dark apartment, he was kicking the door shut behind him and about to turn on the lights when he was pricked by a needle from behind. He crumpled to the floor, his body jerking for a couple of minutes before it became still in the calmness of death. His assailants quickly wrapped him into a blanket and body bag, then gathered up his work papers and computer and some photos from his work table. Much later that night, he was removed and given a final ride out of state. His materials, however, were taken to another location, and deposited as instructed.

The next morning Mandy was up and out running the three-mile route she liked to do when in New York. Up Fifth Avenue across 59th Street, then into the park and up East Drive, cutting west on 72nd Street, then down West Drive and out onto 59th Street and back to the hotel. It was good to be back on the road. There were plenty of bikers out in Central Park, though, as there always were. She had dreamed the night before about corporate dishonesty, particularly involving corporate security directors. She now had a very odd feeling about the corporate security director. Mandy had her doubts about LaSalle's own security director, given the second engine theft ring in five years and both occurring during his tenure. That was why she had the sting conducted quietly, outside his knowledge. *I'll now have to be alert to anything curious about Erik Spenser,* she thought. *Who are you, Erik Spenser? Dreams happened for a reason, after all.*

Back at Allzient for a second day, Erik Spenser was a no-show. The last item on the agenda was to interview James Whitney's supervisor. Frederick Immelt was brought into the room and questioned for some time. Finally, the Allzient team leader asked Immelt the key question in Mandy's mind.

"Did you have any idea that Mr. Whitney was aware of the bribery situation?" he asked.

"Of course, he reported it to me," Immelt said.

The LaSalle team looked at each other and were obviously surprised, as was the Allzient team.

"What? Why hadn't you reported this to management?"

Immelt sprang to attention in his seat and said, "I did. I reported it to Erik Spenser. I told him everything that Whitney had told me. He said he would handle it and that I was not to tell anyone else, and if asked about it I was to deny it had happened. He even made me give him the original Whitney letter. Are you telling me you don't know about this?" he said.

"Where the hell is Spenser today? He was supposed to be here," the Allzient team leader said, leaving the room to try to find Eric Spenser. While he was out Mandy asked Immelt some questions.

"Did Mr. Whitney give you any details?" she asked.

"No, he told me he had a file and was prepared to deliver it with everything he had. I told him I had to report up to management and that he should hold on until I got back to him," Immelt said.

"What happened after you told Spenser?" she asked.

"Nothing. We all became distracted when the merger announcement came out and I didn't do anything else.

Next thing I knew, Whitney had gone around me and sent his whistleblower letter to senior management."

"Then did you speak to Spenser again?" Mandy asked.

"I tried to, but he didn't return my calls."

The Allzient team leader came back into the room and reported that Eric Spenser was nowhere to be found. He hadn't come into the building. Immelt was dismissed and the Allzient and LaSalle teams talked over what they had just heard.

"I guess that's why you didn't disclose the bribery. Your corporate security director stopped Whitney's report from getting to you, so you truly didn't know about it," Mandy said, looking at the senior Allzient person in the room, with everyone nodding their assents.

The rest of the conversation was uneventful, and after establishing Allzient's concurrence that the bribery matter would be resolved as soon as possible, they left for La Guardia to return to Chicago midafternoon.

CHAPTER 2

MANDY called the Washington, D.C., anti-corruption unit at the Department of Justice, her former office, and asked for Stewart Simons, her former boss. Mandy had struck up a good friendship with the support staff at that unit, and they were happy to hear from her and to connect her to Stewart right away after briefly catching up with each other.

Stewart Simons came on the line and said, "Mandy! How nice to hear from you. Are you ready to come back yet?"

"Hi, Stewart! Please keep answering my calls that way. With all the stuff I've got going on here, sometimes I think DOJ would be restful. These days I need to constantly finger my St. Dymphna card." She actually had the St. Dymphna holy card from her grandma Betty in her hand as she spoke, who'd once given it to her to help her cope with her tormentors. St. Dymphna was an Irish saint from over a thousand years before, the patron saint of those afflicted with nervous or mental disorders. Grandma's strong French-Canadian Catholic religious beliefs made her prone to handing out holy cards if the opportunity presented itself. A powerful good luck totem like St. Dymphna was nothing to laugh at, despite what Stewart Simons then did.

Laughing at her comment and remembering her use of St. Dymphna while in court on corruption cases, he said, "I'm sure LaSalle's acquisition of Allzient has to be frozen in place now that you have bribes and dead guys, so you can probably relax."

Mandy said, "Wait, DOJ knows about those things already?"

Stewart slowly said, "Mandy, James Whitney had supplied a whistleblower letter to us within the last couple of days, so he was all over our radar screen, and before we could get our bearings, he turned up murdered."

Mandy said, "How do you know it was murder?"

Stewart said, "I can't tell you too much of that since it's an ongoing investigation. We're doing what you used to do—investigate. Once we learned of his death, we had the FBI collect the Union Station closed circuit surveillance video and spotted Whitney awaiting the boarding call for the Northbound Amtrak Acela train. As we watched the video, we found him seated with his backpack sitting next to him. The side pocket hosted a mini-water bottle; I think it was a Dasani brand. Whitney briefly left his backpack to walk over to the newsstand about twenty feet away, and when he did so, someone briefly appeared in the screen and replaced the water bottle with a matching Dasani bottle. That person was in sunglasses and had a hoodie, so we can't identify him, but he must have known a lot about James Whitney to be able to switch the same kind of water he liked to drink. That water bottle turned out to be pretty special. It was doctored with an extremely dangerous substance, maybe a nerve agent. Anyway, as fast as he appeared in the picture, he also disappeared. When the boarding announcement finally came, Whitney grabbed his backpack and got to his seat on the train."

Mandy asked, "What job did this Whitney guy have at Allzient?"

Stewart said, "He was a financial controller for Allzient's transportation group, and had a New York office in the fleet transportation group of the company. Anyway, he'd been in Washington, D.C., to meet with his lawyer about the whistleblower letter he'd submitted to his employer, apparently with no response so far. They were deciding what to do next, and the result was to go up the line to DOJ. Whoever poisoned him must have judged that Whitney had passed into a new category of risk, one he would come to regret. Whitney's revelations about Allzient's bribery activities were going to interfere with its merger opportunity, he must have known."

Mandy said, "What about the guy in the hoodie? Any sign of him after that?"

Simon answered, "He was caught on outside cameras heading to the Metro entrance, and we haven't been able to spot his path after that. Baltimore PD was called to the station when the train arrived. A nearby passenger noted that after the train departed, Whitney opened his water bottle and took a long drink from it and replaced it in his pack. No more than a minute later Whitney started to wheeze and cough, then seized up. Finally, he crumpled against the window side of his seat and stayed there, apparently as dead as could be, until the Amtrak conductor came to take tickets and discovered his body. Whitney did not respond to the efforts to wake him, and the conductor concluded that a serious medical event had taken place with the passenger. As the train was two minutes out from the Baltimore stop, the conductor radioed ahead for medical assistance."

Mandy asked, "Was the crime scene searched?"

"While the Acela train was in Baltimore and passengers were disembarking and embarking, the body of Whitney was quickly whisked away to nearby Johns Hopkins Hospital's emergency room. Just a quick interview with the woman who'd seen him in his collapse, and nothing illuminating had been reported. Nothing had led Baltimore police to conclude the train was a crime scene, so it was allowed to go on its way. Whitney was declared dead after five minutes of time spent trying to revive him in the emergency room."

"Have you gotten the details of the bribery the whistleblower alleged?"

Stewart said, "We've been getting cooperation from Whitney's lawyer."

"Can you share details with us?"

"I don't think I can go that far. If Allzient shared that detail with you, assuming they have it, it would be between you and them."

Mandy said, "OK, well, I was just calling to pull you in on this. We'd relied on Allzient to contact the authorities, since it was their employee. But once the employee turns up dead in the middle of our deal, I believe it's no longer just an Allzient matter."

Stewart said, "While technically this is Allzient's problem with us, and not yours, I'll have to deal with them. That's true, but I'm happy to talk with you about this as we go forward, unless there's something sensitive."

Mandy replied, "Sure, that would be fine with me. One question I have for you, though, is whether you've ever seen a scenario like this in corporate corruption. We both saw stoolies get whacked in the mob cases regularly, but in corporate bribery, have you ever seen behavior like this? I haven't. And wouldn't you see management reacting immediately to a whistleblower letter instead of ignoring it? There's only downside for a company to do that, don't you think? Especially one involved in a merger."

Stewart said, "No, I haven't seen this before, and you know that yourself from your years here with us, like you're saying. But if you think about it, there is hardly any daylight between a stool pigeon and a whistleblower, looking at it from the other side."

Mandy said back, "I know that there is resentment and anger in every case with a whistleblower. That's standard in these things. But something's not right here, Stewart. I know you have a process to follow, but I'm concerned that there may be something else going on. Something that we're not seeing."

"Mandy, are you going somewhere with what you're saying?"

Mandy said, "I think you ought to pull the FBI in on this and see what they can sniff out. Do you know Steve Baker in the Chicago office?"

Stewart said he didn't, so Mandy explained Steve Baker's able handling of an ongoing engine theft sting and that he was very familiar with LaSalle. She urged involving him because of that.

After the call she made a beeline to Rick's office to warn him about the impending bad news that the feds were in the picture already.

Mandy Doucette's job was to make sure laws were observed and there were no company people going off the reservation and causing legal problems. She was like the law department's *Internal Affairs* section of a police force. Considering that role, her mere presence was enough to unsettle others. In-house lawyers were, as a group, not particularly well-liked anyway among the business managers.

That suited Mandy just fine. It left her free to pick her friends and to make do with them. As a teenager, she'd worked with the harbor master at Wilmette Harbor north of Chicago, just a short distance from her home. In what turned out to be a life-altering event for her, she'd caught a coworker filching funds from the harbor master's petty cash fund and turned him in.

She remembered her actions like it had been yesterday, even her words to the harbor master.

Mandy had said, *"He's been taking a portion of the funds received. I've seen him do it a number of times, but he didn't notice me. What are you going to do about it?"*

When the harbor master told her he would figure something out, dismissively, it pissed her off. She thought to herself, *Are you going to let this guy get away with it?*

She decided he was weak and spineless, or maybe worse, so she called the Wilmette police herself and reported the theft. In part, she came to regret it. On reflection, she thought, *What were you thinking, that you could just go over the harbor master's head and become a vigilante?* He'd been prosecuted and given a suspended sentence as a first-time minor offender without a prior record. But he was a very popular high school junior and had turned his friends into a support group who harassed Mandy mercilessly after the incident. At New Trier High School in Winnetka, she was plagued by attempts at revenge.

She could recall telling her sister Reggie what she found. *"I opened my school locker the other day and found a noose hanging inside. Threatening notes are showing up all the time on my desk and I get sneers and insults in the hallway. I can even go into a classroom and see someone has left an insult to me on the chalkboard."*

But the other part of that history that never bit back at Mandy had to do with the harbor master himself. It turned out that he'd collaborated in the thefts for a share. He eventually served time for his part, and Mandy took note of her own satisfaction with making it happen. One time Reggie said to her, "I would be willing to bet that was when you wanted to go into some form of law enforcement."

She'd retreated into a shell and resented people who wouldn't stand up to the bad ones. Reggie was her lifeline who kept her from sealing herself off from the outside world.

Reggie had said to her, *"Mandy, you have to be strong about this. High school will be over soon and we'll go our way and they'll go theirs. Don't get yourself tied up in knots over it. Remember that we're twins, so I have actually been getting some of the same treatment as you. I'm ignoring it and I want you to do the same."* Reggie had worked to keep Mandy able to interact with people, since the harbor master debacle had pretty much soured Mandy on people in general. She loved Reggie for that, but at times she was also rubbed raw by the constant pull Reggie had on her to keep her from sinking back into her funk. Of course, it probably wasn't so much fun for Reggie doing that, she guessed. She had always been resentful of Reggie for being Grandma Betty's favorite. Grandma pretty much was open about that, which Bob Doucette thought was not to his mother's credit.

Mandy had indeed decided that her future was in some form of law enforcement. She thought to herself, *I could feel pretty good being a cop or a lawyer; it would be better to go after the other side.*

Eventually, her path led to the Justice Department, where she spent three years in a prosecutor's role in its anti-corruption unit, and following that the three-year stint she had as chief compliance officer at LaSalle.

Wednesday morning started abnormally for Mandy when she arrived at work to find Emily Jenkins waiting for her in her office. Mandy was usually the only person on the floor when she arrived each day. Emily was not someone to be taken lightly. She started right in on Mandy.

"Good morning. I understand you're running a sting operation on my Kansas City engine plant. Is that true?"

Mandy replied, "I didn't realize it was *your* engine plant. I thought it was *LaSalle's.*"

"Cute," she spat back at Mandy. "It's part of my goddamn strategy that this engine division performs well, because if it stumbles, it will reflect badly on our strategy. And that means me, and my incentive comp. I want you to tell me that this play of yours will not end badly."

Mandy said, "Not sure what you mean by *end badly*. If we disrupt or catch the theft ring we think is operating out there, that will not be ending badly in my humble opinion. That's what we're trying to do."

"We have a corporate security director here. Why isn't he running this instead of some lawyer?"

Mandy said, "I was told he was here for the earlier case, just like this one. Now it's reoccurred, so the general counsel said I should get involved and oversee it. That's all I know. I'm not trying to make anything stumble."

"I am also told you're now the gatekeeper for the Allzient deal with the sudden bribery problem that's come up. What's your plan for dealing with that?"

Mandy said, "That's mostly a problem involving Allzient and the federal government. Seeing as how they've ignored the whistleblower's letter and let it go to the DOJ, and now the whistleblower has been murdered, it's out of our control. What's still in our control is to find out everything about Allzient's details and to try to get due diligence back on track. That's what I plan to do."

Emily popped up out of her chair in Mandy's office and barked out, "Make sure you do. Just don't kill my deal."

Emily Jenkins whipped out of the office and headed down to the elevators, her reputation preceding her. She encountered no others in her short burst. That was because no one wanted a close encounter with her. In her late forties and very attractive, and divorced with no children, she was the most ambitious of the female executives Mandy had dealt with at LaSalle. She attended all of the board meetings and was known to get close to some of the directors. Mandy knew that this annoyed Ed Rosen, the general counsel. Neither Ed, nor Mandy, for that matter, was happy that an officer might be improperly cozy with board members. There were plenty of pairings between CEOs and senior officers in corporate America, but she'd never heard of an officer getting together with a director. She thought to herself, *Why not? We've all got the same equipment and urges, right?* Mandy was pretty sure she'd caught a whiff of Emily Jenkins' coziness with board member Harold Menzies, with it tipping over into some sheet-wrestling. She thought that would not be an illogical place for Emily to end up, using the internal radar that frequently made her suspicious of her fellow employees. It was sad, but true, she thought to herself—people sometimes sank their own ships.

This wouldn't be my first rodeo with troublemakers, she thought to herself as Emily strutted down the hallway away from her, looking like a Wretched Witch. It happened to be her nickname. *Now there's a woman who's out to get me.* She made a quiet decision right then and there to put Emily under the electron microscope for further examination, like her sister Reggie used in her pathology lab.

Back in her office on the top floor of the building, Emily Jenkins was fuming about the insolent redheaded compliance officer she'd just confronted. She had no use for attorneys anyway, especially sassy ones. Her nightmare scenario was to be trapped in a room with an internal auditor and a compliance lawyer. She even had one of those Velcro lawyer dolls in her office. She liked to rip the head, arms, and legs off when one of the lawyers set her off, which had just happened. That done, with the doll ripped to shreds and strewn around her office, she headed off to a meeting with all of the officers. She'd call Harold Menzies, her board member confidant and supporter, and try to stir up some real trouble for Mandy fucking Doucette.

Rick dropped by Mandy's office and gave her a heads up, asking if she'd heard from the general counsel Ed Rosen.

"No, why?"

"Emily Jenkin's on the warpath over you and complained to Ed over the engine theft sting, and now the bribery matter."

Mandy said, "Sounds like something that evil bitch would do. Why hasn't Ed talked to me directly about it? And what did you say about it?"

Rick said, "That you're the best one to handle it, that's all. Don't let her rattle you. Everyone knows her for what she is. Emily's just Emily, and her ambition is probably going to lead to her own demise one day."

"If that's true, why is she roaming freely among the prison population?"

"What exactly did she say, anyway?"

"She warned me that anything that hurt the engine business would hurt her and her incentive payments."

Rick said, "Bullshit. I handle the Compensation

Committee materials, and I know the engine division performance hasn't been in her incentive package for a couple of years. She's using that to get you out of the way on Allzient. That's my guess."

She immediately went up to Ed Rosen's office and got his assurance that he was behind her when it came to Emily Jenkins, who was paranoid that her strategic house of cards may be blown down.

"Why would I want to blow down her house of cards?" she'd said.

Ed said, "Emily views these things as her babies, and she's worried that you're not up to the challenge. But I told her to be calm and you would handle it."

Mandy thought to herself, *The right person to handle these? I've got more experience with these kinds of things than all the other lawyers in this department combined!*

But all Mandy said out loud was, "Thank you. I appreciate you having my back."

That night Mandy had another call to catch up with Reggie, who was still in Pennsylvania dealing with the bodies and with the burial site.

Reggie said, "These two have been in the ground a while. It's a very shallow grave they were found in, and it's easy to see why something partially dug them out. I can't even tell if they were put in the ground at the same time. It's two white guys with lots of tattoos, mostly looking Eastern, as in Russian. No IDs. Acid all over the bodies. Nasty. Tattooed like those thugs in that Viggo Mortensen movie *Eastern Promises.*"

"I think I prefer whistleblowers."

Reggie said, "Speaking of that, how does it work with them?"

Mandy said, "Whistleblowers are protected under the law, first of all, but you probably know that. But did you know that they're encouraged to report up through their internal channels first? But if they don't, or try to but then don't get results, they have the avenue to report directly to the Justice Department."

Reggie said, "People don't want Uncle Sam in their face, huh?"

"Yeah, and they don't want to pay crippling fines either."

"What does *crippling* mean?"

"Easily in the hundreds of millions."

Reggie said, "I get it. That's a lot of money, no matter who has to pay it. Not as bad as acid in the face, though, I guess. What about your acquisition? How does that work?"

Mandy said, "It's bad enough dealing with your own sins, but when you're the buyer in a deal, you get the acquired company's past sins as if they're your own. I don't think people understand that. Why would they, if they're not knee-deep in this stuff? No free passes are given to big corporations, just because crimes were committed under a prior owner. Anyway, I don't know what this is going to lead to. All I'm usually supposed to do is address and minimize risk, not go crazy and go outside my patch. But I was told this is now going to be my problem; how do you like that? Nobody told me of any restrictions on what I can do, so I'm just going to do what I think is needed."

Reggie said, "You're not going to pull another one of your vigilante tricks again, are you? Like with the harbor master? You know how that turned out, and we're both still paying the price for that."

Mandy said, "Look, I just got a royal ass chewing from Wretched Witch. She was waiting in my office when I got here and tore right into me over the engine theft sting I'm doing, then she threw in Allzient. So, I could use some support, not lecturing, dear sister."

Reggie said, "Wretched Witch's the one you were warned about, right? She's like two or three levels above you?"

"Yes, and now she has me in her crosshairs."

"You need to cool down and not antagonize her. She can do you real damage, especially if you lip off to her. And I'm not trying to lecture you."

Mandy said, "Sure feels like it. Taking shit's not my strong suit."

Reggie said, "You don't need to tell me that. I've been trying to keep you calm my entire life. I don't want to see you provoking someone who can kill you off if it suits her."

Mandy decided that her sister was indeed in lecture mode, and it had not been the right thing to call her, so she decided to switch directions.

"I've been trying to understand all of this. The mystery of Allzient and how it could have a bribery mess in its lap and not address it, is beyond me. Letting someone get killed, or God forbid killing off the whistleblower itself, is really outside anything I've seen before. That brings in the federal government and pretty soon everything will be revolving around its initiatives and DOJ will be controlling everything. Meanwhile, Wretched Witch has a vendetta against me for multiple reasons. And finally, we haven't been able to pursue the due diligence that might help this situation."

Reggie said, "See, that's what makes finding two dead bodies so straightforward and enjoyable."

CHAPTER 3

MANDY WOKE UP the next morning worrying about the upcoming marathons. Mandy and Reggie were marathon runners trying to complete marathons in all fifty states and in the ten Canadian provinces, as well as complete the "marathon majors"—Chicago, New York, Boston, Berlin, London, and Tokyo. The sisters had participated in the track team at New Trier High School and ran in cross-country races of five kilometers for years before graduating to the longer endurance events. Their track coach encouraged them to find races in the community and to push themselves for time and distance.

Mandy could remember the drumbeat of the run and its hypnotic effect on her. As she started out on her run that morning, she thought about the agony of the training for a marathon. *Those new longer distances steadily build up on you, from the little 5K all the way through the full marathon distance. You can't just jump off the couch to run one of those marathons without that buildup. Each new distance would make you push yourself harder even though you just wanted to give up. Every time you passed the last run's distance, you'd have to focus on a tree or something and just push yourself to get to it, then do that over and over again until you could see the finish line. And when you crossed that finish line you felt as if you could not possibly run another step.* That's the way she was feeling right now, the challenge she took on repeatedly and had no one to blame but herself. It was a self-inflicted wound, if you looked at it through the negative prism. *Was this what she was doing with the other parts of her life, she wondered?*

The marathon project was one that Mandy had lobbied Reggie to do with her, and it intensified after Mandy's episode with the theft at the harbor master. She was definitely on such a personal quest that Reggie sometimes wondered if the two were connected. There were plenty of people who took up long-distance running because of something else going on in their lives. Sometimes it was dealing with an addiction, or trying to suppress some tragedy or oppression in their life. Maybe Mandy was still suffering from the old harbor master episode. Reggie had said to her at one point, "Look, if this is what we have to suffer through just for you to get over the harbor master incident, I'll give you my St. Dymphna card too so you can have two."

To which Mandy had replied, "Look who's talking? Now you do triathlons. That wasn't my idea. Maybe you need to keep your own St. Dymphna card and you can borrow mine."

In the office that morning, Mandy and Rick went through their thoughts on the task at hand with a due diligence checklist. It was one that the department had used to sort through the tasks that needed discussion. Nowhere on that list appeared the word *murder*. They were in unexplored territory as far as that went.

The department always operated under a veil of secrecy, given that it was constantly involved at some stage of an acquisition, divestiture, bond offering, or some secret event. One of the perennial concerns was making sure everyone, not just in the law department, but throughout the headquarters group, respected confidentiality and followed the law—no trading, tipping, or talking. Now that the deal was announced, and the death and bribery were made public, there was an imminent media deluge Mandy saw coming. So instead of worrying about their own people keeping the deal secret, as would always be a concern during due diligence, this time it was different. With everything public, now the task was damage control on how the news affected those who watched the company—stock exchange, market analysts, shareholders, and employees. She shot off an email to Rick about the need for LaSalle's public relations and investor relations staffs to be briefed and prepared to answer the likely questions.

She'd had enough for the day, so Mandy packed up and headed out on a cold walk on lower Michigan Avenue past Billy Goat Tavern in the already-dark March evening. It was always a challenge to get past the smell of frying cheeseburgers at Billy Goat's without succumbing to the temptation, so she gave herself permission to do so and in she went. She felt like she needed a drink, anyway. The first thing she saw was Rick Crawford on a barstool watching her as she came in. She planted herself next to him and promptly ordered a white wine.

He started right in, with a John Belushi delivery: "Did you know that Billy Goat Tavern is a chain of taverns in Chicago, with the first right here on the Michigan Avenue location in 1934? This used to be a favorite haunt of newspaper reporters like the late, great Mike Royko."

Mandy said back, "Yes, thank you Rick Belushi. And just so you know, Billy Goat was a Chicago legend long before inspiring Belushi's *SNL* skit."

They could both hear choruses of *"Cheeseborger, Cheeseborger"* from the rowdy patrons in the tavern, followed by *"Chips, chips, no fries."* But the most entertaining Billy Goat factoid was the one from 1945.

Mandy continued, "It was the legendary Curse of the Billy Goat of its owner, William "Billy Goat" Sianis," she said, pointing to the old photograph of Billy Goat and his goat on the wall behind the bar. "He threw the curse on the Cubs after being ejected from a World Series game. He'd tried to bring in a real goat to the park—even bought a ticket for him. Supposedly the curse was that the Cubs would never have another World Series victory, and it still hasn't."

Suddenly, Rick wasn't in receiver mode. In short order he angrily pulled a gob of toffee out of his mouth and was throwing it in the ashtray, along with a gold crown that was stuck to it. In the process, he knocked over the salt shaker and a small pile of salt ended up on the bar. Mandy quickly took a pinch and threw it over her shoulder.

"Sonofabitch," he said. "I know I should never put those in my mouth." Mandy avoided his eyes so she wouldn't laugh at him.

Rick said, "What was that you threw over your shoulder?"

"Some of that salt got spilled. It should undo the bad luck."

Rick said, "What bad luck?"

Mandy said, looking at him like he was crazy, "From the bad luck you just got from knocking over the salt shaker."

Mandy liked Rick a lot and they were at an equal level in the department, so that made things easier. She had worked with him now for three of his ten years in at LaSalle. He'd switched from a busy career at a Wall Street firm that had sapped his life force. He'd switched to in-house practice to save his marriage and family life, and led the department's acquisition activities. He lived in Winnetka, a North Shore Chicago suburb where his wife had gone to New Trier High School. His four kids were spread across grade school, middle school, and, of course, New Trier. He had that New Trier connection with Mandy and Reggie in common. A frumpy-looking guy in his mid-forties, with blond hair and a curious smirk on his face most of the time, he was given to alternating fits of rage and self-deprecating humor, depending on the inspiration. Despite his appearance and fickle demeanor, he was a brilliant lawyer. She still remembered like it was yesterday when she once closed his office door and was startled by fluttering hand-drawn cartoons taped to the door, all labeled with the caption *CRAWFORD'S WORLD*. Without taking the time to examine them, she'd said, "What are these?"

And he told her, "Somebody's idea of humor. Someone waits until I have a bad moment, and then creates a *Crawford's World* cartoon and tapes it up there."

"Hmmm, how long has this been going on, and who's doing it?" was her reaction.

"Long time. Don't know," was all he'd said.

Seeing this fit he was throwing, she wondered to herself, *should I be entrusting this situation to Rick, who might go off the rails at any moment?* Then she thought to herself, in a moment of unexpected self-reflection, like suddenly seeing what was right there in front of her in her blind spot, *Maybe I'm like that too, and maybe that's why I'm drawn to Rick as a friend.*

As he fingered through the ashtray looking for his crown, Mandy said, "Well, getting back to the matter at hand, there's a lot we have do here to get this back on track. I know you're thinking that we've only got three months to identify and to resolve our issues with the indemnities. You'll have big *Emily problems* if this drags out. I've got compliance problems that will be dumped in my lap if this goes forward. So, either way, we're motivated. Or just plain fucked."

Looking at her with an indecipherable expression on his face, Rick asked, "What about men? Anything going on there?" He knew it was a little intrusive to be asking a question like that, but after all, they had worked together for a long time now and he felt he knew her enough to be able to be asking her about that. They were pretty good at confiding in one another too. Clearly, it would be an easier discussion for Reggie to have with Mandy, but Rick had said it, so she had to react.

Mandy said, "Wow, that's a sharp change of subject. And did you just run a conversational red light and plow right onto a private road? Since you seem to have a sudden unforeseen interest in this, yes, Reggie's got a coworker who she's been getting close to. I haven't met him yet, but I've warned her about office romances, and the FBI even has an anti-fraternization rule." She took a second, scrunched up her face, and said back to him, "Hey, wait a minute, did you mean Reggie, or me?"

Again, she thought to herself, *Is this erratic change of topic proof of unpredictability? Also, not a good trait to have in someone you're relying on.*

Rick said, "Well, I meant you, actually. Hope you're not offended by me being nosy."

She answered, "No, no, that's OK. Uh, uh, I'm actually not in a relationship right now. There was someone I met kayaking on the river a while ago, but I couldn't see that working out. He was a White Sox fan anyway. Just kidding."

If you were a Chicagoan, you tended to be either a Cubs fan or a Sox fan, usually having to do with what side of Chicago you lived on. It was no different than the Yankees-Mets or Dodgers-Angels rivalries in New York and LA. It was kind of stupid, but a very real thing, and what was irritating the most was someone claiming to be a fan of both at the same time.

Rick said, "No, I get it. That's valid. Well, if you're

interested, I've got some investment banking buddies who are single."

She thought to herself, *And would it make sense to take recommendations from you on that topic either?* But what she said was, "Well, I'll let you know about that, but right now I'll just take a rain check. The kayaking guy actually just left me a message about dinner, so I'll probably take a chance. Maybe bring him a Cubs hat."

Just down the bar from them some other patron dropped his knife on the floor. Seeing this, Mandy said to Rick, "See that down there? In our house, if you dropped a knife, it was a real ordeal. One of Grandma Francesca's many Italian superstitions was that no immediate family living in the house could pick up the knife, or bad luck would attach to whoever picked it up. My mother, or grandmother, if she were there, would shout, *Don't touch it! Bad luck!* It was not unusual for a visitor to our house, like the mailman, to be ushered into the kitchen and asked to pick up one or more knives that lay on the kitchen floor. Friends, delivery men, even the occasional passersby were recruited to perform the service and Grandma would touch the horseshoe to break any bad luck that might have just arrived. Visitors always questioned the red chili peppers hanging in the foyer—a standard good luck totem to reverse any bad luck. My mom, Gabby, and Grandma Francesca wore little horns—necklaces or earrings—for good luck." Grandma's superstitions held a total grip on the family.

Rick said, "What if you unconsciously picked the knife up? Would you go *poof?*"

"You'd have to touch a horseshoe. That's why we have

one over the door, so it's always in the same conspicuous place. That knife this guy over here just dropped," Mandy said casually, "that's a nonevent. Has to happen in the home."

"So, you're very superstitious, just like your grandma Francesca?"

"Yup, just like the rest of my whole family. Why else do you think I take the St. Dymphna holy card with me and hold it?"

Rick said, "Yeah, that's pretty out-there. I've gotten used to it, but for a while I was bothered. How did your fellow prosecutors react to that at DOJ, or did you hide it?"

Mandy said, "The DOJ guys were OK with it. They even had their own little peculiarities, if that's what you think about St. Dymphna."

"Is that what that salt throwing you just did was all about?"

"Of course. Spill salt, and you better throw some over your shoulder to counteract the bad luck from the spill."

Thinking it was time to change topics again, and desperate to get away from superstitions, Rick said, "By the way, I've got the Cubs tickets for opening day. How about you and Reggie joining me for the game?"

LaSalle had maintained four season's tickets for the Chicago Cubs just behind the Cubs dugout on the third base side of Wrigley Field. Mandy and Reggie had grown up in Wilmette, so as Northsiders they were naturally Cubs fans.

Mandy said, "Love to," and picked up her stuff to head home.

Later on, Mandy, in her two-bedroom apartment on the fifteenth floor of her River North building, was looking out the south windows to the Loop. Mandy gazed at the night cityscape, and was missing her sister. The identical twins were twenty-nine-year-old, blue-eyed, shoulder-length redheads with modest but insistent freckles. Mandy remembered her youngest sister Prudence saying, "Even your freckle placement is identical with Reggie's!"

They had lived together while undergrads at the main Northwestern University campus in Evanston, and during grad school at the near-north downtown Chicago campuses of Northwestern — Mandy for law, and Reggie for medicine. Once grad school was over, they went off to Washington, D.C., together. Mandy snagged a job with the Justice Department's anti-corruption enforcement unit, and Reggie pursued postgraduate studies in forensic pathology at George Washington University. Once Reggie was done with that, she found work with the FBI lab in Quantico, Virginia, while Mandy went into the corporate law department at LaSalle located in Chicago. Mandy had spent an exciting three years at the Justice Department, but she decided to head back to Chicago when Reggie had to relocate to Quantico from Washington. The market for corporate compliance lawyers had mushroomed recently, and she thought it time to get out of DOJ. It was the first time in their lives that they were separated, and they missed each other terribly. Mandy kept a two-bedroom apartment so Reggie could stay with her when she came back to Chicago. Reggie did the same in Quantico.

Due to their marathoning, they were in excellent

shape from the constant year-round training and racing. The fifth and sixth children out of ten, they'd been each other's best friends, confidants, and sources of comfort since birth. Their middle place in the family resulted in them being organizers of the other siblings, and sometimes counselors and detectives. *Finding things, mediating fights, helping solve math problems, you name it.* Their mother Josephine, was of Italian stock and their father's ancestors were French Canadians who emigrated to the Midwest. The family had settled in the northern suburbs of Chicago and all of the children were raised there. Though most still resided somewhere in Chicagoland, a few had drifted out of the Midwest. The sisters' father Robert had been a successful corporate lawyer. He'd progressed to a general counsel position in a large telecommunications company in Chicago, eventually being named CEO and a member of its board.

Before starting their brood, their mother had gotten a master's degree from Loyola University in early childhood development and worked with new expectant mothers. Josephine, known as "Josie," despite her multiple-degree education, couldn't shake the superstitions ingrained in her by her mother Francesca.

Mandy recalled one day as she and Reggie were returning home after school, a mailman, leaving the house at the same time, said to them, "Knives just lying on the floor? You guys live in a pretty wacky home, I think."

Mandy and Reggie looked at each other and just kept going. *For those who don't know, no amount of explaining will suffice.*

Their grandmother on their father's side, a flamboyant octogenarian, still smoked a pack a day and talked with her hands, weighed down by gaudy gold bracelets and big rings. Mandy remembers Grandma Betty with her fire-engine red long nails as exotic. These days, she had a room in a retirement home in downtown Evanston. Mandy expected to see her soon at the Easter dinner in Wilmette, with the usual drama she brought to every family event.

Robert was prone to assigning nicknames liberally. The sisters became the "Deuce." Eventually, for obvious reasons, they became the "Red Deuce." Grandma Betty was "Phwing" for reasons that would become obvious. Their mother, because of her constant chatter, was "Gabby."

CHAPTER 4

MANDY AWOKE the next morning at 5:00 a.m. Reggie would be undertaking a similar routine over seven hundred miles away. After thinking about the prospect of responding to the kayaker's dinner invitation, she replied to his email with a gentle decline. The kayaker's name was Patrick Carney, and she had to admit that she was attracted to him. Her message offered some hope for him, though, saying she was pretty busy now, but he should get back in touch in a couple of weeks.

Mandy lay awake for some time, unable to get her mind off Wretched Witch, the due diligence list, and trying to sort out a game plan for the day. Instead of going running, she got her first cup of coffee and worked on *The New York Times* daily crossword puzzle while eating a bagel, before finally heading out to the office.

Crossword puzzles kept her word skills sharp, as well as satisfying her need to solve mysteries. Growing up, she had shown rare dissimilarities in interests and skill sets from her twin sister. Mandy's word fascination ripened into the love of reading and debating, leading her to become an English major at Northwestern before setting out to become a lawyer. Of course, it had helped that she had a lawyer as a father. Mandy was also a dogged arguer and frequently found herself arguing on behalf of one or another of her siblings with her parents. In fact, it was usually on behalf of Reggie. Her encounter with the Wretched Witch about "whose engine division was it anyway" came to mind as a little mini-argument she'd just had.

Mandy had run into a bit of trouble in Catholic grade school. She was fiercely protective of Reggie, and when Sister Anne once challenged her for something, Mandy jumped up and yelled, *Leave her alone. She didn't have anything to do with it.* That had earned her a prominent placement in the troublemakers' ranking kept by the nuns each year. No student wanted to know what happened if you gained the top spot, since expulsion was one of the possible outcomes.

Reggie, though, was a science person who had been an avid butterfly collector as a young girl. It was not uncommon for one of the Doucettes to open the freezer and to find a butterfly frozen to death in a plastic baggie. There would be charges of cruelty to animals made by the siblings against Reggie, but she would calmly assure them that it was the most humane way to kill a specimen. Reggie had an extensive butterfly collection on the wall of the room she shared with Mandy. She loved examining living and dead creatures, and went on to excel in science classes. From there she double-majored in chemistry and biology before going into medicine, all at Northwestern. It was a natural path for a person who loved to solve biology mysteries to pursue forensic pathology, which is what she did.

One day in the department's refrigerator, Mandy mistook some item in there as a frozen butterfly, and it brought her back to the years of Reggie's beginning hunter stage. She was still in it, but well beyond beginning stage.

Mandy and Reggie shared a common nonathletic hobby too, though. They were dedicated genealogists, who had spent considerable time researching and documenting their family's roots. They could trace back to the sixteenth century their French ancestry from the Normandy coast, where their émigré ancestor was a French carpenter, through the Acadian part of now-eastern Canada. From there, their ancestors had been chased out of Nova Scotia by the British to Louisiana, then a firm possession of France and a safe haven. After eventually returning to the area near Quebec City on the St. Lawrence, their adventurous ancestors made it up to the Midwest. At Easter, the sisters were anxious to pin down Grandma Betty on some of that history to fill in some missing blanks.

Mandy was going through the Allzient organization chart, along with the detailed business description. This was part of the acquisition package prepared by Allzient's banker, and used by the LaSalle team to bid on, and win, the deal. Part of Allzient's business—in fact, the main attraction to LaSalle—was its alternative energy operations. These operations included an electric vehicle fleet business that was aggressively contracting with government agencies who were looking to replace their aging gas-guzzling vehicles. Even the U.S. Postal Service was becoming a customer. Allzient had an office in New York to service U.S. customers. She also noted with interest that Allzient had acquired a Chicago-based company, Spruance Corporation, nearly a decade ago. She had heard her dad mention Spruance once upon a time.

Mandy's other tasks for the day were fairly routine: prepare an annual code of conduct update to the board's Audit Committee and handle outstanding code complaints. She thought to herself, *I've got enough hot potatoes. Why do I have to handle this Allzient mess?*

After an hour she got her first phone call of the day from her sister. "Whatcha doin'?" Reggie said.

"Trying to sort out what code of conduct cases can be pushed to the side or dumped on others. Here's what I can't figure out. These people who get mixed up in code of conduct violations are just shocking to me, but they're supposed to be highly ethical corporate employees who respect and obey the code of conduct and the law."

"Did you think that the people in companies were all going to be angels? Wasn't that who you prosecuted at the Justice Department?" Reggie said.

"I guess so, but I used to think that when I left Justice and got into a corporate law department, I could have a breather from the dark side," Mandy said.

"Remember what Uncle Jim told us? All of his clients were guilty, and when you asked him how he could stand it, he said he just focused on getting them fair trials. Who knows, maybe that's why he drinks so much. I can just see him going to Cook County Jail and visiting his shackled clients and preparing to defend them, and all day long listening to lies and denials."

"Well," said Mandy, "that doesn't describe how I think about all corporate employees, though. I think corporate employees are honest for the most part. You only hear me complaining about the bad ones, but I don't put them all in the same category. *I'm pretty reasonable, actually.*"

Reggie said, "I'm glad you don't. You need to have some fairly high confidence level in your fellow man to be able to make it through one of your days."

"Unlike Uncle Jim, at least I can take comfort that I represent the corporation, and not the employees. Not that it stops the employees from assuming that I represent them. Just think about that idiot in Wretched Witch's strategy department I had to throttle in last year's acquisition. I caught him saying out loud that he was going to have his cousin buy some shares in that company before we released the announcement. He told me I should be protecting him instead of lecturing him. I told that arrogant little inside trader that I represent the company, not him. Now that I think about it, that's probably why Emily Jenkins can't stand me."

"You're overthinking this, and you're really becoming cynical," said Reggie. "I can tell when you get going on this code of conduct stuff. You tend to dwell on the darkness. Lighten up. There's always happy hour, or you can go running. By the way, those two bodies I've been working on turned out to be former Allzient employees. We interviewed their families and it turns out they were originally Spruance employees."

Mandy yelled, "Shit, Reggie! When were you going to tell me that?"

"Sorry. I forgot, but I just remembered."

"Ugh! Well, fill me in please," Mandy asked.

"We think they're Russians, for sure, based on tattoos, dental work, surgeries, and even stomach contents. Our guys have matched them up with missing persons reports. One of them was with a warehouse company in New Jersey. The other was a security manager in a New York high-rise office building. Now they're trying to trace back their history to see how they got here and who they may have pissed off so much. There's a lot of speculation that this is Russian Mafia-related, but I don't buy it."

"How did you go make the connection?"

"I met with the families and got some DNA samples from their children. They matched."

"Why couldn't the families look at the bodies and confirm identification?"

"Well, I didn't tell you this detail before, but before the bodies were dumped, their faces, fingertips, and tattoos had been doused with acid. Nobody was going to want to look at that mess, much less be able to make a positive identification."

"Ugh. That's sickening. And you wanted to do this job. Why?"

"Hey, I love this stuff. Remember when we were kids and I would always dissect insects and try to figure out why something died? It's my thing. What are you talking about anyway? You don't like people and you can't stand dishonesty. That's all you've got all day long. How does that make sense? At least dead guys don't lie."

"I guess we're both trying to solve mysteries." Mandy said, shrugging.

Mandy decided she'd go for a noon run, since she'd skipped her run that morning to worry about things. *Lawyers are, after all, professional worry warts.* In the company's fitness center at the river level, Mandy, dressed in her black tights, Patagonia vest, and Hokas, headed out east along the Chicago Riverwalk. Past the tourists waiting to board one of the Chicago architectural boat tours, she ran until she reached the marina in the inner harbor on the left and Buckingham Fountain in Grant Park on her right.

In a moment of recognition, she realized that her body was not fighting the forced activity. When the body fought it, every rise felt like a small mountain. She wasn't feeling that; she actually felt energized at each rise encountered.

Approaching the south part of Grant Park, she hugged the lakeshore and encircled the Shedd Aquarium, Adler Planetarium, Soldier Field, the Field Museum, and finally McCormick Place, before heading back north. She kept up her pace and felt no slackening of any of her equipment—quads, hamstrings, or calves.

CHAPTER 5

IN MANDY AND REGGIE'S CALL the next morning, Reggie said, "I started trying to figure out cause of death on those two bodies from Pennsylvania. So far, I've only found small puncture wounds on both bodies, so I'm suspecting some drug or strong chemical. But I haven't found any telltale chemicals. I don't think these are Mafioso hits. Those guys don't get elegant with their handiwork. It's usually a blunt instrument—shotgun in the face, large caliber bullet in the head from behind, and slit throat—nothing fancy. Pretty interesting," Reggie said.

"You'll figure it out. What are your plans for Easter?"

"I'm coming out and plan to work out of the Chicago office and stay a week. They're thinking of setting up a satellite lab in Chicago. This will be a trial. Can I stay with you?"

"Of course you can. You know you don't need to ask that," Mandy said.

"Well, if you have any overnight visitors, I wouldn't want to get in the way."

"Ha, ha. Is that your way of shaming me for not having a boyfriend?"

"Maybe. A colleague's joining me after Easter. You'll like him."

"Is he a colleague, or a colleague *with benefits?*" Mandy asked.

"No comment," Reggie answered.

"You know what I've told you about not doing your *business* in your own backyard, right? And don't you have a non-fraternization policy at the Bureau?"

"Yeah, but that might change."

"The policy?"

"No, the circumstances."

"Are you telling me you're leaving the FBI?"

"No, but he might be."

"I need to meet this guy. Does he have a name?"

"He would be Dan Aleri. A nice New York Italian boy. Mom will be pleased. Think he'll know about the knives, or not to throw a hat on the bed?"

"That's your job to find that out."

The CEO's office early the next morning was crowded with Emily Jenkins, Ed Rosen, Rick Crawford, and Mandy. Mandy was busy thinking to herself about the main player in the room. CEO Jim Kerwin was a lawyer by training, but had been in general management and out of the practice for many years, but loyal to his legal sensitivities nonetheless. The Board of Directors was satisfied with his overall strategy plan results, but anxious that time not be lost in completing the pieces. LaSalle's stock price had been battered as it was going through its makeover, shedding some businesses and adding others that built the new strategic composition. LaSalle's evolution had been going on for over 150 years, and Jim was just its latest custodian. Jim knew that the stock would suffer while the deals were taking place and for some time after, until results became stable for a few quarters. That was to be expected, and the board was patient for the process to play out, as long as there were no unusual problems. What was not in anyone's calculus was a scandal. That was most definitely an unusual problem, but one that Mandy felt Jim Kerwin was up to the challenge to lead them through.

Jim led the discussion. "Well, we certainly didn't need this, and I don't look forward to calling the chair and delivering this news. Ed, what kind of feedback do you have?"

Ed deferred to Mandy, who reported on the New York trip. She said, "From the meeting that took place, we think the whistleblower made a good claim. Even did the right thing in reporting, and we got surprised to learn that he sent his letter to the DOJ. We also satisfied ourselves that management didn't know what was going on because the corporate security director blocked the process from working. And now he's missing."

Emily said, “I don’t like where any of this takes us, whether it’s the cost or the customer impact, or the delay. Can we at least make sure we’re completing the rest of the due diligence work?”

Jim said, “We should be pressing ahead with the diligence, of course, and I’ll update our directors on the situation. I don’t like the delay any more than you do, but I think we have to let this play out. Where do we stand on keeping quiet publicly on this, and when could we see making something public?”

Ed Rosen said, “I think that the issue is already public. We need to say something immediately, and be prepared to respond to analysts and to shareholders. I’m surprised the media isn’t all over us already.”

Kerwin said, “Rick and Mandy, maybe you could let us discuss this in a smaller meeting please?”

Mandy and Rick left the room.

Emily Jenkins blurted out, “Is Mandy Doucette up to this challenge? We need to make sure we have our best on this issue.” Emily had obviously persuaded Jim to push Mandy and Rick out the door so Emily could feel free to bash them.

Ed said back, “She came out of the Justice Department unit that handled anti-corruption cases, so I’m glad she’s on the case. Believe me, she will be like a dog on a bone with this, and if there is any odor that she doesn’t like, she’ll run it down until she gets to the bottom of it. I have heard it from others that she was known as a deal-killer at the Justice Department.”

When the meeting broke up, Emily was the first out of the door and rushed down the hall toward her office.

Rosen followed her out after a couple minutes and nearing her office overheard her speaking in a loud, agitated voice to someone on her cell phone. The only words he heard were, "...she may be a deal-killer. There's got to be a way to keep her from doing any damage." Rosen popped his head in the door and she noticed him, immediately cupping her phone mic and saying, "What is it, Ed?"

"Sorry for interrupting. I just thought you'd like to have another discussion after what Jim just asked."

Emily said, "Let me finish this call and I'll come by." She closed her door and continued her conversation.

Rosen nodded and moved off down the hall, unable to hear any more through the closed door. He was now on alert that some difficulty lay ahead.

"Harold, is there something you can do about this?"

Harold Menzies said, "What would you like me to do?"

"I don't know, get her moved off this or something? Ed said she would sniff out whatever is there. I don't know what else is there, but maybe if she finds something she'll try to kill the deal."

Harold Menzies said, "Let me think about that. Meanwhile, keep your head down on this. We want to get this done, but you can't be seen to be disregarding serious problems with an acquisition you're leading. It could end up *you* being removed from the project, rather than the lawyer."

"OK, you're right. It just pisses me off that I'm at the mercy of someone who has the reputation she has."

They hung up and Harold Menzies decided to make a call or two. His first call was to Chairman of the Board David Renfrow, in which he reported that he'd learned from Emily Jenkins that a bribery claim had been made against Allzient by a whistleblower and that it might be endangering the deal. Menzies also related that he understood an internal lawyer known for killing deals was assigned to deal with the bribery issue.

"David, we cannot afford to let this deal slip out of our grasp. Getting this deal done will be a game changer for us. They need someone managing this problem who has the skill to salvage the deal and not make it go up in smoke."

David Renfrow said he would speak to Jim Kerwin about it.

Harold then made a very discreet call to someone he knew could take care of the situation, but the solution could be extreme.

"Apparently there's a bloodhound that was let loose on the Allzient deal. I don't care what she finds out about that bribery thing, but if she catches a whiff of us and pursues it, you know what kind of havoc she could wreak."

Later that day Chairman David Renfrow called Jim Kerwin and let him know about Harold Menzies' concern about Mandy Doucette.

Jim said to David, "May I ask how it is that Harold Menzies is learning of these staffing issues?"

David replied, "We can't be beating around the bush on this—it's too important. Harold got a call from Emily Jenkins. Look, Jim, I'm sorry for getting into the weeds on this, but can you assure me that Amanda Doucette is able to handle this?

Jim said, "I trust Ed Rosen to put the right people on this. I don't share Emily's concerns, and must say that Emily has a record of burning through any people she sees as obstacles, regardless of who they are or what the issues may be. Let's let this play out."

They hung up and Jim Kerwin fumed privately in his office about Emily casually going around him to speak to Harold Menzies. In his mind a decision had just been made for him that it was time to look closely at Emily Jenkins. *What was it they called her? Wretched Witch?*

CHAPTER
6

A FREAK SPRING STORM brought four inches of wet snow into the city overnight, so Mandy's day started with a treadmill run in the apartment building fitness center, instead of the usual lakeshore run. She was thankful for that fitness center, just as she was for the one at work. Chicago's weather was unforgiving. While on the treadmill, she had her regular morning call with Reggie. It was pretty interesting, seeing that she was making some progress on the two buried bodies in the shallow grave in Pennsylvania.

"Have you figured out cause of death yet?" Mandy asked.

"Poison. I know that sounds too subtle for Mafiosos, like I was saying before. I've got a lot of tissue samples to analyze, but I did find pinhole puncture marks."

"As in snakebite?"

"No, as in injection."

Mandy said, "Ugh. What about Paris? How are you doing on your long runs?"

The Paris Marathon was high on their list of international races. They were trying to get the marathon majors done, and had already completed Chicago, New York, and Boston. The rest were international — London, Berlin, and Tokyo. But they had chosen Paris for the next race since Mandy had a planned code of conduct training session in the Paris suburb where LaSalle's office was located. They had three weeks to taper after their longest training run, and still three more long runs yet to finish training for the race distance.

"I'm where I'm supposed to be. Don't worry. By Easter I'll be even with you."

Mandy's way to the office was slushy along Ohio Street, and she opted to turn south on Rush Street and to head to lower Michigan Avenue again. Her building had an entrance on that level, and she could avoid walking at a forty-five-degree angle into the wind on upper Michigan Avenue. Every time she made the trip on lower Michigan Avenue, she imagined the encounter the cinematic Dr. Richard Kimball had with his nemesis Dr. Charles Nichol in the film *The Fugitive.* There was certainly nothing inspiring about lower Michigan Avenue, though. It was just a down and dirty sublevel in Chicago, and the less you were in it, the better. Cars, trucks, homeless, and cops, all hidden from the sunlight. Up in her office, she looked out on the lock where the Chicago River met Lake Michigan as a few ships were lining up to pass through. This view always mesmerized her and let her think through problems.

She was ultra-sensitive to the aftershocks that would follow a deal crater, if that's what happened, and she didn't want that coming back on her. The proponents of the acquisition tended to take aim at anyone in the company, usually the lawyers, who caused an acquisition to fail. Even when it should fail. The proponents had a lot at stake if deals failed, usually because they had missed some key issue. Besides that, this deal seemed to make strategic sense, unlike some of the deals that hadn't work out too well. Mandy walked down to Rick's office and found him on the phone with his dentist's office, trying to get an appointment for the replacement crown. He finished that and looked at her.

Rick said to her, "Ed's calm, but Jim and Emily are pissed — at Allzient and at us. They want this to get done, assuming the Allzient house isn't burning down. After their meeting yesterday, Ed tells me that he and Emily had a one-on-one heated meeting in his office, with Emily ranting and raving about lawyers and claiming that we're trying to kill this deal. What do you think?"

Mandy said, "Fuck it. Let's get in her face right now."

They ended up with Emily Jenkins in her corner office on the twenty-fourth floor.

Emily said, "Word that the process has slipped into disarray is filtering back to me through the investment bankers. This looks like it's turned into a clusterfuck! Do we have any control over this, or are we going to be held hostage by Allzient?" she asked.

Mandy said, "You know we have murders here, right? So far, three? Along with a now-public bribery case?"

Rick turned red and jumped in, saying, "Goddamnit! We're going to have to slow up on the acquisition for a while until there's some clarity. I can't see Allzient being able to attend to what they need to while this distraction is occupying them. In fact, we need to start worrying about whether their business is going to disintegrate if this goes public and they get roasted. Won't their customers want to wash their hands of them for the corruption? And is this what you want to buy—a company that has just sabotaged itself?"

Emily, a little subdued by his outburst, calmly said, "I don't think I need a lecture on what I want to buy, Rick. There's still value because of the proprietary technology they've developed. I've worked my ass off on this deal, and I'm not going to see it get killed off because of some minor legal bullshit. If we can salvage the deal with a purchase price cut, maybe we can separately assure their customers that we'll pick up the pieces. Harold's going to be irate if we let this deal slip through our fingers," Emily said.

Mandy said, *"Harold?"*

Emily recovered from her slip and said, "I meant Jim, and the board."

Mandy sat there shaking her head, and said, "Bribery of foreign government officials is not *minor legal bullshit.* It's a huge problem that the DOJ will pursue with intensity. We've put our whole compliance program on hold while this is moving, but maybe we can resume our activities while Allzient works through the situation. I want to cut the department loose to pick up what was pending, and to move it along."

They agreed that the regular compliance matters would be resumed. This included the board reports and presentation for the upcoming meeting. As they were leaving Emily's office, they could see the dyed-green Chicago River below and the starting of the annual St. Patrick's Day Parade down State Street. The green dye certainly concealed a lot of ugliness and filth that was the true nature of what they were looking down on. Just a street or two to the west at the Clark Street overpass, a plaque marked the spot of the tragic sinking of the SS *Eastland* in 1915. While it was an unimaginable tragedy claiming almost 850 lives when the ship rolled, a shocking discovery was made while the recovery operation was underway. On the river bed at that spot, a one-man submarine was found carrying its dead captain and his dog. The Chicago River was full of surprises.

Mandy said, "Just as the freak snowstorm melts away, in time for the parade and my long training run." As they left, it wasn't lost on Mandy that an act of corruption was holding up a deal in a city and state that had been renowned for corruption. And it wasn't lost on Emily Jenkins that she had just heard a useful piece of information on Mandy Doucette that she would have to pass along.

As Rick and Mandy were climbing into the elevator for the ride down from the twenty-fourth floor, Mandy looked at Rick and said, "She's shacking up with that guy. I can smell it."

Rick said, "What guy?"

"Harold Menzies. You heard her. That was a big, hairy slip of the tongue. I'm betting she's trying to figure out a way right now so that she can cover her tracks. We have a senior officer doing the horizontal bop with a board member. Do you disagree?"

Rick said, "I don't have your bloodhound skills. Let's

just watch her and see how she behaves. Please continue with your pending matters. Do what you think's necessary."

"Well, I've had a lot of experience in sniffing out liars, and she's shaping up to be a big one in my opinion." To herself, Mandy said, *Wretched Witch, you're going to have a companion soon, courtesy of me. I believe Rick Crawford just said to have you watched, and he didn't say how.*

Rick and Mandy parted company and went to their respective offices.

In her office, Mandy called Special Agent Steve Baker, her FBI contact on the engine theft project and said, "Steve, I need to have an investigator do some work on some issues. Do you have a recommendation on a private investigator I could go to? Somebody you're familiar with? Maybe an ex-agent?"

Steve said, "Yes, I've got a great guy you can use. Ray Hanson. He used to work in our unit. Let me text you his contact information."

Steve texted the contact information and Mandy called the investigator and gave him the assignment of shadowing Emily Jenkins, with the added request to bug her phone. Mandy knew this was very risky of her, but felt she had to fight fire with fire. She doubted that any reasonable interpretation of Rick's request would imply the ability to sic private investigators on a senior officer of the company. She was doing it anyway.

Mandy puffed out a breath in exasperation and pulled out the list of pending code of conduct matters to review. Her first item was an ongoing sexual harassment complaint against a senior vice president in the manufacturing unit.

She read over the summary of the complaints. The first had begun as an internal audit item that ripened into embezzlement and an embarrassing affair between two coworkers. The workers were let go and the subsequent lawsuit was settled.

The second item was an embarrassing incident involving a cleaning lady walking in on a midlevel executive with his pants down and a helpful porn website up on his computer. The employee was given a warning, but not before his supervisor suggested that they all just turn their heads, saying, *"Look, it's only a cleaning lady."*

Mandy had asked him, "Have you read the code of conduct?"

"Of course I have," he'd said.

Mandy pulled it out and reread to him two sentences.

"This code applies to conduct in general no matter who was affected by a violation."

Then, "It's every employee's obligation to participate in monitoring and helping enforce the code." The supervisor had nothing else to say.

The last item was the straightforward case of fraud and embezzlement in the engine division. For some time, the Kansas City engine manufacturing operations had been reporting the disappearance of large amounts of engine parts. It suspected an internal theft ring. Mandy had pulled in the FBI, since it involved interstate commerce and there would be jurisdiction. A very quiet investigation had been ongoing for almost a year, and it was time to try to have some arrests made.

Mandy also reviewed her training session schedule, which called for meetings in the LaSalle offices in Prague, Istanbul, Paris, and Milan in the next month. These meetings were standardized and the attendees had been notified to attend, so there was no reason not to get them done. The training sessions schedule had been laid out to the Audit Committee of the board the previous year, and she had to be able to say they were on track for completion so that her department's plan was on track.

That night when she got home there was a brown envelope with her name written on it at the apartment building's concierge desk. She opened it and it was a photo of her parents' house on Linden Avenue in Wilmette. The house she had grown up and lived in her whole life. She turned it over and in black magic marker were two words: ***BACK OFF.*** She felt a shiver go through her body and she turned to look out the window at the street. She didn't know what she was thinking she would see, but she was certainly shaken by this. She wrestled with what she should do. Call the cops? What would she tell them and what would they do about it? In the end, she was too petrified to do anything about it, so she did nothing.

The next day, the three problems were handled as far as they could be. The only thing that had to be wrapped up was a sting to round up the engine parts theft ring. Mandy had to catch up with the plant manager and with the FBI and Missouri State Police agents who were involved. But it turned out there was still one surprise left in the week. Looking at her emails, she saw she had one from Randy Haggerty, her contact at the Kansas City plant, saying he had urgent news for her. She called him immediately and was put right through, even though Haggerty was in a meeting with several people.

"Mandy, we did the raid today. The FBI and state cops busted a facility full of engine parts, and they got two drivers and loads of data. And wait until you hear this. They also got a name from one of these guys they busted, who agreed to cooperate to get immunity: Willis Traynor."

"What? Our corporate security director here in Chicago?" Mandy said.

"That's him. This is going to send some shock waves through your building. They're serving the arrest warrant this morning. Maybe as we speak. I'm surprised Ed Rosen hasn't gotten to you yet."

Mandy thought a little about the engine theft sting operation. She'd met with her contacts at the Justice Department office in Kansas City and the Missouri State Police in a video conference, and worked out the details of the operation. This had started several years ago in another engine plant, and with the help of the corporate security head in the investigation, the inside theft gang had been caught and prosecuted. This had been before Mandy's time. But it had recently occurred again in Missouri, and the company had been concerned with the similarities between the episodes. Once these details were worked out, local plant management working with law enforcement was set to spring the trap.

Mandy said, "This is huge, Randy. Congratulations. Is Special Agent Baker working with you there?"

Steve Baker was the special agent running the operation on behalf of the FBI. A Chicago-based agent, he was running the operation out of the Kansas City office. Randy said he was there and that they were debriefing this morning and trying to work out charges and to secure evidence. Mandy said she'd call back soon. She went up to Ed's office and got caught up on what had happened. He was busy laying out all of the plans for the arrest and the media coverage that was sure to follow, as well as a department meeting to fill everyone in. Mandy called back to the plant to talk to Steve Baker. He came on the line, and she congratulated him and thanked him for pulling this off. She could tell he was riding high with a big bust like this. They talked about how it had gone down and, most importantly, how Willis Traynor had gotten caught in the net.

Baker said, "Traynor had been arrogant and overconfident. He'd been involved in breaking a similar ring five years earlier in another LaSalle factory in Ohio. So, he'd actually *gone to school* on the earlier incident, and then tried to run his own ring."

Earlier that day near the close of business, federal agents descended on the LaSalle headquarters building and arrested Willis Traynor on charges of grand theft involving interstate commerce and wire fraud. This was occurring simultaneously with the arrest of several employees in the Kansas City operations, as well as the interception of a semitrailer delivery of engine parts to a warehouse outside of St. Louis, Missouri, but on the Illinois side of the Mississippi. That made it interstate commerce and was a solid basis for federal jurisdiction. The warehouse arrest had netted a truck driver and three men occupying the warehouse and unloading the goods. The Justice Department, Missouri State Police, and FBI, in coordination with LaSalle management, issued a joint news release announcing the arrests and charges. The next morning's *Chicago Tribune* and *Kansas City Star* carried the following article:

> It was announced yesterday that a joint operation by the U.S. Justice Department, the Federal Bureau of Investigation, and the Missouri State Police, working in close coordination with LaSalle Enterprises, Inc., a Chicago-based multinational corporation, had concluded with the arrest of at least six individuals. The arrests included employees of LaSalle Enterprises' Kansas City engine plant, as well as the company's corporate security director. After an undercover operation of two years' duration had netted a roll-up of the theft operation, law enforcement and the company were surprised to see that the corporate security employee involved had been instrumental in the earlier arrests on similar circumstances in another LaSalle Enterprises operation in Ohio. Those arrested will be charged with various felony counts related to grand theft involving interstate commerce.

Mandy continued to be in a state of disbelief that the head of security was involved in the theft ring. Not just involved, but its architect. Whatever had driven him to betray the company must have involved some level of desperation. The fallout from the episode would be significant, and Mandy was relieved that the security function did not report up through the law department. It would, of course, have to be incorporated into the report she was preparing for the Board of Directors. Would the failure of the company's compliance function to stop a repeat engine theft ring cause management or the board to lose confidence in her? Who was going to suffer from this?

Mandy thought there could be some real corporate embarrassment in store here, but it was a big relief to have the bust done and to eliminate a theft ring, not to mention lifting the proverbial middle finger to Wretched Witch. Mandy received a call from CEO Jim Kerwin during the day to congratulate her on bringing in the theft ring, so she was riding high for the moment. That was welcome, but she still had to wonder about the corporate security officer. Not that there was any connection between LaSalle and Allzient on this issue, but she wondered what the odds would have been that both companies would have problems with their corporate security heads at the same time. It certainly proved one point—just because you were the head of security didn't mean you were ruled out of being a troublemaker. Mandy took the coincidence to mean that she should continue looking at Erik Spenser as closely as possible. In fact, now that she was thinking of Willis Traynor of engine theft fame as the architect of the whole scheme, maybe that was how she should be thinking about Spenser. Had he been an architect or a worker bee?

CHAPTER 7

MANDY WAS AT HOME and needed to shake off LaSalle and get distracted. She called Julie, a fellow kayaker friend in River North, and they popped up to North Avenue to have dinner and then go to a Second City show. That always got her mind off her troubles, even though she had to sit shoulder-to-shoulder with over a hundred people in a small room. Second City was a national treasure, she thought.

Julie said to her, “Have you seen Patrick Carney?”

“No, but I had an email from him inviting me to dinner. Why”?

“I saw him a while back, and he asked about you. He even asked for your contact info, so I shared it with him. I hope you don’t mind?”

"Sure. But I had to put him off for a while due to work pressure."

Julie said, "Well, I wouldn't put him off for long. Patrick would be quite a catch."

Mandy said, "Why is that?"

"Handsome, successful author, independently wealthy, interested in you. Want me to keep going?"

"Nope. I get it."

The next morning Mandy saw another email on her phone from Patrick Carney. This was the second time in a month he was making an attempt with her, and she thought she should take a chance. He apparently wasn't going to give up. He was asking if she'd like to go out on the river this coming weekend. She thought about it and decided it would be good medicine for her. She sent an email back agreeing, and they met at the river spot they had used for their trips on Saturday morning.

Patrick was waiting for her when she came down the ramp and he helped her get the kayak down in the water. It was a two-seater.

Patrick said, "Why the two-seater?"

Mandy said, "It's what my sister and I use together. Why don't we both get in this one and leave yours on your car?" They boarded and headed out into the river, with Patrick in the rear seat.

"It's been awhile. How have you been?" he asked.

"Good. Busy, but good. My sister and I are going over to run the Paris Marathon next week. What have you been up to?"

Patrick said, "Marathoners! I'm impressed. I was skiing in Colorado. I have a place in Aspen, and a lot of friends out there who ski with me. Other than that, I've been doing a lot of writing."

Mandy said, "What kind of writing? I guess I didn't know that about you."

"Well, we really don't know much about each other, do we? I'm a novelist. We've kayaked together in the group, but not had the chance to get to know each other. That's why I suggested this, when I couldn't get you out to dinner last month."

"I'm glad you were persistent. How long have you been writing?"

"Off and on for eight years, I guess. I'm fortunate that I don't have to have a regular job."

Mandy said, "And why is that?"

"The family business, or what was the family business a long time ago, has left me pretty independent financially."

"What business is that?"

"LaSalle Enterprises."

Mandy stopped paddling, turned around, and stared at him. Patrick steadied the kayak and looked at her. "What's the matter?" he said.

"That's where I work. Didn't you know that?"

"Really? No. I had no idea. What do you do there?"

"I'm a lawyer. Been there three years."

"My father's a lawyer too, in a patent firm. How do you like it there?"

"It's a great company. A lot of history in Chicago. Very international. In fact, before going to Paris I'm visiting some of the foreign operations for work. How was your family involved?"

Patrick said, "My great-great-great-great grandfather founded the company in the 1840s."

"Seriously?"

"Yup. Seamus Carney came out west after working on the Erie Canal, just off the boat from Ireland. He left County Kerry in the 1830s, when jobs were scarce there. He started a company when he came out here and did many projects, including building bridges over the river, the Galena-Chicago Railway, the lake tunnels, and on and on. The company grew and changed from that into the major company it is now."

The kayak drifted north when they took a paddling break, and Mandy asked why so, since the current seemed to be heading to the south.

Patrick answered, "That's because the river has a complicated current going one way on the top and below the surface another current going in the opposite direction. The Chicago River has its surprises, that's for sure. Sneaky, huh?"

Mandy said, "Yeah, kinda reminds me of some other problems I have." Patrick wasn't sure what to make of that; she'd said it almost sotto voce, so he decided not to pry.

They'd resumed paddling and were heading north to paddle around Goose Island, passing under bridges one after another.

"His son Patrick, was my namesake. I'm actually Patrick Carney VI. The sixth. Patrick the First died tragically in the Great Chicago Fire in 1871."

"That's terrible."

"There were over three hundred people who died in that fire. It destroyed seventeen thousand buildings and torched over three square miles. Anyway, his body was never found."

"So, what happened to the company after that?"

Patrick said, "We're coming up to Ward Park on the right. Would you like to get some lunch at the Erie Café?"

"Sounds good."

They tied up at the pier and got a table inside overlooking the river and ordered some food and a couple beers.

Mandy said, "So you were going to tell me what happened with the company."

"Right. I guess the rest of the family kept things going, and they had a lot to do with rebuilding the city after the fire. The company went on to thrive and get into agricultural equipment and eventually other kinds of machinery and transportation equipment. It was the Industrial Revolution, right? Lots of opportunities for everybody, and they hit it big. It's a big company now, not that I need to tell you. Nobody from the family is involved anymore. It went public in the 1940s, but the family has remained a very large shareholder."

"That's an interesting story. I didn't know anything about that."

Patrick said, "How about you? Where are you from?"

"Wilmette, actually. I grew up there and my parents are still in the house we grew up in across from the Bahá'í Temple near the lake. All of the Doucette kids went to New Trier and I went on to Northwestern. Undergrad and law school. The only time I've been outside Chicago is when I worked at the Justice Department for three years a while back. Really missed being here."

"Yeah, that's the way I feel when I'm away too. It's always good to come back home."

Mandy said, "Where did you go to school?"

"University of Chicago. History major."

"Really? What do you do with that?"

"Write books?" he said.

They ate and headed back to the kayak and paddled back down south on the river. It was early for river kayaking, so they saw few canoeists or kayakers on the way.

On their way back to the ramp Patrick said, "OK, let's get this out of the way. Cubs or Sox fan?"

Mandy smiled and said, "Cubs, of course."

Patrick smiled at her and said, "I knew there was a reason I liked you. Can we do something else again soon?"

"Sure. I'd like that. I thought you were a Sox fan, though," she said. And she meant it.

"Nope. Always been a Cub fan, though I don't hate the Sox, like some Cubs fans. Maybe I could call you when you're back from Paris, if that would be OK with you?" he said.

They were just about back at the boat landing when they suddenly heard a boat motor racing from behind and turned to see a boat bearing down on them, then veer sharply to the right of them at the last second, casting a huge wave over them both. There was nothing accidental about it, and Mandy was petrified by what had just happened. By the time they recovered and got to the ramp, the speedboat had disappeared. They got to the ramp and pulled the kayak out and up the ramp.

Patrick rushed over to her once they were clear of the water and gave her a hug that lasted a minute. She was shaking from fear and from cold water, and tried to explain to him that what had just happened was about her, not him.

Patrick said, “What do you mean it was about you?”

“Someone’s trying to scare me off a project, and I’m pretty sure it had to be connected. I’m starting to get really scared.”

She told him about the photo that she’d received and now this.

He said, “I hope you’re taking this to the police.”

She ignored the question, saying, “I’m sorry you got soaked.”

“Don’t worry about me. Just worry about yourself. Come on, I’m taking you home.”

“That’s OK, I’ll be fine, thanks.”

“I insist. Let me get the kayak on the car.” Patrick secured the kayak next to his own on the BMW X-5 and he dropped her at her apartment, taking the kayak down and getting it to her storage unit.

Then he suddenly hugged her again, wished her good luck in Paris, and headed off.

She had a tingle going through her, which she hadn’t had for a very long time. So long, in fact, that she couldn’t remember the last time. Mandy and Reggie each had on and off again boyfriends over the years, but nothing stuck. They were actually closer to each other than they ever had been with the men they’d known. But there was always a chance for that to change.

After she thought about it for a little while, she decided to call Rick Crawford. “Rick, I need a little code of conduct advice.”

"Aren't you the one who gives code of conduct advice? What about?"

Mandy said, "Yeah, I'm the one who gives it, but if I need it myself, I can't very well ask myself, can I? So here goes: If I were to become involved with one of the company's large shareholders, would that be a conflict of interest?"

"Involved how? You mean romantically?"

Mandy said yes. Rick smiled and said, "Well, well... Mandy Doucette. I think we could give the stamp of approval for that. After all, it's a public company, and shareholders don't pose a problem. He's not in management too, is he?"

"No."

"Not a board member?"

"Nope."

"Would you mind telling me who this is?"

"His name's Patrick Carney. He claims that his family founded the company."

Rick said, "The author?"

"Yes. You know him?"

"I don't know him, but I know of him. He's a best-selling author, isn't he?"

Mandy said, "I guess so."

"Sounds to me like you haven't been doing your due diligence. He writes historical fiction, and he's pretty good. And yes, his family was LaSalle's founding family. How did this happen?"

"He called me out of the blue. We'd kayaked together in a group some time ago, and all of a sudden, there he was."

"Well, there's no conflict-of-interest problem with him, so don't worry about that. I guess you don't need my investment banker friends after all."

Rick pulled out his cell phone and pulled up Patrick Carney, then brought up his website, which carried a picture of him.

Rick said, "Don't let that guy get away."

And in a later call with Reggie, Mandy kept up her confessions, saying, "By the way, there may be a guy coming into the picture. We went kayaking. He's pretty good looking and friendly. I'll see if he continues talking to me. I'm not trying to discourage him you'll be happy to know."

"Can you send me a picture of him?"

"Reggie, I'm not out there taking his photo. But actually, he has a website that you can see his photo. Hold on a sec."

She switched over to her text message and texted Patrick's website address to her.

"OK, I just texted his website. Pull it up."

She was quiet for a couple minutes.

"Mandy! Are you serious? This guy's a popular author! And he's gorgeous."

"I hear. I haven't read any of his books. OK, that's enough for now. I gotta get some sleep. Good night." Mandy made a mental note to pick up a Patrick Carney novel next time she was at the airport.

Mandy had been unattached for quite a while and was no fan of work-related relationships. Even the notion of getting close to someone at work was a nonstarter. She'd had some close friends at Justice from her earlier days, but nothing had survived her return to Chicago. As she had warned Reggie, she couldn't have pursued those anyway. Since she wasn't the bar type, it could very likely only be running or some other activity (like kayaking) where she might strike up a meeting. Mandy hadn't really been ready to tell Reggie about Patrick Carney, but she knew she couldn't keep this kind of thing from her sister. It struck her oddly that everyone close to her seemed to be interested in her love life.

Later yet she decided to call Steve Baker for some help.

Mandy said to Steve when he picked up, "Steve, I'm sorry to bother you on your weekend, but I need some help."

"No problem, Mandy. What's up?"

"Ever since I've been involved in the Allzient deal, some scary things have been happening to me, and I think they may be connected to Allzient, but can't be sure. I'm wondering if you can check some things out for me."

"Tell me what the things are and we'll see."

Mandy said, "First, when I started getting into the acquisition I got a picture of my parents' home in Wilmette with the words 'Back Off' on it. Then, I was in a kayak in the river and a speedboat intentionally did a near miss on me."

Steve said, "Where's your parents' house in Wilmette?"

"It's right across from the Bahá'í Temple."

"OK, that's good. I can see if they have surveillance cameras and anything that would cover the spot. Please text me a picture of the photo you received. And when it was taken, if you have that. And where were you on the river when the speedboat thing happened?"

She told him and he asked about the date and time, and she told him.

"Let me see what I can do on these then."

CHAPTER 8

ON FRIDAY MORNING, a man walking his dog through the Watchung Reservation in New Jersey just off I-78 had difficulty getting his dog out of the woods along the trail. He followed the dog off the trail to find him digging at a bag lying on the ground under a pile of dirt and leaves. The dog pulled on the bag until the man was able to see that a pair of legs wrapped in a blanket were sticking out, clothed and with shoes. He called 911 on his cell phone, and two deputy sheriffs from Union County showed up after fifteen minutes and took over from there. The body was that of a middle-aged man, and showed no visible signs of trauma. There was no identification, but the blanket that wrapped the body showed the name of a New York City hotel. The deputies concluded that the body was transported across state lines and dumped at the site. They called in the FBI, which took jurisdiction and called for a forensic pathology team from Quantico.

The team included Dr. Regina Doucette. After the site was checked by a crime scene crew, Reggie had some thoughts. "How far is this from the forest preserve road?"

The deputy sheriff said, "Less than a hundred yards."

"So why would someone go to all the trouble to drive a body from New York across state lines and then do a shitty job of hiding the body?"

"Whoever did it might have gotten spooked and did something half-assed just to get out of there, or the guy might have just been an amateur."

Looking at the body in a cursory way, Reggie noticed an injection site on the neck, with some bruising. With no other visible signs of trauma, she was thinking poison. Maybe like the two stiffs buried in Pennsylvania, except their burial was done in a better way.

Before the body was transported to Quantico for analysis, photos of the body were taken, and agents began to try to connect them to missing persons reports. This led them to the NYPD report which had been filed for the Allzient corporate security director Erik Spenser, who had been reported missing by Allzient.

The Bureau quickly matched the photo of Spenser that Allzient had provided to the body and paid a visit to the Allzient office on the following Monday morning. Once the interviews at Allzient headquarters in New York had uncovered the involvement of Spenser with the company investigation of a whistleblower's complaint, the Bureau made the natural leap to the death having to do with the bribery matter, and pulled in the Department of Justice—specifically the Foreign Corrupt Practices Act unit. The Justice Department had already made the connection and inserted itself into the internal bribery investigation and learned of the role of the recently murdered James Whitney. Things were coming together.

Sunday morning provided clear running surfaces and a sunny, mid-fifties temperature for a sixteen-mile run. Coming out of her apartment, Mandy passed a black SUV idling near her building with blacked-out windows. She thought nothing of it, and headed out toward her usual route, which headed north along the lakeshore in Lincoln Park to Hollywood Avenue, then back south and a long stretch to 57th Street at the University of Chicago. It was a relief to work off the anxiety and to begin to get into her race mindset. A half-dozen of the running group had shown up to run.

Mandy called Reggie while they started running, lagging behind the group so her phone conversation wouldn't bother anyone.

"By the way," Mandy said, "you never finished telling me about the promising Dan from your lab. I need to hear about that."

"Yeah, I'm thinking of having you meet him in Chicago. He's the one coming to the office when I'm there for Easter."

"Whoa! That's a big move, introducing a guy to the twin sister. Does he know it's a test?"

"He doesn't even know there's a twin sister, much less anything about a test."

"Nice. We'll have to decide what to wear." She laughed for a few strides. That was a standard joke between them, since they always dressed alike when they were together. Dressing alike was a lifelong practice for them and provided them with a strong unified front, no matter what the occasion. When one of the sisters went clothes shopping, each of them bought two of everything selected.

They changed subjects and discussed the Paris Marathon route. The start was along the Champs Élysées near the Arc de Triomphe, down the Rue de Rivoli past the Tuileries and the Louvre, continuing to the Bois de Vincennes, a large park on the east side of Paris. Then west along the Seine, passing Notre Dame, the Musée d'Orsay, and the Eiffel Tower, through the Bois de Boulogne and finishing on Avenue Foch on the other side of the Arc.

"The good thing about this route, besides all of those sites, is that it's completely flat, just like Chicago. Especially no climbing the hill to Montmartre," Reggie said.

"There's nothing like a marathon to focus your mind, forcing out all other thoughts," Mandy said. Just then she felt herself be violently pulled back from behind and she and another runner fell onto the grass next to the path while a black SUV roared past them on an internal road in Jackson Park. There was also nothing like doing a long training run while on the phone to your sister and not realize a car was bearing down on you.

Down on the ground with the other runner and stunned by the near miss of the SUV, the other runner apologized to her.

"I'm sorry, but you were just about to get run over. That car was going full speed and you would have been flattened. Maybe me too. He was only inches away."

Mandy said, "God, you saved my life. Thank you."

Mandy could hear her sister's voice screaming out of her cell phone on the ground and she picked it up and breathlessly explained what had just happened.

Reggie said, "Was it intentional?"

"It had to be. This is just a little internal park road. That car had to be going over fifty. I think he was trying to run me over."

"Did you get a license plate number?"

Neither of them had seen the plate number, and the other runner was calling 911 to report what had happened. The SUV had roared off and was nowhere to be seen. Chicago police soon arrived on the scene and took reports, but nothing followed from the incident. The police noted that this was a section of the park where no surveillance cameras were located. No other witnesses were involved, and Mandy just had to let it go.

Their run was done by midmorning and Mandy returned, stretched, and showered. She was still shaken by what had happened, so she slept a while, read her book *The Girl with the Dragon Tattoo* by the Swedish author Stieg Larsson, and watched *Saturday Night Live* that night. Sunday was a recovery day with a lot of reading and some gazing out her windows at the Chicago skyline, except for the shopping spree she had on Michigan Avenue. She picked up three outfits, of course buying two of each.

On Monday morning, Mandy had a visit from Rick with news from the CEO.

"Jim Kerwin and Ed had a call with the chairman, David Renfrow, who questioned whether we could proceed with due diligence. Jim told him we wanted to hang in there because we'd spent a lot of time and money on this so far and it was worth the wait."

"That should keep Wretched Witch happy," Mandy said.

"But get this—the chairman had also spoken to Harold Menzies. He's the big sponsor of this acquisition. Menzies had called him to see how the deal was going and when he found out about the hiccup, he urged that we stick this out. He argued it would either blow over or it would leave us with a salvage opportunity."

Mandy said, "And that's Wretched Witch's handiwork. No question. Indirectly from Emily, delivered through her boyfriend."

Rick said, "Boyfriend?"

"I've already told you Harold Menzies and Emily Jenkins are canoodling together. I'm sure of it."

"OK, so you're the code of conduct guru, so what would that amount to under our code?"

Mandy said, "Well, we don't regulate romance, so I am not about to start an anti-fraternization culture like the FBI has. But on the other hand, looking at it as a conflict of interest, I can get to a problem through that avenue."

Harold Menzies was one of the more respected and outspoken board members in matters of strategic opportunities, even though he had not been with the board all that long. In fact, when the strategic plan had been presented and a list of acquisition candidates had been reviewed, Allzient was not present among the list. It actually had been Menzies who'd raised the name and gotten it onto the candidate list. Emily Jenkins had gotten behind the Allzient idea and been a crusader for the deal.

Mandy said, "Nobody wants a surprise to turn into a self-inflicted wound, do they? If this deal gets done and we all regret it because of this hot mess blowing up big-time, who's going to pay the price? Wretched Witch? I don't think so. She'll already be moving on to the next shiny object. Harold Menzies? He's retiring soon anyway, right? He won't be around to get blamed. Only we will be here with our hands in our pockets."

Rick said, "I can't imagine Harold Menzies being manipulated by Emily Jenkins. Is that what you're suggesting? Or maybe it's the other way around? Or why isn't it simply Menzies not wanting one of his brainy ideas getting scuttled?"

Mandy said, "Fine, if you don't want to believe me, but I'm telling you that something is not right here. I can smell it. What does Kerwin think?"

"He wants to send an update message to all of the board members and offer to have a conference call if any directors see the need. Otherwise, we can hold off on addressing this until the upcoming board meeting. Kerwin also got Emily's point of view, and you can guess what that was, right?"

"Sure. Charge ahead," Mandy said.

Rick said, "Yeah, and push us into the shooting gallery. She's definitely got her knives out. But I do know that Jim is pissed at Emily for having something going with Harold Menzies."

"Does he want to do something about it?"

Rick said, "He wants us to get to the bottom of it."

"You mean he wants us to be aggressive?"

"I think so. He feels duped by her going around him to a director."

Mandy said, "Let me push Emily up to the top of my due diligence list. By the way, I think someone tried to run me over on my run last weekend."

Rick stood there looking at her with his mouth open.

"Don't look at me in that tone of voice," she said.

Rick said, "Are you saying someone tried to kill you?"

"Yup. Had a witness, called the cops. The whole drill."

"Do you want some protection? I can ask Ed about it."

"I think I'll be OK. I can't really say it was intentional. I'm just going to be super-vigilant from now on."

"Then I'm not going to take up running."

Rick took off and Mandy looked up Allzient on her computer and was able to see the development of its different businesses over the past dozen years. It had been fairly acquisitive, and had been willing to invest in basic science. Its lucrative work in electric batteries, for instance, was impressive and had, in fact, led to its appeal to LaSalle in the first place. With the apparent success of Tesla, it was clear that next-generation batteries would be necessary to be competitive. Allzient's investigation into fusion energy was promising as well, since nuclear reactors would have to make the switch to a cleaner nuclear fuel. Artificial intelligence was also one of its research projects, which sounded like defense industry in capital letters. The early history of Allzient also disclosed its acquisition of an American company named Spruance Corporation that she had seen in her earlier look at the company. Mandy started to look at Spruance, which turned out to have been public, unlike Allzient. Allzient's shares were held privately, so it had no exposure to U.S.

securities laws. She also looked at the Spruance and Allzient senior management teams and boards of directors. Spruance had been an Evanston, Illinois-based company. Given her Northwestern University period in Evanston during undergrad, she was vaguely familiar with that company. Mandy's father's company was also headquartered in Evanston. Maybe he even knew some Spruance people. She spent two days tracking down both companies' histories, including senior executives.

It was now near the end of the week and time to prepare mentally for the eighteen-mile run on Saturday. This weekend also happened to be Easter weekend, so a visit to Wilmette for Easter dinner was on tap. It had been weeks since the last visitation to the rambling home on Linden Street, and she looked forward to seeing everyone, especially Reggie.

Sunday morning Mandy headed to Wilmette on the L—the city's elevated train line. Walking into the family home, Mandy met and hugged Reggie, then the rest of the family. Mandy occasionally felt her repressed tension from her near miss with the SUV coming to the surface to mess with her. This hit her now, probably as a sense that it was OK to have a weak moment in the company of her family. They all piled into cars and headed to St. Joseph's Catholic Church on Lake Avenue for Easter Mass. There was no avoiding church with Mom and Dad. The sisters wore matching white and pink print dresses and were feeling pretty good about it.

Of the original ten children, only six were in attendance. One older brother Tom, and two older sisters Mary and Lacy, were married and living in New York and Los Angeles, respectively, with families of their own.

One of the younger brothers Frank, was off on a trip to London. The rest were scattered around Chicagoland, so it was easy for all to attend.

Dinner was the usual extravaganza by their mother, with traditional ham and turkey, followed by the Easter lamb cake with coconut frosting. When they were growing up, the business of eating was on a shift basis, since twelve people were hard to accommodate and everyone seemed to have different activities. A visit to the Doucette household by a friend was a dizzying affair, with the kitchen in near-perpetual motion at all times. Even the word "meal" was a misnomer in that household. There was constant food preparation and consumption taking place, as had to be the case with that many people. Only for holidays like Easter and Christmas were they all in one room and seated at one table. But with ten kids and two adults, it meant that no single addition to that number at the table would be possible; that meant it would come to thirteen, and having thirteen at a single table was a foundational Grandma Francesca superstition. Over, or under, but no exact thirteen at the table. On the Fourth of July, the whole family would go over to Gillson Park and commandeer a lawn space for the fireworks display.

Mandy and Reggie had to visit their room, which they'd shared with each other and no one else. This was part of the special treatment they'd received growing up and for which they'd been resented by the rest of the siblings. From that room, the twins had operated as therapists, moderators, negotiators, enforcers, and general intermediaries between family members. The room was preserved as if it were still their place of residence.

Bob Doucette had done pretty well financially and was able to provide good quarters for the large brood. Their room hadn't changed much, festooned with the detritus of youth on the North Shore, including a large montage of all of their pictures together, their sports awards and trophies, especially track, and their large collection of sea glass picked from the sand at Gillson Beach over the course of many summers. The impressive butterfly collection Reggie had assembled over the years was on the walls. Also on the walls was an ongoing genealogy chart that Mandy and Reggie collaborated on. This room always revived them when they needed it.

"Remind you of anything?" Reggie asked.

"I'm getting a clear memory of big brother Tom standing in here telling us we were an anchor for the rest of them."

"Yeah. I'm remembering the senior guys threading the toilet paper through our trees in junior year. Who was that guy who had a thing for you? Or was it me?" Reggie said.

"That was Tim somebody. I think he got a law degree too. And I think it was you he had the thing for. You were the one that was nice to him."

Their youngest sister, Prudence, poked her head in the door and said, "Dad said the Red Deuce has to come down for dinner. What are you guys doing up here?" she said.

"Talking about all the crap you got away with as the baby," Mandy said.

"Says you, with your special room all to yourselves."

"Still sore about that are you?" Reggie asked.

"Yup. Are you holding court up here?"

"Maybe. Do you have something to confess or need some therapy?" Mandy said.

She gave them the finger and disappeared downstairs. They followed her and joined in for Easter dinner. Afterward there were games being played, TV being watched, and a lot of helping their mother with cleanup.

After a while catching up with the others and phone calls to those who hadn't come, Mandy corralled Dad on the porch and described what she was working on. When she got to the part involving Spruance Corporation, he perked up and mentioned John Booth. "I remember him. General counsel of Spruance, and a good guy. Down in Sarasota now, if I recall correctly." He never tired of dipping in a toe with Mandy and the general counsel world to get a rush from the old days of constant problem-solving and combat. He was just happy it was her now, and not him.

"Wasn't Booth one of the lawyers in your North Shore General Counsels group?" her mom said to Bob.

"That was a group of local general counsels Dad met with periodically," her mom said as an aside to Mandy.

He nodded, saying that Booth and he had been pretty friendly, and had stayed in touch as Booth had gone to another company for a while, before he retired and relocated with his wife to the Gulf Coast of Florida.

"I might want to speak to him, Dad. Do you have any contact info for him? Maybe you could let him know I'd like to speak with him?" Mandy said. Bob nodded and said he had an email address for him.

He said, "Gabby, can you look in the desk drawer there for my directory?"

She dug around in the desk drawer in the office and

came out with the book. Bob wrote a note with Booth's email address scrawled on it.

"Tell me, are you girls sporting any...."

"No, Dad," they said in unison, cutting him off to avoid the nag. The relationships topic had a prominent *NO TRESPASSING* sign posted prominently on it for their family to see, but that didn't stop the occasional pop-quiz type question from being lobbed. They just had to be careful not to let anybody into that discussion.

By the time they left, the sun had long set.

Bob said he was taking Grandma back to Evanston and if they wanted, he could drive the sisters downtown rather than them having to take the train. They said their goodbyes and hopped in his car.

Once in the car, Mandy said, "Grandma, you have to shed some light on a couple of things for us so we can complete our chart."

Grandma Betty said, "What chart is that, sweetheart?"

Reggie said, "It's the chart we've been working on with all of the family genealogy."

Grandma waved her hand up in the air and said, "Oh phwing! Who cares about that ancient history?"

Bob said, "Ma, they're interested. So are the rest of the kids. So just hear them out."

"Fine. What do you want to know?"

Mandy said, "So what was great-great grandpa? A lumberman or did he own a hotel?"

Grandma Betty said, "Both, of course. After he paddled his way to the western shore of Lake Superior and portaged out west, he built a small stopping house on Otter Tail Lake, Minnesota. That's what they called hotels those days in the wilderness. Then the Chippewas raided it and burned it down. He got out alive and high-tailed it to Fort Ripley down the Mississippi for protection. He became a lumberman then and that was it for him. He just stayed there and lived out his life in Little Falls on the Mississippi River. Why are you so interested in this?"

Reggie said, "The first reason is that we're going up to Duluth this summer to run Grandma's Marathon and we'll be right where he dragged his birch bark canoe out of Lake Superior to go west. We're just trying to fill in all of the blanks."

Mandy said, "The second reason is that we're trying to understand what our ancestors were like and maybe help explain why we are the way we are."

Grandma Betty said, "How can that tell you why you are...whatever you said?"

Reggie said, "The more we can put together, the better chance of reaching an explanation, even if we don't exactly have a cogent question. Maybe it has to do with understanding how everybody is, and take it from there. Take, for instance, if a person was very adventurous and wanted to know if there was a family member in their genealogy that would be the source of it? That would be nice to know."

Grandma said, "You're talking about yourselves, then. OK, I get it. Well, I hope that helps. Now can you get me back upstairs?"

On her way up the elevator, Grandma Betty said, "Cogent. That's a good word."

The sisters took Grandma upstairs and delivered her back in the care of the home. The Clark House was a stately brick building for the elderly in the heart of Evanston that provided excellent care, if you could afford it. Bob could afford it. Back in the car on the way downtown, Bob said, "You know, Phwing probably has a lot of info squirreled away somewhere in there. Maybe someday you'll be able to get your hands on it."

He dropped them off downtown and headed back to Wilmette, and they returned to the apartment.

Mandy said, "I forgot to mention to you that Rick invited us to the Cubs' home opener next week. He's got the company's four seats. Do you think you could make it while you're still in town?" Reggie looked at her and raised her eyebrows. "Of course, that would be fun. Do you think I could invite Dan?"

"I'll find out. Meanwhile, what's going on with your double murder case?"

"I already told you cause of death is still unknown, technically, but you already know I think it's poison. At least we know they were formerly with Allzient. I've got multiple tissue studies going on and suspect some type of poison. But this other thing is that I don't think they're locals. The dental work looks like Eastern European, maybe even Russian," Reggie said. "And now I've got Erik Spenser, your missing Allzient security director, freshly murdered. It's possibly all connected."

"Russian murder victims buried in Pennsylvania. Both former Allzient. That's interesting. And Spenser was found in northern New Jersey. Those three buried bodies and the dead whistleblower, that's four murders so far. Hmm."

Reggie said, "I noticed that you didn't share with Mom and Dad your near miss with the SUV on your run. Are you keeping that from them for a reason?"

"I'm just not sure what happened there. I have a

feeling about it that it wasn't an accident, but I don't want to spook them by saying anything unless I'm sure."

"We better be very careful. If someone's after you, it could be that's not the last you'll see of it. Come on, you've had the scary photo, the speedboat, and now an SUV. Can't you see this pattern?"

"Yes, I've got your organization working on it."

"Oh."

Starting Monday morning, Mandy began the process of hunting down former Spruance executives through old SEC filings from those final years before it was bought by Allzient. She confined her efforts to the CEO William Blount and the president, CFO, and some senior vice presidents. She quickly saw that Blount had passed away, as had the president, and had little luck with any of the others. She asked a paralegal to try to track down those few, and then she prepared to reach out directly to John Booth. She typed an email to him introducing herself as Robert Doucette's daughter and describing her position in the LaSalle law department. She said that she hoped by now he may have received a message from her father, asking for his help. Without going into too much detail, Mandy explained that she was dealing with the company that had acquired Spruance, and that he may have some history that would help her. That done, she asked if he could spare her some time for a visit, to discuss the history Spruance had before Allzient.

By Monday afternoon, Booth had replied to her email and said he'd be happy to spend some time with her.

"Bingo!" Mandy said after getting his email.

They agreed on a Thursday afternoon visit, which allowed Mandy to avoid an overnight trip and to get back the same day.

In the afternoon, Mandy had a call with Steve Baker.

"Mandy, I've got some results in on the two threats you had. We were able to get a look at the Bahá'í' Temple's security cameras and we located someone we can't identify, but can see how he was dressed. He was taking a photo of your parents' house, but then he moved out of the picture quickly. Then we were able to locate some security cameras around the river and saw the speedboat incident as you described it. We got the name off the boat but we can't locate it or identify it, but did notice that it looked like the same guy from the photo in Wilmette. We can't see the face, but it looks like the same hoodie."

"What do you make of it?"

"Well, just a minute. I also went back and checked the video from the Union Station waiting room and see that the guy switching the water bottles with James Whitney looks like the same guy as in these others."

He continued, "All I can say right now is that it all looks connected, and you should be very careful. I'm going to report this to Stewart Simons in case it has anything to do with the Allzient case. Let me know if anything else happens."

"Thanks, Steve."

CHAPTER 9

THURSDAY MORNING started early for Mandy as usual, but instead of a run, she was off to O'Hare. Reggie hugged her, and Mandy hopped in a waiting car as Reggie ran up to the lake. The flight to Sarasota was uneventful, and the cab ride to Booth's home on Siesta Key was a twenty-minute ride. Booth lived in a house set inland on the key. Mandy wondered why he would not have a beachfront location if he were going to come all this way. When she knocked on the door, his wife let her into the home that opened onto an open-air room on the backside with a private dock and a boat. *That explained why,* she thought. The wife was a cheerful woman wearing a very-Florida Lilly Pulitzer outfit with sandals. John Booth invited her to sit, and they drank iced tea. Iced tea was still a long way off in Chicago, she told him.

"Yeah, but it's almost Cubs' season," he said. John was in white shorts, a Ralph Lauren Polo shirt, and boat shoes. He looked like he was ready to jump in the boat.

"Well, in fact," Mandy told him, "I happen to be going to Wrigley next week for opening day." They talked Cubs-Sox stuff a little, and he asked her if she'd like to get in some boat time for their talk. She took her bag and climbed aboard, and Mrs. Booth cast them off. John piloted the boat out of the serpentine canal system that served the island. They found their way out onto Roberts Bay and began a long, slow meander down the coast, pointing out some porpoises and gators along the way. He said it was too warm for manatees now, and that a cold snap was needed to lure them in.

Booth did some tour guiding for a bit, and finally turned to her and said that he missed having the regular contact with her dad. Of course, he said, at least Bob had grabbed the brass ring and become a CEO, leaving the practice of corporate law behind him.

"Of course, my main time with your dad was when he was in the law business, and we had lots of contact back then. Our group of general counsels helped each other a lot. I think we all got a lot out of that, whether it was having contacts or understanding how others were handling the issues that came up."

In fact, he laughed, "I recall one meeting in a restaurant that your dad's staff had set up. It had been his turn to host a meeting. When he got to the restaurant, he realized they hadn't reserved the meeting room like they were supposed to do, and someone else had it. Your dad instantly had the manager pull all the potted palms throughout the restaurant and make a plant wall, sealing off one end of the dining room—voilà!—an instant meeting room. It was a very elegant solution. If you have that same inventiveness and initiative as your dad, you'll go far."

Mandy said, "That sounds like my dad. With ten kids to manage, he was always dealing with the unexpected. I think I've learned a lot about thinking outside the box from him."

"Well, let's see if I can help you out here. Tell me what's going on, and what you need from me."

They were just barely moving south down Little Sarasota Bay and heading toward Venice, with the pilot describing the near miss the area had when Hurricane Charlie passed through just to the north five years before. Booth pulled out a tray of sandwiches his wife had stowed in the boat galley and poured some iced tea. They nibbled as he steered and Mandy talked. She went over the company history and strategy briefly, and then she started in on Allzient and why it was attractive to LaSalle. Booth interjected that he was very familiar with LaSalle as one of the original companies from Chicago and knew that years ago it had competed with John Deere and International Harvester. He hadn't followed its latest evolution, but knew that it had morphed from old-line agricultural equipment maker into diversified transportation and energy equipment. She started in on the energy equipment and the battery technology, and explained that Allzient has been appealing for that reason.

Mandy knew that there was a thread there back in the Spruance organization, and was curious about the history with Allzient.

She said, "Confidentially, we were just starting to do the post-announcement due diligence on this. No sooner did we make the acquisition announcement than Allzient got hit with a whistleblower letter over bribery. I'm really trying to dig into Allzient's history and find out what I can about that side of things. I would appreciate anything you could add about Spruance and Allzient."

Booth said, "Ouch. That's a nasty surprise to get. Well, Spruance's connection with Allzient was really the brainchild of one of our directors, a guy by the name of Armand Moines. I think he single-handedly engineered that deal happening. An interesting guy, to say the least. Years earlier he'd also gotten us connected to the CIA in a strange episode."

Mandy said, "That sounds interesting. Tell me about the CIA thing first, if you don't mind."

Booth said, "Sure. One morning in late 1999, our CEO Bill Blount was anxiety-ridden over the mounting paranoia about Y2K. I'm sure I don't have to explain that to you, and by now it's widely regarded as a baseless fear. But back then it caused a lot of people to obsess over the *what-ifs*. Meanwhile, into that hectic day an unannounced visitor shows up, referred to us by one of the Spruance directors, Armand Moines."

Booth explained that Armand Moines was a board member of some three years' service who had wide contacts and international experience. Obviously, he had more extensive experience than Blount knew about.

"The visitor's name was Philip Ray, as I recall. He produced a business card introducing himself as a CIA employee, and was there to ask for our help in giving jobs to ex-CIA agents. It wasn't every day a CIA agent wandered in, so we heard him out and promised to make introductions for him to let him explore opportunities in European operations. He played the national security card with us, and I guess we felt we couldn't act like we had no interest in helping the government. Nor could we rebuff someone one of our directors sent to us for help."

Mandy said, "That's wild. What was it like having the conversation with the CIA guy?"

Booth said, "I can practically remember exactly how the discussion went."

He then related the conversation as best he could.

Bill Blount said, "I couldn't imagine what interest the CIA could have in a visit with us, so thank you for making that clear right up-front."

Philip Ray said, "Of course. Everyone's surprised, I can assure you. But we hope you will hear me out on this, because the government really considers this as a matter of national security. We've been in the process for some years of bringing out our human assets from the former Soviet republics and wished to place them in continuing employment in private industry. I'm not at liberty to give much detail on the subject beyond that, but if you have a willingness to participate, we would love to give you more information."

Blount thanked Philip Ray for coming in and explained that he needed to join a conference call with the Spruance management team over the Y2K problem and offered to let John Booth continue the discussion. They shook hands and Blount left his office, with Booth remaining with Philip Ray.

Booth said, "Putting people into the organization would really be a human resources topic, working with our local business management teams. I would be happy to get the right people to have the kind of discussion you need and you can take it from there."

Ray said, "Yes, I understand that. The Agency would

appreciate anything you could do to help with this. I myself don't know the backgrounds of the individuals, but if there's a next step to be taken here, I will arrange for it and hope there is some opportunity. All we ask is that this connection with the Agency be kept to your knowledge only, for the protection of the people."

"Right. I'm not in a position to deal with the specifics either. Placements within Spruance are dependent on the skill sets, and what needs we have for different operations. So let me check with the right people here and I'll be happy to get back in touch with you and put you in direct contact."

Booth then said, "After Ray left and Blount finished his Y2K meeting, we discussed the idea and called Armand Moines to get his take. Moines explained that he'd had involvement with the Agency in the past, and thought we owed it a hearing if for no other reason than to show good corporate citizenship. Moines vouched for Philip Ray, but encouraged a contact with Langley if that seemed in order."

Mandy asked, "Did you go along with that?"

"Yeah, I guess we did go along with it. Blount dropped the matter in my lap and asked me to work through human resources to see if any open positions in European operations were a good fit, and they left it at that. I took the next steps and it led to potential spots being identified. They made a decision not to identify the background of the CIA contact with this issue, as Philip Ray had requested. If anyone was to know about backgrounds, it would be left to Philip Ray to develop resumes for the prospects."

Little did John Booth know that he had just opened the door to a trail of violence and intrigue that would leave its imprint a decade later.

Mandy said, “What happened after that?”

“I think we eventually hired some of his people into various spots in Spruance’s European operations in mid-level posts in manufacturing. Beyond the two of us, no one was any the wiser about the CIA connection.”

Mandy interrupted, “You’re saying you found positions for spies in your company?”

Booth said, “Ex-spies, technically, but yeah, I guess you could say that. When you say it that way, it does sound incredibly stupid.”

Mandy said, “And wouldn’t your defense department business have made it dicey for you to be hiring spies?”

“Well, I guess it never struck me that way, since it was the government that came to us and requested it in the first place.”

He continued with his story. “Within six years, both of us were out of the organization. Bill retired and sadly died a couple years later. I left Spruance for a short stay with Northwest Engineering, until its family-connected lawyer was ready to take the general counsel position, and then I also retired and moved down here. But a few years after the visit by Philip Ray, we began to explore strategic partners, at the urging of the Board of Directors. As a matter of fact, as I recall, it was Armand Moines who had been the strongest advocate and even pointed us in the direction of Allzient. Corporate earnings and strategic plan implementation were not being realized and the board was impatient to return some value to shareholders through an increased stock price. Just before we left, Spruance was merged with Allzient. Had it not been for Moines, I doubt Spruance would have ever been acquired by Allzient.”

Mandy asked, "Why did the board want to sell?"

Booth said, "That was really near the end of our careers at Spruance, and Blount and I were trying to go out with a real victory for our shareholders. The board wanted to seek a partner to help us take our technology advantage to the next level. Back then we didn't have the people needed to really do that, as far as leveraging it for commercial value. So, we weren't looking to sell. We wanted to buy. That direction to be bought was really Armand Moines' influence—being acquired by Allzient, specifically."

Mandy said, "Did you have any knowledge of Allzient's ethics back then, or if there was anything shady about their practices?"

"Nothing that I can recall, but remember that we wouldn't have been looking for something like that. We were turning out to be the seller, not the buyer. If anything, it would have been the reverse, and we would have been put under the spotlight in due diligence by Allzient, as the buyer. Allzient was a private company taking over a public U.S. company."

Mandy asked, "Just out of curiosity, why would you want to do a short stint after Spruance and before retiring?"

"Well, I did it as a favor to a friend that was running Northwest, but after I was there for a while, I got some real sense that something wasn't right with their business practices, so once I started asking questions, the family owners replaced me. I don't know what happened with them after that."

Mandy said, "Doesn't leave you with a good feeling."

"Yeah, not the way I wanted to end a career."

By this time, Booth was heading back north. He asked Mandy when her return flight was leaving. When she told him, he suggested taking her up the coast and he could let her off right near the airport at the Ringling Museum dock. It was a short cab ride from there to the airport. She agreed and took a LaSalle annual report and proxy statement from her bag and put it on the deck. "As a former public company general counsel, I imagine you like seeing these disclosure docs for shareholders, so I thought I'd leave them with you."

He picked up the proxy statement and paged through it, stopping at the list of nominees for election. LaSalle, like many public companies these days, put photos of its directors in the proxy statement. Booth scanned them until he stopped at one photo in particular and stared at it for some time. "This guy looks very familiar, but I don't recognize the name—Harold Menzies. That Spruance director I mentioned, Armand Moines, who was very much the proponent of the Allzient deal, looked a lot like your Harold Menzies. I remember being surprised about Moines' level of interest in the Allzient deal. I mean it's one thing to support looking at a possible partner, but it gets a little befuddling when someone seems quasi-obsessed with it. Maybe it's just me, but I thought I detected some interest above the usual."

"Are you saying Menzies looks like Armand Moines, or that Menzies *is* really Moines?"

"I'm not sure. I would have to dig out a photo of Armand Moines to look at it. I shouldn't shoot from the hip," Booth said.

"Do you know who these CIA people were who got hired, and what they did or where they went?"

"I don't know about the people we hired," Booth said. "I'll go back and look for Moines' photo and give you a call when I can get it and compare it to this Menzies photo."

By this time Booth had reached the Ringling Museum dock. He let Mandy off after she connected with the cab company. She shook his hand, thanked him, and said she looked forward to hearing back from him. He wished her well and asked her to pass along his best to her dad.

Mandy got to the airport and after getting through security called Rick Crawford. "I've just finished talking with the former general counsel of Spruance Corporation, the company Allzient bought before we thought about buying them. There's something very curious about this. Before they sold out to Allzient, they were paid a visit by the CIA looking for help in placing some ex-agents."

"Oh, man," he said.

"And they apparently hired some of them. That means there could have been multiple intelligence agents placed into Spruance, which then got purchased by Allzient, and is now on the verge of being acquired by LaSalle. That makes this a security risk deal, and the Arthur Ross obsession may be coming to fruition."

Mandy kept going. "And there's something else curious about a director—one of ours. Do you know much about Harold Menzies? You know, Wretched Witch's boyfriend?"

"Not really, but I'm sure we can find out if we need to. Tell me what you need and why you need it. Poking around into directors can be dangerous business and requires going up to Rosen, if not Jim Kerwin. Maybe even the chairman. And if I were you, I wouldn't go around cavalierly referring to an officer as Wretched Witch, or to her as Harold Menzies' *boyfriend,*" he said.

"OK, I hear you. But maybe she shouldn't go around badmouthing the company's lawyers. And maybe Ed Rosen should do a better job of standing up for his lawyers. So, John Booth sees the picture of Harold Menzies from our proxy statement and says it looks a lot like Armand Moines, from the Spruance board."

Rick said, "Shit. Let's talk about this when you get in tomorrow."

Then she called Reggie and told her about the day.

"Do your FBI buddies have a way to find out CIA personnel stuff?"

"Ah, Mandy, what are you up to with the CIA?"

"If I told you, I'd have to kill you."

"Very funny. Never mind. I'll ask Dan. Do you want to tell me what you need first, or just find out if my 'buddies' have a way to find out?"

"Let's go with the latter, please. See you in about four hours." Mandy's own FBI connections from the engine sting matter could possibly help on the Moines and Menzies question, but she needed to think about how to approach that so that it didn't go somewhere she didn't want.

Mandy's flight back seemed to be half the time it took her to fly down. She was in deep furrowed-brow mode. When she got to O'Hare and turned her cell back on, she had an email from John Booth. "Found something. Call me tomorrow a.m. P.S., I'm an early bird." She also had a text from Reggie: "Dan has an in."

CHAPTER 10

ALL WAS WELL in the River North apartment, with Reggie sound asleep by the time Mandy walked in. A note on the counter read, *morning run?* Mandy turned in and set an alarm for 4:30 a.m., the usual wake-up time for a weekday run. Her mind was racing and when she finally dropped off, it would probably only give her five hours' sleep.

When the alarm went off, she dragged herself out of bed, threw on some running clothes, and found Reggie waiting with coffee for her. "Thank God."

They headed east to Michigan Avenue, then north on the usual route.

Mandy said, "I'm dying to find out what John Booth found in his digging through Spruance photos. This thing is spinning off in a direction I wasn't expecting."

"Would you like to hear the latest on my dead bodies?"

"Tell me."

"My friend Dan has come to the conclusion that the nerve agent that was used on them was most likely Novichok. And by the way, it appears to be the same stuff used on James Whitney."

"Holy shit. So now it's *friend* rather than just *colleague?"*

"Don't change the subject. Did hear me just say *nerve agent?"*

"Yeah, what about it? It's poison, right?"

"It's a nerve agent, meaning something that the KGB uses."

Mandy said, "OK. That's something to get excited about. Now back to the colleague?"

"Yeeeeesssss, it's that same Dan Aleri. And he's thirty-two and unattached."

"So, when are we meeting with Mr. Dan? Wait, did you just tell me we're in a mess involving the KGB?"

"Looks like it."

Mandy stopped to think about the newest puzzle piece. *So that adds a KGB-style assassination aspect to a company loaded with spies.*

"He suggested a drink tonight at 7:00 p.m. at the Signature Room. He wants to do the tourist thing and to see the night skyline."

"I'm in, as long as we make it short, because we have a twenty-miler tomorrow, as you recall. I suppose you don't want to hear my speech about fraternizing with colleagues again, right?" Mandy said.

"As you lawyers like to say: *Objection, your Honor—asked and answered,"* Reggie replied.

Reggie also said her FBI guys could get some spook

stuff, so she asked what Mandy needed. "I need to find a guy by the name of Philip Ray. But don't push the go button just yet."

On the way out the door, Reggie hit Mandy with a surprise.

"Did you say that car that almost ran you over last week was a black SUV?"

"Yeah, why?"

"Because when I ran yesterday, I noticed one idling about a block away from the apartment when I went to run. Then I saw another one in Lincoln Park."

"Was it the same one?"

"I don't know. I didn't exactly want to go taking down plate numbers. Let's just keep our eyes open. I'm pretty sure the driver knew I had spotted him, though. I made it a point to glare at him before I continued."

They kept their eyes open, but saw no suspicious black SUVs on their run.

When Mandy got into the office that morning, the first thing she did was to drag out the proxy statement and look at the photo of Harold Menzies. Then she called John Booth's number, remembering that he was an early bird. He answered on the second ring. "I hope you had a good flight back."

"I did, and I gather you had a successful look in your files?" Mandy said.

"Well, I did find some photos of the board members from trips we used to arrange, and although I didn't find many with Armand Moines, I did find a couple. I'm not particularly good with faces, but in looking at the proxy statement photo of your Mr. Menzies, I believe he's either a brother to Armand Moines or *is* Armand Moines. These photos may be ten years apart, so I think more work is needed on this. I've also dug out the contact info for our former human resources vice president, Beverly Barrow, and would be happy to pass that along if it would help. I can't find anything on the mysterious visitor Philip Ray that I told you about."

"Do you have a photo of Armand Moines that you could email to me please?"

"Let me do that right now. Hold on." He went offline and emailed her the photo. He came back on the call and she pulled up the photo.

Comparing the two photos, Mandy said, "I would be willing to wager that your Mr. Moines is our Mr. Menzies alright. If you can please send me the contact information you have for Ms. Barrow, I would appreciate it, and if you don't mind doing one more thing for me, please call Ms. Barrow to tell her I will be calling her. And thank you very much for this."

"Anything for Bob Doucette's daughter."

Mandy went to Rick's office as soon as he arrived, and asked him if he'd like the latest.

"Sure, but would you like to see my new tooth first?"

"Not necessary."

"You're not likely to get as good an offer as that for the rest of the day. Nobody better tempt me with any toffee again either."

"Don't look at me. I'm completely toffee-free. You don't happen to make a habit of this dental emergency thing, do you?" she said.

"That's confidential."

"Well, let me show you something about our Mr. Menzies, if you don't mind." She laid out the proxy statement next to the photo she had gotten from John Booth. "I give you Harold Menzies and Armand Moines. In my opinion, one and the same." He stared at them awhile and said, "Well shit."

Then she told him the Philip Ray CIA agent story. She had no more on that, except that Allzient could have some shady characters in their operations, based on what John Booth had told her. She told him it might be beyond her ability and resources to try to dig into this. "I do have somebody who can reach out to find out about Philip Ray. Do you want me to go there?"

"Oh, yeah."

Rick picked up the phone, called Ed Rosen, and asked if he could join them. Ed came in a few minutes later, with Rick motioning for him to close the door behind him. He did, and twenty or more pieces of paper taped to the back of the door fluttered. Ed said, "What the hell is this?" Both Rick and Mandy said, "Never mind," and he sat down. Rick pointed to Mandy, who regurgitated the whole previous day, ending with the two photos. Ed said, "Jesus! This can't be happening, whatever it is."

Rick wanted to tell Ed about the threats Mandy was getting, but he bit his lip because Mandy didn't want to reveal it right now.

Mandy said, "We need to think this out and figure out how to proceed. I think by Tuesday we need to come up with something and take it to Jim Kerwin."

Ed said, "Why not Monday?"

Rick said, "I think it has to be Tuesday. Monday afternoon we're all going to the Cubs home opener." Mandy stared at him. "Sorry, it's important," Rick said.

Ed shrugged his shoulders and said, "Tuesday, then," and got up and left.

Mandy said, "Speaking of the Cubs game, do you have the fourth ticket free? Since we're asking Reggie's colleague to help us with the FBI, it would be a nice gesture to take him to the game."

"I do. Consider it done."

It was a ten-block walk to the John Hancock building from their apartment, and they made it quickly in a forty-five-degree night, wearing matching black jean jackets and red outfits underneath. Along the way, Mandy updated Reggie.

"I got the go-ahead on Philip Ray, so you can sic your colleague on that. And Dan's invited to the Cubs home opener."

When they got to the ninety-fifth floor and the lights of the city in a 180-degree panorama hit them, they were slightly stunned, as usual. One could never quite get over this view, even if it was touristy. They found Dan sitting at a small table. When they walked up, he was the one stunned, and he struggled to get the next words out of his mouth. "I guess this is something you didn't tell me about, right? Which one of you is Reggie?"

Reggie raised her hand and said, "Dan, Mandy; Mandy, Dan Aleri. And you're right, I didn't tell you I had an identical twin sister. It's too much fun seeing people react like you did." They all sat down.

Mandy said, "Don't worry. A lot of people have that reaction."

"I mean, it's fine. I just wasn't prepared for it. And, frankly the two of you are stunning together." He looked around and said, "By the way, a lot of people are looking over here. I'm sure they're not looking at me."

Reggie said, "Yeah, we get that a lot."

"Let's have some wine. Lots of wine." He ordered two more glasses and said, "I hope white is OK?"

They drank wine for a while and had plates of tapas that served as dinner. They talked about families and backgrounds, the sisters' running, and Dan talked cycling. The sisters talked about the family growing up in Chicago and the family roots back in Minnesota, and before that Quebec. Dan filled them in on his family's New York and Italian connection. That pretty much finished off the evening. Before they headed out, Reggie said to Mandy, "You can thank Dan for agreeing to see if the Agency can shed any light on those names, by the way."

"Right. Thanks for the help, Dan. Oh, and you're invited to the Cubs home opener Monday afternoon."

"Thanks. Do they let Mets' fans in?"

"Sure, there's always the chance of a conversion experience. By the way, if you're visiting our apartment would you throw your hat on the bed?"

"Oh, God no!" he said. "That would be a ton of bad luck for whoever slept there. Is this some kind of a test?"

Mandy said, "Maybe. I think Gabby and Grandma would approve."

Reggie said, "I'll fill you in on the family's Italian superstitions later, but it sounds like you have already been indoctrinated."

Dan walked them back to their apartment and said

goodbye, looking a little awkward. Reggie raised her hand and said, "I'm Reggie."

"Right." And he wandered off to the Chicago Avenue Red Line stop to catch a train to his hotel. Dan made a mental note to himself that if he were going to get to first base with Reggie, he had to have the skill to identify her from her identical sister without Reggie having to raise her hand.

Mandy said, "I like him. But I hope he knows what has to happen before he can have a serious relationship with you."

Reggie said, "You mean your approval?"

"No, wise guy, I mean that anti-fraternization problem thingy."

"Right. Yes, you've said that."

"And I do approve of him."

CHAPTER 11

BEVERLY BARROW was a human resources director in a division of a paper company in Minneapolis, Minnesota. She had moved around some in the years following her service with Spruance Corporation. On Monday morning, April 2, Beverly's phone rang with a call from Mandy Doucette. Beverly acknowledged the message from John Booth, her old colleague at Spruance, about the call she was likely to get from Mandy, and said she was happy to help.

"John was always a pleasure to work with, and of course law and human resources always worked closely together, sometimes on things that we considered the underbelly of corporate America, in my opinion. If only human resources were just doing training and handing out bonuses, life would be wonderful. It's the disciplinary stuff and firings that make it ugly," she said.

"Tell me about it!" Mandy said. "And I agree with you. John's a pleasure. I found out that my father had known him in Chicago for years, so there are a lot of connections. I don't know if John mentioned what I was interested in talking to you about, but I'm hoping you can help me."

"He explained. What is it you need?" Beverly said.

"My company is in the midst of due diligence on an acquisition of Allzient. We're trying to track back through some hiring details that John thought you might remember, even though it's been ten years," Mandy said.

"Well, let's see how good my memory is. Fire away."

Mandy gave her the scant info she had, attributing it to a favor that had been asked by one of Spruance's directors Armand Moines, to take a look at some prospects in Europe for employment. These were people who Armand was trying to help.

"I remember that, because a request coming from a director through the general counsel was not normal. There were a half-dozen or so and they may have all been hired, but through the company's German or Polish subsidiaries, I think. Spruance was expanding those units at the time, as I recollect. I don't recall names, but might be able to contact some former associates and get them."

Mandy gave her contact information, thanked her, and said goodbye.

Mandy was dressed for a baseball game, since this was the season opener and she would be heading out soon with Rick to go to Wrigley Field. They were going to rendezvous with Reggie and Dan at the Ernie Banks statue outside the main gate. When they got there, they had to squeeze through the teeming Cubs fans trying to get in. Reggie and Dan were waiting at the statue, and introductions were made. Rick complimented the sisters on their matching outfits, and in they went to get their seats. The sisters had their hair up and stuffed under Cubs hats, with their matching red chili pepper earrings clearly visible. Mandy leaned in close to Reggie and said, "Did you get a Cubs hat for Dan?"

"Nah, he wouldn't wear it anyway, if I did. He's a Mets fan and by New York constitution hates the Cubs."

Dan looked over at them and said, "Nice earrings."

The spectacle of opening day took the normal three-plus hours, with the Cubs coming away with an unexpected win against the Nationals. No foul balls came their way, even though they were sitting in a target-rich foul ball area three rows above the Cubs dugout. Rick had predicted getting bonked by one. Their seats were in the sun and spotting any foul balls would be an exercise in looking up into the sun and trying to avoid getting hit. But his luck held and they were spared, though he did get doused by a spilled beer from someone trying to get a foul ball. None of the others were caught in the dousing. Mandy thought to herself, *Would this be a Crawford's World inspiration moment?* After the game, the four made it around the park and across Sheffield Avenue into Murphy's Bleachers for a beer. They found a spot and huddled with Coors Lights and talked over the day, waiting for the L crowd to diminish so they could get on a train without getting smushed. Everybody pulled out their cell phones to check messages.

Rick said, "By the way, my compliments on your matching red chili pepper earrings. Are those the good luck charms you were telling me about in Billy Goat's, Mandy?"

Mandy said, "You're being very observant, Rick. I like that. By the way, the human resources person from the old Spruance Corporation just sent me an email. The guy she thinks we need to find is named Erik Spenser. I didn't tell her we have him *in custody-ish*. Or to be precise, Reggie does." She looked at them and raised her eyebrows, saying "....and we're off." They finished their beers and headed for the L. Mandy, Reggie, and Dan got off at Chicago Avenue. Rick stayed on, still smelling like a brewery.

The three ate leftovers and sat around the kitchen table, with Mandy saying it was time to lay this all out and to see if there was anything that suggested any new steps, so she laid it all out for Reggie.

"First," she said, "we've got a whistleblower, now dead from a nerve agent.

"Next, we've got bribe payers and bribe payees. Still needing to work on that.

"Next, we've got a seller who knew about, but didn't disclose the corruption to us and let this blow up in both our faces. We now know it was their dead corporate security director that short-stopped the whistleblower letter from being disclosed.

"You found two buried stiffs that you're now saying were killed with a nerve agent. So maybe we have four people killed with the same stuff?

"We've got a CIA guy making a weird request to hire

ex-spies as a favor to Uncle Sam, but we don't know who, where, or how many. We don't know about the CIA guy either.

"We've got one board member at Spruance who was very interested in helping the CIA guy. Why? That same board member may have been very interested in Spruance selling out to Allzient. Why? We've got a LaSalle board member who was very interested in having LaSalle acquire Allzient. Why? That same board member is having a toss with a LaSalle officer. Zowie! I should know more about that soon."

Reggie interrupted her litany. "What do you mean you *should know more about that soon?*"

Mandy said, "I've got a private investigator shadowing her."

"What? Are you crazy? You're having one of your own senior officers investigated? Did someone approve you doing that?"

Mandy said, "Kinda. Let me continue." Reggie raised both her arms in surrender.

She continued, "Those two board members may be one and the same, using different names. We've got a LaSalle officer who wants to push to get this acquisition done before we've been able to figure all this out. Why? And she's the same officer entangled with the very interested director. Finally, we've got the itch to talk to the seller's customers to make sure they're calm, but we don't know who they are yet or whether the seller will let us talk to them."

"That's a lot of stuff," she said. "Did I leave anything out?"

Reggie said, "How about somebody tried to kill you with a boat, then an SUV, and I've seen SUVs lingering?"

"Oh, yeah. And I think I forgot to tell you that someone left a photo of our Wilmette house with a message to *BACK OFF!*"

Reggie said, "No way!"

Dan had sat through the review and took his opportunity to leave for the night, giving Reggie a kiss on the cheek as he was on the way out the door.

"Yeah," said Reggie to her sister when Dan was out the door. "I know. That was more than a *colleague* move."

"Sure was. At least he knew which one of us was you. Not sure how that would have gone over if I'd gotten the kiss."

Reggie said, "In the best tradition of the Doucette sisters, I would expect you to ward him off if he were going in for the target."

Mandy just shrugged her shoulders at Reggie.

After the run the next day, Reggie packed up and headed back to the airport to return to Quantico, on the lookout for black SUVs but seeing none.

After Reggie left, Mandy checked her phone and saw she had a text message from an unrecognizable phone number that said simply, "GET YOUR NOSE OUT OF BUSINESS THAT DOES NOT CONCERN YOU, OR ELSE!"

She immediately forwarded the text message to Steve Baker and asked him if he could add this to his list to look into.

CHAPTER 12

LOOKING OUT her apartment window on the Potomac River on an almost-spring day, Reggie said in her early call with her sister, "My assignment for the day, if I understand it correctly, is to ask Dan to see if there's anything that his CIA source can tell him about Philip Ray, Erik Spenser, or Armand Moines. You don't want anyone raising questions about your director Menzies. Have I got that right?"

"Yup."

In the FBI office in Quantico, Reggie asked Dan if he wanted to grab a cup of coffee, and they sat down in the cafeteria. Reggie asked Dan if he could send up a few names to his CIA contact and see what came back.

"What am I supposed to say the context is? You don't just ask about agency people without that," he said.

"I think you just tell them the names have come up in companies that are involved in a matter the FBI is handling," she said.

"Hmmm. OK, I'll do it, just because it's you, but don't be surprised if we get nothing back and there's some strong pushback just from asking the question. But if I do it, will you go out to dinner with me?"

"OK. Who's paying?"

Dan said, "That would be me."

"Is that a date?"

"Well, that might technically be against Bureau policy."

Reggie said, "Then what is it?"

"Let's call it an expression of gratitude."

"Well, if it's me being grateful, wouldn't I be the one doing the paying?"

"OK, let's call it a date. Just don't tell anyone in the office"

"OK."

Mandy and Rick paid a visit to the general counsel later that morning and briefed him on where everything stood. There wasn't much to report, since there hadn't been too much going on that they could see. It was possible Allzient was moving right along on the whistleblower issue with the Justice Department, but they currently had no window into that unless Mandy wanted to call Stewart Simons to try to get something out of him. That didn't sound like a good idea, based on what he'd told her. It sounded like he'd call her if he wanted our input, but not the other way around. Maybe it was time to learn more information. He knew that Emily Jenkins wanted to make contact with Allzient customers and to stroke them some, and Rosen said he was OK with that as long as it didn't complicate things.

Then she asked him about Harold Menzies. "We're not sure how he fits in. We also had this mystery man from Spruance from a long time ago who we're trying to look into, but that's not the same as looking into a current LaSalle director. What do you think?"

"How would you want to do it?" Rosen said.

"I'd like to have an expert look at the two photos we have of him and the other guy Moines, and get an opinion of whether it's the same guy. Looks like it to us. If I get support for that, then see what comes back from the look into Moines we're doing now. If he's got something interesting going on, then we put Menzies through the same screen."

"OK, but I'm going to mention this to Jim so he's not surprised."

"Don't do that. Let's just go with the *better to ask for forgiveness than for permission*. By the way, were you the one who recruited Menzies to the board?" Rick said.

"No, I think Harold's name came from Jim or from his predecessor, and it was because of some familiarity they had with each other from an industry group or a referral from another common friend. I know that his background in government contracts was considered his special appeal," Rosen said, then added, "And you guys are going to get me fired for keeping Jim in the dark."

Rick said, "We just think we shouldn't taint the process. Imagine the dumb shits we'd be if we told the fox about the hens we were bringing in?"

"Do you know if a search firm was used to vet him and to get his resume? Would that still be available if it was?" Mandy asked.

Ed didn't remember. It'd been too long.

He said, "You could look at the director's five-year history in the proxy statement every year, so if you go back to the start of his board membership, you can look to that proxy statement to see where that takes you. Anything farther back than that in time, and they'd need a report from a search firm. Be alert, though, to the possibility that Harold Menzies and Emily Jenkins seem to be very close. As the main proponent of the Allzient deal on the board, he seems to have bonded with Emily, the main proponent in management."

Mandy said, "I've been saying that all along. There's no *seem to* about it. I'm glad you've finally seen that too. I think both of them see this deal as their crowning achievement, so they may present a united front to stand in our way. It's worth pursuing. I think this is very important to know about."

"I'll keep that in mind, but I'm pretty sure Jim Kerwin would go ballistic if he knew one of his officers was consorting with one of his directors. Are you sure of that?"

"Almost."

"I don't want to hear more on that unless and until you get to *absolutely,* but I can assure you that Jim Kerwin wants to know what she's doing with Harold Menzies," he said.

"I'm going to find out."

Ed said, "You do that. Do whatever it takes."

Mandy had a twinkle in her eye.

Later that day, Ed got in to see Jim Kerwin to discuss Harold Menzies. He asked Kerwin if he could reconstruct the way that Harold Menzies' name had come up and what kind of checking was done on him.

"I would have left that to you to check, but I think I got his name from a list of directors who were referenced in some work on government experience, but it's a blur now. Might be that I met him at one of the meetings of the Chicago Council on Foreign Relations. Why are you asking this?"

"We're trying to put to bed questions that have come up since we started unraveling some of the oddities in the deal. This turns out to be one of them." Ed said.

"What kind of oddities? I don't like *oddities* involved with my directors."

"We are just seeing that there's too much alignment between he and Emily on this acquisition than we would expect to see between an officer and a director."

Jim said, "That's your word for it—*alignment*. I love that. Well, you know I've already gotten wind of that and am not happy about it. How can we get a high degree of confidence that it's happening?"

"You mean besides just flat out asking her? Or him?"

Jim said, "Yes, I'm not confronting either of them without more. This upcoming board meeting is his last. Maybe we let him ride off, then lower the boom on Emily. *She's not getting away with this.*"

"I've actually got Mandy working on just that."

Jim said, "Do whatever it takes."

At the Langley, Virginia, offices of the CIA, an aide asked if he could have a word with Sherman Haskins, the associate deputy director for counterintelligence. He was told to come to Haskins's office at 11:00 a.m. When he was shown in, he said, "Sir, we had a ping with the names Philip Ray, Erik Spenser, and Armand Moines being put through on a query in our system. The alert was tagged to contact you if those names popped up as being of interest."

Haskins, a balding, thin man of just over six feet and wearing tortoise-shell eyeglasses, said, "Talk to me."

"Well, they came up in a query from human resources management. Is this something to worry about, sir?" the aide asked.

"Get the trail back to how this started. When you have that and who in the Agency received the request, ask why the request was made. Tell them that no answer should go out to the requester. Let me know what you find."

The aide left, and Haskins thought through what might be going on. *The Philip Ray name of mine hadn't been active in years. The last time that name had any activity was when it received a callback from a Chicago lawyer agreeing to consider candidates for the exfiltration project. The handoff to their human resources people had taken place, and six or more individuals had been employed by the company. Some of those individuals employed had remained employed, others having moved around and been dealt with harshly. It might be time for more to go away, like he'd done with the other two who had moved. It was a very big problem if exfiltrated agents decided to free themselves from the world he had created for them. Would they then consider themselves liberated and able to unburden themselves of what they had been up to? If they did that, which they had been told not to do under any circumstances, did they think there wasn't going to be some consequences? For now, he was content with the remaining people he had in place within Allzient.*

The person known as Armand Moines had also dropped out of the picture once he had maneuvered his company to be acquired by a German company. He was now known as Harold Menzies. It may be time for him to have a discreet conversation with Harold Menzies about the need for him to move on. One certainty on Menzies, though, was that he couldn't be made to *go away* like the others — Menzies would have to be a survivor.

Later in the day the aide called him and reported that the pinged request had come to human resources management from an FBI pathologist working at the lab in Langley by the name of Dan Aleri. He had a cell phone number that he passed along. Haskins made a subsequent call to the head of human resources and was rough with him about his people searching the system at the request of outside people. FBI was very definitely outside people. He made another call and asked for a listing of all calls made by or to the cell phone number he'd been given. While he was waiting for this information, he called another number that was answered immediately: "This is Harold."

"We need to talk. Someone has eyes on you. They've dug up the old Moines name."

Harold said, "We just have to keep this together for a couple more weeks, then I vanish into Shanghai."

Rick paid Mandy a visit, and found her office strewn with papers in piles. She was at her work table.

"What's all this?" he said.

"This is the Allzient mess with its European customers. You told me to try to figure it out, so that's what I'm trying to do."

"What have you got so far?"

"I have it down to three Allzient customers in Europe with transactions involving electric vehicle fleets. There are contract documents and accounting records. I need to get someone from internal audit to help with unraveling the connections and understanding the accounting docs. What's up with you?"

"I started a few things, and now I have to figure out what to do next," he said.

"OK, let's compare notes."

She told him how she had reviewed things with Ed Rosen and he'd informed the CEO about Harold Menzies and Emily Jenkins, and he had authorized them looking into that however they needed to do it. She also explained the look into Armand Moines and the name of the mystery CIA guy, and to see if they could locate the people hired by Spruance. They also had the name of the guy hired by Spruance from Beverly Barrow—Erik Spenser—and knew he became the Allzient corporate security director. Mandy reminded him that she had an outstanding schedule to do code of conduct training sessions in Europe, and that if that schedule matched up in some way with what Emily Jenkins wanted to do with the Allzient accounts, maybe they could combine a trip and she could tag along. Recognizing that Allzient had to be approached before doing that, they decided to reach out and to start that process.

They called Bob Thereaux, LaSalle's outside counsel, and asked him to request approval of Allzient through their counsel, noting that nothing would be said about any questionable activities. LaSalle wanted to make contact with these customers, who in many cases LaSalle already had some relationship with, to assure them that any present transactions would be unaffected. He would get that going right away. Within the hour Theroux let them know Allzient had approved it, but wanted the details of the contacts made.

They then called Emily and let her know that they were cleared to have dialogue with Allzient accounts. Emily would be having those conversations, not the lawyers. She said she would put together a proposed itinerary and coordinate with Mandy.

Finally, they discussed the Moines issue. Rick asked, "If we could burden Reggie with another request for help, could we get help on identification? The FBI has facial recognition technology to compare the Moines and Menzies photos."

Mandy said, "Sure, let's call Reggie."

When Reggie answered, Mandy said, "Careful, I've got *Mr. Gold Crown* guy here."

Rick gave her the finger. She instantly reflected on getting shown the middle finger twice within two weeks now, once from her youngest sister and now from a colleague. Mandy knew Rick well enough to know he didn't mean anything by it. He actually enjoyed his own misadventures, ironically.

"OK, I'm all ears then."

Rick said, "Hi, Reggie. I know we're asking a lot from you, but can we add one more thing?"

"Give it to me," Reggie said.

"We've got two photos. One of our current directors named Harold Menzies, and another of a director of the Spruance Company whose name came up from years ago. That's the Armand Moines who we asked you to look into. These men in the photos look a lot alike and I wonder if the Bureau's facial recognition software could be used to see if they're a match. We're separately trying to run down the Spruance guy's identity and background, but if we can conclude they're identical, this gets a lot easier, not to mention getting a lot weirder. What do you think?"

"Send them over. I've got guys who can feed them in and get a quick read." They signed off, and Mandy pulled up the photos and emailed them to her sister.

"When do your code of conduct training sessions start in Europe?" Rick asked.

"Week after next. There are four cities in four countries, with the last one being Paris. Reggie's coming to meet me there so we can run the marathon."

"Better you than me. If Emily visits the Allzient customers, since Allzient has approved, maybe you can meet up, as you suggested," he said.

"Hanging with Wretched Witch in Paris? I can't think of anything more fun than that."

Rick changed subjects.

"Ed told me Jim Kerwin suspects a Jenkins-Menzies linkup and wants some reliable confirmation of that, and he wants me to do that."

Mandy said, "I guess he's becoming forgetful, because

he asked me to do it too. And now you're asking me to get that reliable confirmation?"

Rick said, "Yeah, I guess so. How would you do that?"

"I've got a guy."

Rick got up to leave, and on his way out said, "Do it your way. I leave the details to you. But be very, very careful."

Mandy thought through what had just been said. *What the hell! I'm not a private investigator. Isn't what they do dangerous? What if I was to get myself shot or poisoned? I would only have myself to blame for that. The smart thing for me to do is to let them think it was their idea to hire a PI. But could I really trust anyone else to do it? Or is this just too much action to pass up? To be continued.*

CHAPTER 13

MANDY was approaching her trip to Europe as an exercise in personal hell. Not because she disliked Europe, or that she felt any misgivings about her subject, or even because she had problems with any of the people she had to deal with. It was because she had to be in large group settings in each location, when she really only felt comfortable in groups of four or five at the most. Also, the area president of the European business had been known to disparage the people sent over from the corporate headquarters, and nurtured a culture of independence that made the job of everyone from Chicago very difficult. Mandy's time at the Justice Department had suited her very well, since she worked in a unit of five attorneys. She hadn't been a managing attorney, so that helped. It was uncomfortable to be in a group setting in the first place, but to have to manage others was not something she relished. Being an introvert, which she guessed she was, was never easy in a business setting. It provided the ever-present risk of being publicly shamed.

Mandy had spent three days preparing for her training swing through Europe, which started after a Sunday Alitalia flight to Milan that left her jet-lagged Monday morning. A quick shower and short nap made her somewhat functional, so that an afternoon with the management team in the Italian office was possible. She would have preferred to have the day to recover and to start Tuesday morning, but she was on a tight schedule. She needed to be in Paris on Saturday morning so she and Reggie could meet up, pick up their race packet at the expo, and get situated and calm before the race.

The sessions were at the LaSalle offices in Milan, Istanbul, and Prague, in that order. Each of the sessions involved gathering the top management team of twenty or so people per office. A standard presentation deck of slides was used, and questions and answers followed. The topics were the usual ones from the code of conduct—compliance with law generally, maintaining confidential information, and avoiding various kinds of abusive behavior. Some good questions from her audiences at least gave Mandy the idea that they were listening. She could only wonder how much was being absorbed, though, since the whole U.S. legal system was not user-friendly to international employees. And, of course, some people were culturally opposed to some U.S. policies and practices, with the dismissive attitude that Americans made everything into more than it needed to be.

Once the presentation was over, some individuals wanted one-on-one guidance, which was a pleasure for Mandy. Not only was it a clear signal that understanding had taken place and it was being digested, but it let her be natural and comfortable dealing with individuals rather than with groups. She would help with that however she could. Once that was all past, the top management would take her out to dinner and show off some sights the locals were proud over. In Milan it was the Duomo, LaScala, and Da Vinci's *Last Supper.* In Istanbul it was the Blue Mosque, the Hagia Sofia, and the Bosphorus. Prague had the town square and the St. Nicholas Clock Tower.

On Friday afternoon she flew to Paris in less than two hours. A quick car ride into the city center and the Hotel Raphael on Avenue Kleber, and voilá, she was just a couple blocks from the race start on the Champs Élysées and the finish on Avenue Foch. She spent the afternoon wandering the shops on the Champs Élysées and Avenue Georges V.

Just after arriving a call came in on her cell phone from Klaus Juergen, the managing director of LaSalle's German business based in Frankfurt.

Klaus said, "Mandy, I hope you're well. I'm sorry for calling you without warning, but I need your help."

Mandy said, "Klaus, so good to hear from you. How did you know I'm in Europe?"

"I didn't know, but when I called your office, they gave me your cell number. Where are you?"

"I'm in Paris right now, just finishing up a compliance presentation trip and waiting for my sister to join me for the marathon Sunday."

"Mandy, let me get right to the point. We have an

emergency here. Our finance director Horst has done something stupid. He received a call from someone he believed to be Jim Kerwin, who directed him to wire one million euros to a bank account in China related to a transaction you were working on. He said the company needed to carry out this transfer based on your recommendation in the deal, and that it was highly confidential and he needed to do it immediately. Horst said he needed to get the wire approvals, but was told he needed to act immediately, then he could get a hold of you to confirm if he needed to."

Mandy said, "I don't know what you're talking about. I made no recommendation. That's ludicrous. We have procedures for authenticating transfer requests. Did he authenticate it?"

Klaus replied, "No, he just went ahead with it based on Kerwin's strong insistence. He had met and spoken with Jim Kerwin numerous times and was convinced it was Jim he was speaking with. He initiated the transfer and then he felt a pang of panic and regret and came to see me about it. He's really tearing himself up over this."

Klaus said, "We contacted his office and were told that he had made no calls to this office. I think we've just gotten scammed. I need to straighten this all out with Chicago, but is there anything you can do to head this money transfer off?"

Mandy said, "Klaus, email me the details of the transfer and let me get to our Treasury Department to try to stop this money transfer. It might be possible to intercept the wire before it's received."

After hanging up, Mandy called her friend in the LaSalle Treasury Department and started a chain of events that led to the cancellation of the wire transfer so that no money was sent. After concluding what needed to be done, letting the general counsel know what was going on, and reporting back to Klaus, Mandy realized that this might just be another of the various actions intended to discredit her and to have her removed from the project. *Was that some paranoia that she was now experiencing, or was it speaking the truth?*

She made a mental note to herself that she had to add this to Steve's pile.

Reggie arrived the next morning. They took a cab ride along the entire racecourse to get familiar with the route. Then they went to the race expo and got their race packets. With a whole day to rest, and for Reggie to recover from jet lag, they had an easy Saturday. They spent hours at street side cafes drinking coffee, eating croissants, and watching Parisians come and go.

Race day was a perfect sixty degrees and cloudless, with little humidity. In other words, *a great day for 26.2 miles on the streets of Paris,* as the race website had promised. As race start time approached and nerves got high, they thought they would be hearing the French national anthem, *Le Marseillaise,* but instead they were treated to the Black Eyed Peas pumping *I Gotta Feeling* until the starting gun went off. How un-French was that?

After that, it was four hours of wonderful Paris streets and sights for another notch on their marathon belts. Mandy took the first few miles to get her groove going and to gain an ability to talk while running at the same time, and she could talk lightly to Reggie. After that, it was the usual battle of the mind-over-matter runner fighting off pain and exhaustion and powering through to the next level. Paris was a good course for getting settled in and just crunching out the miles. It was mostly straight and practically flat, and spectacularly scenic. Mandy and Reggie would take that any day.

One reality they had about the race, and always had for that matter, was that wherever they raced, everyone in the competition could have been dropped into any other race in any city in any country, and they would be indistinguishable from anyone else. For Mandy, even though she was in the largest crowd imaginable, her group dynamic fear was not triggered. She never felt that in a marathon crowd she was anything other than a single person, or at most a duet with Reggie, trying to get through an athletic event. Masses of struggling humans having every conceivable challenge possible, from crotch rash to surprise heart attacks, and yet the mob soldiers on to get over the finish line and recover. Hell, some people even ran barefoot, which they could never understand; it was somehow comforting to see them pulled over by the side of the road as you passed them, pulling broken glass out of their bare feet. The sisters crossed the finish line on Avenue Foch with a respectable 3:58 finishing time. They stumbled back to the Hotel Raphael, showered, and checked carefully for any *equipment problems.* No blisters, lost toenails, rashes, pulls, or any other injuries. They rested in the room, then went out to a local restaurant for lunch, catching everyone's stares at their identical appearance, enhanced by wearing their finishers' medals. This was a reward of sorts after months of training.

"What was your favorite running costume among the runners today?" Reggie asked.

"It would have to be the *Moulin Rouge* dancer group, I think. How about you?"

"I liked the mimes with the white painted faces best. But my runners-up were the squad of French Foreign Legion runners."

"What was up with those water-filled balloons they gave out at the aid stations, instead of cups? You lost half the water when you chewed open the balloon. I miss getting cups of ice-cold Gatorade. But at least they didn't hand out bananas with the peels still on, like in New York. Whose idea was that? To have thousands of people throw banana peels on the racecourse?" Mandy said.

Reggie said, "My biggest relief was that I spotted no black SUVs or threatening-looking characters along the course, not they would have had a chance to spot us among twenty-five thousand runners moving in the mass."

In the morning Mandy went to the office and Reggie went to Orly to fly back to Washington, D.C. Mandy's session was much like the others, except that the French were more resistant to the message, and Mandy had to work harder to emphasize that this was corporate policy and not negotiable. All Reggie had to do was watch movies for eight hours.

Mandy was reminded of a colleague's joke once told at a management meeting:

> Three managers were told of a procedure they had to follow. An American, a German, and a Frenchman. The American said, "That's great, and then we can add this and do that. It'll be great."

> The German said, "We'll do precisely that, without variance." Then the French manager said, "Why do we have to do that?"

To her relief, no such reaction greeted her when she was through, and she looked forward to getting back to the Chicago grind, as beautiful as Paris was. And she was also relieved she was done with all the appearances in front of large groups.

Once that was over, she sent a message to Emily Jenkins suggesting dinner. Emily had scheduled her visits to the Allzient customers to coincide with the end of Mandy's trip in Paris. They had dinner at the Raphael that night, and Emily filled her in. She'd visited the customers in the three countries involved in Allzient's bribery, and found their managements to be cautious and verging on hostile. Mandy was relieved that she hadn't had to attend with Emily, as they had earlier planned. Emily had felt that a lawyer's presence would be ominous to the customers, and she was probably right. But even without a lawyer around, they were difficult. They were outspoken on the activities that had been uncovered and had indicated harsh consequences on their employees. They weren't so direct about continuing business with Allzient after what had transpired, or more importantly, with LaSalle if the acquisition went through. Regular, agreed-upon transactions had taken place and goods had been delivered. Service agreements were in place for ongoing maintenance and for updates to software, so there was an uneasy continuity in their relationships. Emily thought that her visit was slightly helpful at best, and neutral at worst. She was glad she had done it, but wasn't sure how much it would help the decision-making process to proceed with the transaction. When they finished dinner and went to their rooms, Mandy had a feeling that Emily was preparing to blame the deal going south on the lawyers. She wasn't sure what made her feel that way, or what she could do about it, if anything. Emily hadn't said anything overtly. She simply gave off the vibe that the concerns about the bribery were an overreaction.

Once back in her room, Emily made a call to Harold Menzies. He was six hours earlier in the evening than her with the time change. He picked up on the first ring. "Hello beautiful. How's the city of light? I'm missing you."

Emily said, "I miss you too, darling. Can't wait to get back. I just had a barely tolerable dinner with fucking Raggedy Ann, and tomorrow I have to fly back with her. I'm telling you, I just smell her trying to poison this deal. I have to find a way to nudge her off the road."

Harold said, "It's better you don't do that. I'm in a better position to deal with her. Please treat her with kid gloves and let me handle it. You just keep me informed on what you see and hear. Can you do that?"

Little did Emily know that Harold had already tried to deal with Mandy on the road, and not just nudge her off, but that had not gone according to plan. Now Mandy was on the alert. The subsequent attempt to deal with her when she was on her own in Lincoln Park was fruitless. Her watcher had been spotted right away outside the apartment, and later in the park he had been stared at from a distance. Stared at sufficiently long to lead to an abort decision. The last thing they wanted was a Chicago squad car giving chase to the watcher. He'd had a number of things done to try to shake her off the case, including implied threats to her family, anonymous text message, a brush with a speedboat, and an elaborate million-euro money scam. Nothing was working. The woman was not easy to scare off.

"I'll try. I better get to bed. I have to catch the early flight tomorrow. Love you."

"Love you too. Sweet dreams."

Once the call ended, Menzies put the phone down and turned to face his roommate and said, "Amanda Doucette. You haven't been able to deal with her? I think she's a big risk, so you must deal with her decisively."

The next morning, Emily and Mandy both headed to Orly for their return flight. A dinner with Wretched Witch was enough for Mandy; now she had to share a flight with her. Luckily, she found out at the gate that Emily was in first class and Mandy was in business class.

CHAPTER 14

ERIK SPENSER'S CONTROLLER had spent all of his evenings looking at the James Whitney materials taken out of Spenser's apartment. He thought he had finally sorted out everything that Whitney had squirreled away on the thumb drives he'd kept at his apartment. Whitney had even been helpful enough to keep photos of the documents and accounting entries found to support the findings. Spenser had copied all of it. He'd also gone through the email accounts Spenser had hacked of the lawyers involved, and was pretty sure he knew who all of the players were, and what they had done and were planning to do. Finally, he sorted through all of the photos Spenser had collected one way or another, and was painstakingly trying to match the photos with the names of the players. Once he knew the names, he could do quite a bit with what he had, but every bit of input was helpful. All of this had been possible because the manager who James Whitney first communicated his belief about fraud and bribery taking place had contacted Spenser, as corporate security head. Erik Spenser had instructed him to do nothing just yet, and let Erik investigate. If the manager was questioned about why he had not reacted to James Whitney's approach, he was to deny any knowledge. It was that simple.

Erik Spenser had learned a lot more, and now his controller had to decide what to do next. If action was needed, it was now past the time to have Erik Spenser ask for any authority, since he was out of the picture for good. He would have to use his other assets to go after Amanda Doucette.

He slogged through the rest of the Whitney materials and isolated the individuals who he thought had been the players. In each of the three European customers he had identified a single person, and two bribe-crazy Allzient employees, for a total of five. That would clear the decks in the bribery matter, except for the lawyers.

In Spenser's Brooklyn apartment, the Whitney files had been strewn over the dining room table, according to what his team had reported to him. Dining room table was really a misnomer. It was the only table in the apartment, and the other furnishings were minimal and utilitarian, to say the least. Erik Spenser was, of course, a pseudonym. His true name was Russian, but he'd given it up when he was exfiltrated out. Becoming Erik Spenser had been easy, because his controller at the CIA had been kind enough to provide him a new identity with a complete back story with all of the necessary documents and credentials. So that had made an entrance into Spruance Corporation's German operations seamless. Given the assist he'd had, he could begin his new life in his new home and working in his new company in a corporate security position. Life had gone on for him and he became comfortable with his new identity, taking pains to establish his value to Spruance and to learn as much as he could. The security office work he did was ideal for his purpose. The day came when he discovered a note in his coat pocket addressed to his former Russian name. The note carried a place, date, and time. The note simply said "be there" in Russian. And so began a long process of adapting to a new reality, as he was finally being activated to begin his responsibilities. As those responsibilities took on shape and depth over the years, he'd learned how to prove his value.

"Philip Ray" had known that Spruance had technologies which were in development and in various stages of commercialization at any one time. Erik had acquired them and passed them along at regular intervals to his new controller. It was a turn of the tables from what he had done while in the service of the Americans while in Russia. Now, he was taking information from European companies and passing it along. Allzient was another of them. He didn't know where it was going or how it was being used. He wasn't going to learn either. His family remained there, and while he had no contact with them, their well-being was dependent upon his performance. His controller reminded him of this from time to time. He was also given bits and pieces of information about his family, enough to prove to Spenser that they were being watched.

His days with the company were thrown into uncertainty when Spruance was unexpectedly acquired by Allzient. The transaction took months to complete, and he was eventually folded into the combined structure of the two companies while a routine process of organization changes took place. Redundancies in positions were eliminated, but he was a survivor of that process. His controller continued to prod him for information. He was eventually advised that he would be transferred to an Allzient office in New York City, and he would be given assistance in relocation and work visas and everything else needed. Since he was in a security function, he had access to a great amount of information and organization facilities. He was well situated to do anything that he was instructed to accomplish. These instructions were delivered by the usual method, wholly separate from his company supervisor's instructions and the so-called "job description" and "goals and objectives" by which he was evaluated each year. It was a human resources extravaganza that occurred at the end of every year and that he detested. But it was all part of the game that had to be played with perceptible enthusiasm. He even had performance interviews with his supervisor that resulted in ratings that were tied into an annual bonus payment.

He was expected to take training sessions, including on subjects such as diversity sensitivity, avoiding inappropriate conduct, and protection of proprietary assets. An endless march of modern corporate correctness.

For a few years he was coached by his controller on what was expected of him in the new Spruance-Allzient combined company. He excelled at following both sets of expectations. On the one hand, his comfort and security were dependent upon his performance. On the other hand, his personal safety and his family's well-being were also dependent upon following the instructions given him by his controller. He'd wanted to believe that this was a balancing act he could maintain indefinitely, but in periodic flashes of terror, he confronted images of facing disaster and his whole world crashing down around him. Best he put his head down and *keep on keeping on,* as the Americans said. His head was down now, all right. It was now part of a bag of bones in a shallow New Jersey grave.

The controller, formerly known as Philip Ray, and now known as Sherman Haskins, sat looking over all of the Whitney stuff. He was furious at Spenser for not having picked up on this bribery nonsense earlier. Had he known about that, he could have cleaned it up and prevented someone like Whitney stumbling across it. Once Whitney stumbled across it, and did what he did, it was a runaway train. He had ordered Whitney killed and hoped that he could clean up the rest of the mess. Of course, if he did the first and couldn't do the second, what would he have created? He could look into Whitney's lawyer's files to see who all of the players were and what he might be able to do about them. Yes, he would do that.

A while back he had instructed Spenser to deal with the two strays from the group of six who had been brought out of Russia and placed into jobs in Spruance. Those two had left to take jobs in America—one a warehouse manager, the other an office security manager. He had been told to dispose of them and to be prepared to do the same to their families if needed. He'd taken care of the two and dumped them together in rural Pennsylvania, after pouring acid on them to erase their identification. He figured that was enough. He wasn't going to try removing teeth or take out the family just yet. The controller was content to move forward with the remaining four assets remaining in place in Allzient, and when the merger took place, he would have at least four people in place to begin moving into more sensitive positions.

Now, though, he had to finish figuring out what to do with the bribery gang and how it all worked. After three days he thought he fully understood it. Whitney had not really created a roadmap to what he knew, either because he was sloppy and disorganized, or because he didn't want to serve it up on a silver platter to anyone.

Whitney's findings, as the controller reconstructed them, led him to conclude that bribes had been paid to three main buyers in three countries. The Spanish electric utility company had purchased twelve hundred service vehicles. One of the Italian cable television companies had purchased over five hundred vans for their service departments. The Parisian post office had purchased eight hundred vehicles. All these contracts had been issued with full prices reflected on the purchasers' versions of the paperwork, but with the pricing divided between the cost of the vehicles at 80 percent of the total and a service cost of 20 percent of the total, with different payment directions for each portion. The seller's versions reflected only the 80 percent amount as the full price. The sales head managed this personally. Whitney had dug into this and discovered it.

Spenser apparently had known Whitney discovered some discrepancies, but didn't know the full story until now. He knew enough to get authority from his controller to deal with him and to get the means to do so, but he had questioned why he should have taken that ultimate step. He was concerned now that the bribery had gotten to this whistleblower stage. Once it was known, could he recover from it? That was why he had instructed Whitney's supervisor to hold the letter and not to report it. Spenser was struggling with what to do next, and he expected to learn that from his controller, but instead he'd been told to hold on and that he would receive instructions. He had to have a plan, because to have no plan would put things in his controller's hands, and that could end very badly for him. His failure to identify and to clean up the bribery might have sealed his fate, regardless what he did about it now. His memory of the controller's instruction to let nothing get in the way of the LaSalle acquisition of Allzient reverberated in his head, because the bribery had certainly done that.

Spenser had been focusing on the two insiders at Allzient who had engaged in the bribery and fraudulent bookkeeping. They were reckless and unworthy of the riches they were collecting. The controller made his decision. It wasn't worth the effort to toy with the bribed officials or with the fools who made the bribes anymore. The controller's concern now was that the wound had to be cauterized and not spread to what was really going on.

He looked at all of the outside lawyers involved in the case. There were Washington lawyers who had represented James Whitney, but he was dead now. Allzient was going to have to deal with this, that was for sure, but its outside lawyers were preoccupied with completing the sale to LaSalle, and the Whitney matter was now a sideshow which threatened the acquisition and needed to be eliminated. Now that Whitney and Spenser were gone, he should leave that alone.

The more Sherman Haskins thought about it, this whole bribery situation with all of its offshoots should just be allowed to take its course. What he should do is protect against those looking to go any further than the bribery matter. The LaSalle lawyers may be the obstacle to getting the deal closed and may have to be dealt with. He had isolated three people on the LaSalle side: Rick Crawford, Bob Thereaux, and Amanda Doucette. He quickly dispensed with Bob Thereaux, believing him to be much like Allzient's lawyers — they were all in service of getting the deal done. So, they could provide progress, and should be allowed to continue. That left the two inside lawyers at LaSalle, one of whom was the primary deal person and in charge of managing this transaction. Crawford seemed to have overall deal responsibility, so he should be left untouched. The redheaded woman named Doucette was in his crosshairs, though, and became his primary focus of concern. Her role, apparently, was to turn over all the rocks and to see what crawled out. If she didn't like what she saw, she might be able to influence the outcome. This was the one Erik Spenser had fingered as the real problem, and in fact the one Harold Menzies had told him about.

He had to concentrate on Amanda Doucette.

Mandy was efficient at overcoming her jet lag upon the return from Paris. Staying up the entire flight back to Chicago and then getting a good long sleep in the normal pattern kept her disruption to a minimum. She could allow herself three days to sleep in after the marathon anyway, a routine resting period before resuming her running.

She had a text message from Reggie saying that it was important that she and Rick call her about the facial recognition they'd requested. Reggie, of course, was just back too, and recovering as Mandy, but clearly, she'd learned something important. Mandy visited Rick's office and found him working through his due diligence list and taking stock of where the process stood. He invited her in and asked her how the trip to Europe had been and the race as well, though to be honest he cared little to nothing about those races.

They had already discussed the aborted theft attempt with the impersonation of Jim Kerwin and the supposed recommendation by Mandy, the latter being a deliberate attempt to undermine her and to get her removed. Rick had made sure that was passed along to Ed Rosen, and it would have to be reported to the internal audit department and ultimately to the Board Audit Committee. Mandy would have to use that incident to warn management to the risks of that happening again.

"Looks like Reggie wants to talk to us," she said. "Shall I call?"

"Yes, please. Anything to get my mind off this list and what remains to be done."

When Reggie got on the phone, she said, "There's good news and bad news. What would you like first?"

"Let's start with some good news," Rick said.

"We matched the photos on the face recognition software program. Your two people are really one—Moines is Menzies." She explained that there was no identity that popped up, and she admitted that she had only asked about the technical question of whether there were separate persons or only one person in the photos. If she was going to try to find out about identity, that would be another process and require more inputs.

"If that's the good news, I hate to hear the bad news," said Mandy.

"Well, my friend Dan got a reprimand for poking around with the CIA and those names you wanted checked. He didn't hear back from his contact, who happened to be in the human resources department. When he tried to follow up, he was told there could be no answer given. He got the distinct impression that his contact had gotten into some difficulty. He was finally contacted by someone senior who told him not to poke his nose into Agency business."

"Someone *'senior'* as in who?" Rick asked.

"He didn't give a name. He just said someone in the counterintelligence section."

Rick and Mandy made faces at what they had just heard.

"I'm sorry, Reggie, we didn't mean to get anyone in trouble. But just out of curiosity, what would make counterintelligence come into the picture?" Mandy said.

"Beats me," she said.

"Thanks a lot for doing those things. We'll leave you alone now and see what we can make of this," said Rick.

They ended the call. Rick said that he thought Rosen should hear about Moines and Menzies. Mandy said that they couldn't let the CIA counterintelligence issue drop, but that neither Reggie nor Dan could be pushed into a space that was dangerous for them, if that was what it was.

She said she had an idea about the counterintelligence

issue and would noodle on it, and then she added, “You know it has bothered me since the beginning that things seemed too out of the ordinary just to be a garden variety bribery scandal. Now I’m pretty certain that we’ve got some higher-level things going on here. If you throw into the pictures the harassment and threats thrown my way, it paints a picture of something really much bigger. We’ve had the CIA and now counterintelligence. There’s some kind of national security smell to it and I can’t seem to put it together yet.”

Mandy also let Rick know she had a good recommendation on an investigator to use on searching for Armand Moines and for Philip Ray, and he agreed she should initiate the work. She promptly called him and gave him the assignment, mindful that she had already given him the two that she had not shared with Rick—Harold Menzies and Emily Jenkins. He asked her to direct his findings back to her and gave her everything she knew about all of the names.

Before she left Rick’s office, she said to him, “Do you know you have on one black shoe and one brown shoe?”

He said, “They’re the same shoe, aren’t they?”

“Yeah, but people usually wear two of the same color.”

“You know I’m color blind, right?”

Mandy said, “I don’t think I knew that. Maybe you should stay away from identical pairs of shoes in different colors.”

“Thanks.”

Mandy decided to bounce a question off Special Agent Steve Baker, so she called him.

"I have to ask if you could shed any light on something we've learned about a curious FBI call."

"Try me."

Mandy explained the outreach her sister had tried through Dan on the CIA agent's name back from the Spruance days, and that a very blunt message came back from the CIA counterintelligence office, waving off any contact with the CIA. She asked if he could imagine why the counterintelligence unit would suddenly be involved.

Steve told her that his guess was that if someone at the Bureau was poking their nose into Agency business, then the Agency discipline that was threatened would push back to its counterpart at the Bureau to get the caller waved off. "But I'm just guessing."

"I'm really in over my head here, but are you telling me our question took us into a CIA counterintelligence area? That it was the counterintelligence section that was threatened?"

"Sounds like it. Do you want me to look into it?"

"Like I said, I'm in over my head. I don't want any blowback against my sister or her friend, beyond what they've already had. But I think something's going on here that's beyond our understanding, and needs to be looked at. So yes, and thanks for offering to do something, and congratulations again. I hope you can get back to me soon on this," Mandy said.

"No problem. We've been instructed to alert our management if and when we see the CIA getting involved in domestic business. Maybe that's happening here? I'm going to see if our counterintelligence chief would get on a call with you and me and you can tell him what you know."

CHAPTER 15

ALAN FRENCHE'S OFFICE was on the top floor of the J. Edgar Hoover Building in downtown Washington, D.C., the FBI Headquarters. He'd been the director of counterintelligence at the Bureau for ten years, and was amazed at how much the job had changed from routine human activities to cyber intelligence. His background, like that of most of his senior colleagues, had been experience in the former, rather than in cyber. In the intelligence community the name for it was HUMINT (Human Intelligence). Finding, observing, interfering with, and ultimately shutting down a foreign intelligence operation was his specialty, and he had to rely on teams, if not hordes, of young techies to get a grip on cyber intelligence. He wondered how long it would be before he was replaced by the cyber warriors, and after that by artificial intelligence. He much preferred human intelligence. No single approach by foreign actors was used, even though cyber methods were the lion's share of the action these days. Eternal vigilance was called for to make sure nothing slipped past the guardians of the country's assets. All of that rested on his shoulders.

He'd been called by Special Agent Steve Baker from the Chicago office, who was finishing up a large interstate theft ring bust for a Chicago company. Baker told him he needed some of his time and wanted a call with a Chicago lawyer he'd been working with, and would be in Washington in the next couple of days and wanted to meet. He, Baker, and Mandy had a call that morning at 10:00 a.m., in which Mandy was asked to lay out what was happening.

She started out with a look back a decade ago. "Another Chicago company ten years ago had a visit by someone claiming to be a CIA agent."

Right away, Frenche was troubled by the Agency being active in the United States, without anything further being said. The CIA was, by its charter, unable to conduct any intelligence activities on U.S. soil. That was the province of the FBI. The CIA could only be engaged in the United States if another U.S. intelligence agency requested its involvement. The director of national intelligence was extremely concerned that the boundaries among the intelligence agencies were observed carefully. If Frenche happened upon a violation of this boundary, he was duty-bound to report it. Though calm on the outside, Frenche was boiling on the inside. His counterpart at the Agency, Sherman Haskins, was a deceitful snake, and Frenche suspected him of pulling some typical Agency tricks. This was something that he needed to put an end to.

When Mandy was done with her account, Baker said, "Mandy and the LaSalle people have been good to work with in the engine theft case. I know you want to know of any CIA activity taking place in the United States, and that was the main purpose of this call, but I also wanted to be helpful to the LaSalle team."

Frenche said, "I'll think about that, but let me dig into it a little, and get back to you soon."

CHAPTER 16

MANDY AND REGGIE talked about any lingering pain they had after getting back on the road and into their routine.

"I'm feeling pretty good," Mandy said, "with pretty good pain—just muscle soreness and a little lactic acid. Should be back to full strength in a day or two." Lactic acid among runners was a pleasant pain, one that signaled muscle soreness, not muscle injury. When talking about their pain after a marathon, they were prone to classify it in one of three categories: pretty good pain, very good pain, or bad pain. The two versions of "good" pain were really just degrees of lactic acid. Any kind of bad pain was some kind of injury, whether it was ligaments, hamstrings, or heel injury. One didn't want that kind of pain.

"I think I might have to visit the chiropractor. I've got some bad pain—hip pain on the right side and a calf-cramping issue. I'll bet the hips are out of adjustment again," Reggie said.

This was a standard postrace discussion, and the problems were routine. What each of them feared was something like plantar fasciitis that could sideline a runner for a long time. Regular visits to the chiropractor to get realigned were a must. Next up was Grandma's Marathon in Duluth, Minnesota, a race that was significant to them not so much because it knocked off another state in their fifty states quest—it did—but due to some family history. According to the family history handed down from generation to generation, a Doucette ancestor had left the family near Quebec City in the mid-1800s, and paddled a birch-bark canoe up the St. Lawrence River and through the Great Lakes until hitting Lake Superior. At the western shore of the lake, he portaged overland to a place they had not been able to track down. Up the lakeshore at the beginning of his portage, he crossed a spot that later became the starting point for Grandma's Marathon, making the start of the sisters' next marathon a multigenerational path-crossing of the family, so to speak. From the point of his landing until his eventual settlement in Little Falls, Minnesota Territory, the history was a blank. This is why the sisters had pushed Grandma Betty for information. Little Falls may have been famous for being the hometown of Charles Lindbergh, but for them it was the Doucette hometown.

Mandy made the comment that "with everything we've accumulated in these ancestry searches, I'm getting a strong picture of the adventurer's spirit. The first

French to escape France in the early 1600s, the refugees after the war with the Brits, the return to Quebec, and the final canoe trip to the Mississippi."

Reggie suggested, "Still got the itch?"

"Oh sure."

Reggie asked where things stood with Allzient, and Mandy ticked off the items.

They now knew that there were three customers involved and two Allzient employees, with no confrontation yet with any of them. But from the LaSalle side, Emily Jenkins had now visited the European customers and assured them that if the acquisition were consummated, then LaSalle would assure an uninterrupted completion of the contracts. No mention was made by her of the corrupt payments.

The seller not disclosing the corrupt payments was now understood, with the statements by Whitney's manager that Eric Spenser had kept it buried. The unresolved issue was Erik Spenser's death. Why had he been killed? Mandy thought to herself, *I wonder if Erik Spenser was the architect of the bribery scam, just like our Willis Traynor was the engine theft ring architect. But would the architect be killed? He would be sitting atop the pyramid, so if Eric was killed, someone else was pulling the strings. Who?*

The mystery CIA agent was still just that—a mystery—and the effort to get information caused a strong knuckle-rap to Dan. This was a growing problem, in Mandy's mind. Although they now thought they knew that there were at least a half-dozen former CIA assets hired by Spruance, as of now only one was thought to be known and until his death had been the chief security officer of Allzient. The two bodies found in Pennsylvania were likely also part of the Philip Ray initiative. Others had been recruited at the initiation of Philip Ray as well, and were now imbedded in Allzient, she thought. This had now grown into major significance in the LaSalle efforts. Mandy had already raised the issue with Steve Baker, her FBI agent-friend, and he was in discussion with Washington, D.C., about what was going on. She had to circle back to him and get up to speed on where that was headed.

The two directors who had interests in hiring a former CIA asset and Spruance being acquired by Allzient, and in turn Allzient being acquired by LaSalle, continued to be of major interest. Shockingly, they were now thought to be the same person. This issue was red-hot in Mandy's opinion, and of primary importance. The files for the Allzient people were being obtained, and a better picture of Erik Spenser could emerge. As to the Armand Moines/ Harold Menzies director or directors, that had to be pursued further as well. Mandy's investigator was snooping into the two (or one) directors to see what could be found, and secretly also seeing if Emily Jenkins was entangled with Harold Menzies.

Reggie suddenly asked Mandy, "This private investigator you hired. You didn't have authority to do that, did you? You went 'vigilante' on me again, right? And then you maneuvered it so Rick Crawford, then Ed Rosen, and then Jim Kerwin all gave a green light to do *whatever it took* to figure out the Emily Jenkins/Harold Menzies pairing? You could say that the thing you got ahead of everybody about was actually authorized?"

Mandy said nothing.

"I thought so. Reverse-engineering your approval," Reggie said.

The businesspeople were still pushing hard to get the deal done.

Mandy asked Reggie if Dan Aleri was troubled by stepping into the middle of this and getting burned, but Reggie thought not. That was good. No need to interfere with Reggie's friendships more than had already been done.

The next day after a good run and some gazing out her office window at the Chicago River and Lake Michigan Lock, she decided on a course of action. She was painfully aware that the report to the Board Audit Committee was looming, and she had received a message from Ed Rosen asking her how her report and presentation were coming. She was to speak to the Kansas City theft ring issue and the corruption surprise at Allzient. That meant that there could be an uncomfortable encounter with Harold Menzies, who sat on the Audit Committee. She would have to discuss with Ed how to manage the hairy parts with Director Menzies in the room. This was taking her into the realm of corporate politics, which she always did her level best to avoid, like keeping your hand away from a flame burning blue. There was a trick in having exposure to the Board of Directors, which her dad had tried to drill into her—it was to always present as narrow a profile as possible, as distinct from presenting a full-frontal target for someone to aim at. This was easier said than done with someone as omnipresent as Ed Rosen, but eminently possible with the occasional presenter like Mandy.

Mandy knew that Steve Baker was another early bird, just like her and John Booth, so she called his cell number and he answered immediately. "Thought I'd check in with you on that strange counterintelligence connection. Have you heard anything back from Alan Frenche yet?"

"Actually, I have," Steve said. "Alan was baffled by it as well, and I expect him to get back to me shortly. From what you explained to us, I've been thinking it might be worthwhile speaking to the Spruance general counsel you told me about. He may be the only actual connection to the person who we're talking about. If that looks like a good way to move with this, would you be willing to invite him and come to Washington, along with him to meet with us?"

"Sure, that would be fine with me. I can call him and ask, but he probably would cooperate, since he was so open with me earlier. The only thing I have to avoid is a conflict with our board meeting, which is going to be a command performance for me. In part, by the way, it will be to strut over our great success on busting the theft ring. Woohoo," Mandy said.

"We will bend over backward to protect your strut," Steve said.

After the Steve Baker call, Mandy got coffee and decided to pay a visit to Greg Carlucci.

"Hey, Mandy. Good morning. What's up?" Greg said.

"I'm waist-deep in this Allzient deal, and there's some strange stuff going on. I just wanted to pop a question at you. I know this is totally out of the blue and I'm only fishing around here, but I wanted to know what happens if you're a defense contractor with a lot of classified work, and you merge with someone who has some security risks."

Greg answered, "That's bad medicine. If by *security risks* you mean people, then none of those people could be allowed anywhere near classified information. We deal with that all the time, as you can imagine. We acquire a lot of companies, and each time we do there's a question of anyone transferring into the defense unit. It would be just like a new hire, so an inside employee from a merger would still need to go through security vetting and would need to get an individual security clearance to work in the unit. There's no dispensation on security classifications. Does that answer your question?" Greg said.

"Think so, but I've got to think about that some more. I might be back. Thanks, Greg."

She continued up to Ed's office. His view ranged from south Michigan Avenue to the westward flowing Chicago River next to the brilliant white marble Wrigley Building, to the Chicago Tribune Building. It was a feast for the eyes. Ed waved Mandy in to sit down. They began to go over the plans for the Audit Committee meeting taking place next week. She would give the overview of the prior year's activities and the statistics from past years, nothing of which stood out, except for the two items that would fall to her to explain — the Kansas City engine theft ring, and the potential bribery and corruption matter that could come to fall into their laps if the deal with Allzient closed.

Mandy told Ed that the engine theft ring was a sore

point, since it had first happened five years ago and here it was again, but this time at the hands of the corporate security director. This was a real black eye for LaSalle, just one that was on someone else's face other than the law department's.

Mandy said, "Personally, I think the engine sting was a perfect outcome. It ended the problem and didn't disrupt the engine division, so Wretched Witch should be relieved."

The Allzient bribery matter, though, was one that had some mysterious potential connection issues with the LaSalle board. Mandy was not sure how to word it in the report or discuss it in the meeting.

Meanwhile, there was still an open question of what the Allzient employee files would show on the critical players.

Mandy said, "I went through the files we got. The two electric vehicle unit employees who were implicated in the bribery ring were fairly undistinguished in their wrongdoing. They were common garden-variety violators, and their trail was obvious. The finance unit employee was the enabler, being the gatekeeper on the accounting and payments functions. There should have been a separation of duties between the payment authority and the financial and cost accounting functions. He somehow was able to short-circuit those controls, and it was easy sailing after that. From a corrective action point of view, it would be pretty straightforward to implement the required system. There may be more discipline for others who might have failed to catch something, but those two were the whole show. They'd been terminated, and Allzient was trying to decide whether to refer them for prosecution.

Mandy said, "So my bottom line on that is that we can clean up the inside part and leave it to Emily to work on repairing the business relationship Allzient had."

The file on Erik Spenser was much more intriguing. It wasn't very illuminating, in that there was no family mentioned, no home connection; it contained a prior work history at Spruance Corporation since 2009, but before that, nothing. There was a hometown of Columbus, Ohio. No primary or secondary school, nor college degree mentioned. He had a Social Security number, a New York driver's license, and a U.S. passport. It was one of the most bare-boned resumes she'd ever seen. There was nothing more to be found at Spruance, since its records had been absorbed by Allzient at the time of the merger. Paralegals were doing identity searches and hunting for any background on Erik Spenser, but coming up with nothing.

After breaking up their meeting, and returning to her office, a message from Steve Baker was waiting asking her to call.

"Mandy, I've heard back from Alan Frenche. He'd like to have you and Mr. Booth in to see him, as I expected. Can you see that through?"

"Sure. Like I told you, it would have to be after our board meeting the middle of next week. Will that work for Mr. Frenche?"

"Yes, go ahead and get Booth. I've blocked out those days for myself as well. I'd like to get this scheduled as soon as possible."

"I'll get back to you this afternoon." And no sooner did they get off than Mandy called John Booth, who was happy to make the schedule work, so it was agreed that he would travel up next Thursday night and be there for a 9:00 a.m. meeting Friday. Mandy immediately called Baker back and got it set.

As an afterthought to her conversation with Greg Carlucci, she paid him a second unannounced visit to ask him what his answer would be if the security risk were a board member. He scowled. "Do you mean the director *had an external risk take place during his term in office,* or the director himself *was the security risk?*"

"The latter," she said.

Greg responded, "Ah, that's a much bigger problem. If the director is the risk, then it calls into question the adequacy of the company's background checking and suggests negligence. Not a good spot for a defense contractor to find itself in. The entity could lose its qualification to possess secrets, and that could deal a death blow to being a responsible bidder for contracts. Are you insinuating that we have such a problem here?"

"Let's just say it's a hypothetical for now," she said.

Sherman Haskins was thinking through erasing the footsteps that could lead to an unhappy outcome. Erik Spenser wouldn't play any further role, of course. Spenser's body had been found, and that was disappointing to Haskins. Whether anyone could make sense of what was known about Spenser and come to a conclusion about his purpose, was anybody's guess. He'd left no breadcrumbs, because his entire loaf had been created by himself in the person of Sherman Haskins. If crumbs did fall, they would lead back to an empty shell. But that didn't stop some clever and driven person from drawing inferences from his existence and coming up with a theory.

He was considering the best way to deal with the Doucette woman. He was also aware of good old John Booth of Spruance Corporation fame. Booth had not seen the old "Philip Ray" for years, but obviously he was a resource that Doucette had dug up. But Booth might have a good memory for faces, and he might just be able to put a face together that bore the name Philip Ray. Maybe Doucette could as well, though he couldn't imagine how she could have seen the face of Philip Ray. Was it possible that Spruance had some kind of security camera that had captured his image when he paid his visit to Spruance long ago? Now what to do about them? He had other people who made up a part of the cast, but they were mostly federal agents. He wished to keep his hands clean of harming them—not because he cared about them, but rather because he was trying to avoid increasing the fervor with which law enforcement types would engage in hot pursuit. And finally, there was Armand Moines/Harold Menzies, who had real talents and value, and who could prove useful in dismantling what he had created and nurtured over twenty years. There was a special connection between them. He would welcome the extraction of Moines/Menzies to a place of safety, as soon as possible.

At 2:00 p.m., that afternoon, Mandy entered Ed Rosen's corner office on the twenty-fourth floor to finish the discussion from earlier. Mandy led off with an explanation. "We stumbled into a set of things that seem not to be associated with the Allzient bribery. There are troubling connections, though. The predecessor company, Spruance Corporation, had been maneuvered to hire some murky characters coming out of the intelligence community, who ended up in its corporate security function. We also learned that a Spruance director urged that hiring to take place, and that same director pushed for Spruance to be acquired by Allzient. In addition, one of our directors was very active in pushing for the LaSalle acquisition of Allzient. Finally, we've concluded that the Spruance director and the LaSalle director are the same person."

"Jesus Christ! Is this Harold Menzies you're talking about?"

"That's him, whatever his name is. Harold Menzies, Armand Moines, or something else," Mandy said.

"Wait now. Back up a little," Rosen said. "You found all of this, how?"

"We were doing our due diligence. The corporate history was right in front of us; I happened to be speaking to my father about it, and mentioned Spruance. He knew the Spruance general counsel. One thing led to another and I found myself visiting him. He told me about a bizarre meeting he'd had with a CIA agent that was requested by the director Armand Moines. I ended up showing him our proxy statement and he noticed Menzies' picture and said that was Moines."

Rosen frowned. "I recruited Harold Menzies."

Mandy said, "I know. I wanted to tell you because this may come out in the Audit Committee meeting next week, and we can't be saying this in that committee meeting with Menzies sitting there. I know you've talked with Kerwin about Menzies' interest in the Allzient deal. What we've just discussed takes us into the twilight zone. We need to know what should go into the Audit Committee preread materials, which are scheduled to be sent out tomorrow. We also need to know how far to go in the presentation next week."

"OK," Rosen said. "Put the report together with the bribery topic. Don't mention this director thing at all. Between now and then, I'll discuss it with Jim. I might want you to join me. I'm thinking out loud right now, but it seems to me that this might be a good topic to convene the Executive Committee to deal with. It hasn't been done much in our history, but this seems tailor-made for it. Menzies wouldn't be there, as it has only the CEO, the chairman, and the other committee chairs. How much more do you think can be found out about this at the board meeting?"

"We have a meeting in Washington, with a senior FBI person, and we're bringing the Spruance general counsel to meet with him after our board meeting. We'll probably know more by the board meeting, but I don't know how much more," Mandy said.

"OK. Stand by in case I need you with the boss. Good work, and Mandy, please thank your dad for me."

"Will do."

CHAPTER 17

AT MIDDAY on Monday, Allzient called LaSalle and informed them of the developments.

Mandy said, "Rick, we have to be prepared with a statement for the media if we're called, and we need to make sure Allzient is prepared to address this as well. It was their employee and their bribery issue. They have to be prepared to talk about the whistleblower's death, and we need to have a position on what this does to the acquisition. Whitney was murdered, then Spenser was murdered; the two bodies found in Pennsylvania were prior Allzient people. We have to assume this is related to the bribery, or to something bigger going on. I'm calling Reggie to find out what she knows, and I'm also calling Justice and see if they'll tell me anything."

A bribery violation and four murders, including a whis-

tleblower, Mandy thought. One nagging question she had was who the hell would be dumb enough to go around killing people for a bribery? It would make no sense to kill a whistleblower if he had already blown the whistle. And why kill the corporate security director? Was he involved? Was this Allzient's own little drama of a corrupt corporate security officer, like LaSalle had with its engine theft ring? *This is all being done to hide a bigger thing; I just don't know what it is. I suspect, though, that it has to do with this CIA thing and the people placed in the business.*

It wasn't long before the murders became connected to LaSalle's acquisition of Allzient and then showed up on national news. A CNN report carried the story of the suspicious death and the body found in the woods, and it being connected to the missing Allzient employee. The story also revealed that his apartment had been broken into. Allzient had been contacted, and CNN had learned that a whistleblower claim had been made regarding the company. It was only a matter of time before LaSalle was approached by the media for a reaction. Much scurrying around occurred among the public and investor relations staffs at LaSalle that morning, trying to have answers to imagined questions they would get.

Mandy decided to call Stewart Simons, even though the last conversation with him had led her to believe that he would call her if he needed her. She didn't know how he'd react to her being aggressive with him. When he came on the line he said, "I wondered how long it would take to hear from you, once the Spenser death became public."

Mandy explained, "We're still in a due diligence

phase, so I need to let our board know what's happening, to the best of my ability."

Simons said, "Well, you were always an aggressive prosecutor, so I don't know why you wouldn't be an aggressive compliance officer, right?"

Even though she knew he couldn't tell her much, if anything, she told him that LaSalle would be happy to help in any way with information; all he had to do was hold up his hand. She also said she was due to give a board update on the subject tomorrow, and if there was anything he could share, it would be most appreciated.

"Mandy, you know I can't tell you anything. Sorry about that, but we're a trying to figure out where to go with this. We're looking forward to seeing you and John Booth next week," he said.

That done, she noticed she had a text message from Reggie asking her to call.

"OK, we just got through discussing the nerve agent that did in the New Jersey body, your Erik Spenser. A massive dose. The kind that would kill instantly. Mandy, what have you gotten into? I dragged out the stuff I had on nerve agents from some training two years ago. This is some scary stuff that's involved here."

She explained that the Russians had developed colorless, tasteless nerve agents decades ago that could be delivered in solid, liquid, or gaseous form. Depending upon the dose, they could be fatal within minutes. The Russians used it in the mid-1990s, and anybody could very well be using it now.

"How does the stuff work?" Mandy asked.

"Well, I don't want to go into the chemistry, because you'd get lost fast. But it causes all of your skeletal muscles to contract and makes the heart and lungs stop functioning, and bang! You're dead."

Mandy shuddered.

"With a less severe dose, and if it's caught early enough, an antidote treatment of atropine mixed with an oxime can counteract the paralysis and relieve the contraction of the muscles. If the person's really lucky, a full recovery can occur, but in between recovery and death, there are a lot of different levels of effect—none of them good: breathing difficulties, crippling, hepatitis, depression, epilepsy, and disorientation. The Russians called this nerve agent Novichok. The Bureau has some of the antidote at the lab."

Mandy said, "Why would someone use that? Why not just shoot him?"

"Gunshots make noise and a mess. This stuff doesn't involve anything obvious, and if enough time passes, all traces of it disappear. You'd have to look very carefully and know what you're looking for. If you don't know, it could be easily overlooked, even by a coroner. If that dog hadn't found the body as fast as he did, it could have left no trace and we would be none the wiser. Whoever did this was trying to avoid detection completely and hoping to baffle forensic analysis. The only telltale mark was a puncture wound. You don't even need to inject this stuff, since it can be ingested as well as absorbed through the skin. My guess is that they had no time and needed to act immediately, so they jabbed him with a large dose and then dumped him, hoping he'd be missing for a long time. They must have been frantic. No time for finesse."

"Yeah, what have I gotten into?" Mandy said slowly.

"I don't know, but it looks like we have the same method being used on all four of the dead. Nobody can tell me they're unconnected."

At noon on Monday, Ed Rosen and Mandy were in the CEO's office as a call was placed to the chairman David Renfrow. Before the call was connected, Jim Kerwin was telling them that he thought this deal and all of its drama was going to overshadow everything positive that management wanted the board to focus on in the upcoming meeting. That was never good. The CEO's goal was always to keep the board confident that the situation was well in hand. It seemed as if a controllable situation had become suddenly uncontrollable, and that management must have done something wrong or missed something. That was the hill the CEO feared he would have to climb, once the board knew what was happening. That hill climb would have to take place in front of all the directors too. Luckily, David Renfrow was always in management's corner, and was patient and calm when a surprise occurred. But boards were always looking to managements to level with them and avoid either sugarcoating or even ignoring a problem.

David came on the line. "Folks, do we have a shitstorm on our hands here?"

Jim answered, "It looks that way. I asked Ed and Mandy to walk us through this, and hope we can be prepared for the board discussion."

Mandy took them through what had happened, and David peppered her with questions. When they got to the Harold Menzies issues, there was no clear path forward that they felt satisfied with, except that David did note that this was the last scheduled board meeting for Menzies, as he was retiring. After the board meeting, he was off the board and of no further concern.

Ed said, "That may be true, but I do feel some responsibility for how I let him come onto the board in the first place, if his background is all that murky."

Jim Kerwin said, "If there was anything going on beneath the surface that he was involved in, and we don't know it, could we be looking at a scandal later? I don't think there is any way to know that before the board meeting, but as you say, let's allow him to ride off and then try to get a real understanding of him. We'll have to deal with whatever comes from that."

Jim added, "I recall meeting Menzies at conferences a couple of times, and he impressed me. I think the idea of bringing him on came from that. Don't fault yourself."

David said he liked the idea of an Executive Committee meeting at the end of the day, including after the annual meeting of shareholders, for them to share this more widely and make sure they weren't keeping all the other directors in the dark. He told them to send a notice for that meeting. Ed felt a big weight being lifted off his shoulders by Jim's taking responsibility for Menzies. They left Jim's office and Ed asked for Mandy to linger after the board and shareholder meetings, in case David wanted her to attend the Executive Committee meeting. Mandy's distinct feeling at that point was that she was getting too much visibility with the Board of Directors. She reflected again on keeping a low profile in the upper echelon of corporate governance.

Tuesday came and went like a flash, with much agonizing over how the presentation would be handled with the Audit Committee the next day, and how they would be prepared to answer questions about the issues being brought to the Executive Committee.

That night Mandy received a call from Ray Hanson, the investigator. She had instructed him to call her day or night, whenever he discovered anything significant.

Hanson said, “Sorry to call so late, but your instructions were to call if anything significant came up, and I thought you should know this. I was tailing Emily Jenkins this evening to see where she was going, and she went to a downtown hotel and met someone in their room. She spent a couple of hours in that room and when she left, she looked like she had been having some fun, if you know what I mean.”

Mandy said, “You’re not talking about playing bridge, are you? Maybe something a little more physical?”

“That’s what I mean.”

“Were you able to find out whose room it was?”

“Yes. It was Harold Menzies’ room.”

Mandy said, “Bingo. Thanks for letting me know. Have you been able to find anything else about Menzies or Moines?”

He said, “Nothing on Moines. But for Menzies, I found nothing else except an address in Washington, that might be his residence. I’ll text it to you.”

“Please stay on it. Especially Emily Jenkins.”

They signed off and Mandy sat there contemplating what to do with her news.

CHAPTER 18

THE BOARD MEETING began early Wednesday morning, and started with the usual standing committees having their sessions in consecutive fashion, so that both the chair and the CEO were able to attend each meeting. Ed Rosen, as corporate secretary, kept the minutes of each meeting. When the Audit Committee was convened, Mandy was invited in and made her presentation. The committee members were extremely interested in what was taking place. It was so outside the ordinary they were mesmerized. On many other occasions where there was controversy, the board members were polite, but outspoken critics of company actions. In this case, they were sympathetic to management. Because of the accelerated deal timing, management couldn't investigate Allzient before it bid. In order to participate, the interested buyers would have to abide by the deal structure. LaSalle couldn't have been expected to see this coming and to swerve away from the train wreck it was becoming. Nor could management have expected to anticipate a murder, much less four murders. The committee was supportive with its comments about how well management had handled things, but emphasized that if any worsening of the situation occurred, it should come back to the board if it wished to abandon the transaction. There was no glory in standing by idly while the stock price plunged, and an abandoned acquisition could be the less harmful path to take.

Only one member chose to suggest that while management did yeoman's work under the circumstances, in retrospect, it would have been better not to participate in bidding unless more pre-bid diligence had taken place.

That comment prompted Harold Menzies to respond, "Look, I know this is my last meeting as a director, so it may be easy for me to say this, but I think it would be a mistake to abandon this deal. No one could foresee these things happening, and acquisitions just don't see this kind of thing. As to walking away, even if the door is wide-open, it would be a tragedy for LaSalle to have worked so hard to get this done, and then have it ripped away from them because of some stupid players who went off the reservation and broke the law. That sounds to me like a lose-lose situation, if it's what happens. I understand that it could get worse, and you could reach the point where it makes no sense to continue, but I urge you to hang in there for a while."

Jim said he understood, and would take it step-by-step.

The annual meeting of shareholders only took thirty minutes. Mandy sat in the room while the CEO made a short speech, followed by answering some innocuous questions from shareholders. The meeting frequently had a smattering of small shareholders and retired employees who asked softball questions. It always amazed management that institutional shareholders chose not to come to the meeting, but this was one of the realities of modern shareholder relations. It was easy in the twenty-first century to have direct access to management and to get questions addressed. One didn't have to attend a meeting and sit through a lot of speechmaking or tedious corporate secretarial peculiarities in order to get one's questions addressed. After all, to attend those meetings, a highly paid employee of a large fund would have to don a suit instead of jeans and running shoes.

Outside the meeting room, several members of the media had gathered, waiting to ask questions. Jim answered as best he could. When asked whether the company would abandon the Allzient acquisition, Jim replied that management was taking it step-by-step and hadn't yet made a decision.

Before the Executive Committee convened its meeting, Mandy was keeping an eye out for Emily. She'd been hovering around the meeting in case Jim wanted her to come in. She wasn't needed, but she still hovered. Harold Menzies gathered his travel bag from the temporary office in the hotel that was set up to support the board meeting, and he was heading out to catch his flight. The board meeting was held in the airport hotel to make it easier for directors to attend and then to head back out to their return destinations. Mandy followed him at a discreet distance and before Menzies descended the escalator he was joined by Emily, who had been loitering in that area. As she followed them, Mandy noticed them touching each other's hands. Once they were aways off from the hotel area, they hugged and kissed. Bingo! Harold broke away and headed toward the security clearance for outbound flights. Emily headed out an exit door. Mandy took all this in and let it simmer in her head, then raced back to the Executive Committee meeting.

Finally, after a long day, all but the Executive Committee members and the lawyers had left. The chairman assembled the committee members and invited the lawyers in as well, giving a synopsis of the events leading up to where they stood. He noted that Harold Menzies was no longer a member of the board, his term having ended when the shareholder meeting concluded. Menzies had said his goodbyes after the meeting and ran off to catch a flight out of town. The chairman then shocked the directors with the possibility that Harold Menzies was a different person altogether than they had thought for a long time. Mandy was asked to give an account on how the identification had taken place.

Mandy said, "We stumbled across the similarity during due diligence. Since we were in a more intense due diligence exercise than normal due to the bribery, we went hard at everything. Mr. Menzies had been recognized by a retired officer from Spruance as possibly being the same director of Spruance, but with a different name. We were able to do some high-tech facial analysis and confirmed it was the same person."

Mandy was dying to spill her guts on Emily and Harold

Menzies, but she kept it to herself. She figured there was another time and place to deal with that. A little voice in her head told her that it was Jim Kerwin's place to inform the board of their mystery director, not her.

A spirited discussion took place. The committee felt that management should try to get to the truth and to meet again to decide on the company reaction. Jim took responsibility for any fallout from having Menzies on the board, since he was responsible for his presence. He had recounted his acquaintance with Menzies, explaining that Harold had approached him at a meeting in Chicago and complimented him on LaSalle's business. One thing led to another, and after some additional meetings, Jim felt he would be value-added as a board member. When he ended up offering him a seat on the board, it had seemed like the most natural thing to do. And, in fact, Harold had impressed his fellow directors for as long as he had been on the board, so that his retirement had been regretted.

Early Thursday morning, Rick and Mandy were at O'Hare awaiting their boarding time. Rick asked, "How do you expect your old corruption prosecutor buddies to treat us in this meeting?"

"I've been gone for a while, so I don't know who'll be there. If Stewart Simons is running the meeting, I'll be relieved. We got along really well while I was there. I can tell you what they'll be looking for though, whether it's people I know or new faces. Justice is always interested in companies with corruption problems acting as submissive as possible, and being willing to take whatever

Justice is dishing out. I'll admit that this an oddball situation, though, since we have Allzient with the corruption issue. We're set to inherit their problems and whatever corrective action or penalty is sought. I'm looking for some sympathy as far as that goes. We need to be able to articulate our anti-bribery compliance program and declare our own clean history. If we get saddled with fines and penalties because of Allzient, assuming we complete the transaction, we need to also assure them that we would introduce a corrective action program to address any weaknesses in the Allzient's compliance program that Justice points out."

"We can do that."

"But then you throw in murders. I don't know what to make of that. That should be of more concern to Allzient than us, I suppose. It should be quite a show."

Rick and Mandy arrived at the Justice Department office. When their outside counsel Bob Thereaux joined them, Mandy filled them in on the conversation she'd had with her sister about Spenser's cause of death. It was a little awkward to have the conversation, she had admitted, because Reggie was bound by confidentiality.

They met with the combined Justice and FBI team, with Stewart Simons thankfully leading the team. Since Mandy had worked with him, he was friendly with her and cordial with Rick and Bob.

Stewart said, "We just finished the meeting with Allzient. It was a difficult discussion, with their security chief having been murdered. I can't get into any detail except to acknowledge that this was not taking the usual path that corruption matters take. Mandy, with her experience at the department, knows and has been saying that." Simons added that it wouldn't go well for Allzient if it had failed to protect Whitney and then he got murdered. He also acknowledged that LaSalle had been in a meeting with Erik Spenser the day before his disappearance.

Simons added, "I regret that this has happened in the midst of you trying to get a transaction done. I'm sure your external audience is expecting some information, if not resolution, for what has been like a bomb going off. I can't help on that. There will have to be a preapproved process with this. In the meantime, though, your company seems to have been truly victimized by this. Do you want to make any comments before I proceed?"

Rick responded, "We truly were blindsided by this. We're very anxious to see what we can do to get past it, and hopefully salvage a transaction. We can tell you what our anti-bribery protocols are, and what we would be prepared to do with this company to install some reliable compliance program features, if they don't already exist. Other than that, we're here to answer any questions you have for us and are willing to cooperate to the nth degree."

Mandy added, "Stewart, I can assure you that we have a robust anti-bribery program. That's my job twenty-four-seven as chief compliance officer. I'm happy to lay all that out for you if you wish. Because of the auction-like nature of the deal, we had limited due diligence. Hardly any chance to turn over any rocks. We were just starting our process when this surprise hit. I'm sure you can appreciate that we aren't sure what kind of due diligence we can expect to get done now, or whether we'll ever be able to get comfortable enough with this to close the deal."

Stewart said, “I’m sure you have a great program, and I understand your dilemma on the deal. Right now, we need to focus on your seller and see what happened here. I would like you to turn over to us anything you have and share any discussions with Erik Spenser. If we need anything else, I’ll be in touch, and if you aren’t receiving updates from Allzient that you expect, don’t hesitate to call me. I can’t promise I can tell you anything, but I’m happy to keep the lines open. We’re also painfully aware that this is not only a serious corruption problem, but a multiple-murder investigation as well. I count four murders, so far.”

Mandy said, “We’ll get you everything we have. As to Spenser, we sat in a room with him for half a day and he only said he was there to make sure he was able to hear anything affecting their security program. The next day he was gone. In more ways than one, apparently.”

The following morning, Mandy went for an early run. She noticed a black SUV parked along Constitution Avenue with its engine idling, and then later near the Watergate Hotel another black SUV, engine idling as well. She didn’t worry too much about it as she got ready for her meeting and met Rick for breakfast. After all, there were black SUVs all over Washington, D.C., with blacked-out windows. They headed over to the Hoover Building, meeting John Booth in the lobby. They were escorted up to a conference room to meet with Alan Frenche and Steve Baker.

Alan Frenche said, “We’ve invited you here today to give us firsthand what you’ve already told Special Agent Baker. Just so you’re clear on this, our focus is looking at any activities happening in the United States that might involve foreign intelligence operations, and where possible, to disrupt them. We try to protect national secrets as well. There's another side of government intelligence operations, one that's supposed to be confined to activities outside the country. When I'm told that there's some of that agency's activity occurring inside the country, I have to be curious about that and make sure I understand what's going on. Does that make sense? OK, and I understand that the Bureau is also now involved in a bribery investigation and related murder case?"

They nodded, and he continued. "First, Mr. Booth, I understand that you were approached by an individual purporting to be a CIA employee and seeking assistance from your company to place individuals in positions within your company. Is that correct?"

"Yes," he said. "He said his name was Philip Ray. It was an impromptu meeting, and we were urged to meet with him by one of our board members. It was very odd, but we met with him, even though we were going through an intense period at the end of 1999. I mean, we reasoned that during the course of your career, what are the odds you'd get an unannounced visit from the CIA?"

"And what did you say to Mr. Ray?"

"We told him we would accommodate his request. We ended up hiring some people in our European operations."

"Could you recognize him if you saw a photo?" Frenche asked.

"I might be able to, though it's been ten years."

"What about the board member who recommended Philip Ray?"

"That was Armand Moines."

"And how did Mr. Moines come to be on your board of directors?"

"I think our CEO met Armand Moines at some industry conferences, and invited him onto the board. Unfortunately, I can't confirm that because our CEO passed away a number of years ago and I have no other resources. I have a pretty good recall on this because it was usually me who got tasked with looking for prospective board members, and it was unusual that a candidate would surface from the CEO."

Rick and Mandy looked at each other. Frenche noticed this unspoken exchange and said, "What?"

Mandy answered, "Well, I may be jumping ahead here, but that was how our CEO said he met our director Harold Menzies, and ended up inviting him onto our board."

Frenche continued, "And this is the person that you believe, and I guess the Bureau also believes, is one and the same person?"

Mandy answered, "Yes, it is. You may know that my sister works at the Bureau's Quantico lab, and as a favor to me she had the photos of the two men compared using the Bureau's facial recognition software. It looks like a match."

"I thought so too," John Booth said.

"Well, if your two directors are really one and the same, and both recruitments took the same pattern, you may be looking at a methodology that's significant. Your company is a significant government defense contractor, is it not Mandy?" Frenche said.

She said, "It is. We have a large Defense Systems Division which designs and manufactures electronic countermeasure devices for combat aircraft, high-tech composite carbon compounds for aircraft stealth applications, silicon chips, and advanced sensors," Mandy said.

"And Mr. Booth," Frenche asked, "was your company also involved in the defense business?"

"Yes, though not to the extent of LaSalle. We were a supplier of exotic metal alloy parts for Navy submarines and aircraft carriers," Booth said.

"And Mr. Crawford," Frenche continued, "does the Allzient business also have defense contracts?"

Rick said, "I think it has a small presence, but it's a big player in the electric vehicle market, and is working hard on nuclear fusion energy and artificial intelligence research. Those technologies may be huge for defense applications."

Alan Frenche said, "Let's come back to Philip Ray. Mr. Booth, do you believe you could give our portrait artist a description so that they could try to draw a sketch of the man?"

Booth said, "It's been a long time, like I said, but I might be able to identify him by looking at a photo. I don't know if I could describe him after all this time. It might be worth trying to look for old Spruance photos of visitors too."

Frenche stepped out briefly and John Booth was called out of the meeting and was led over to a sketch artist. He suggested that Steve Baker be a coordinator and liaison between them and his office. Steve could work up a plan, and in the meantime, if anything occurred to them or if any other curious things happened, they should let Steve know immediately.

Mandy said, "I hope there are no consequences to my sister and her colleague. We imposed on them to ask about the people at the CIA, and who used the Bureau's resources for the photo analysis."

"I suppose there are different channels that might have been used or procedures followed," Frenche said, "but under the circumstances, I won't burn any brain cells on that. But now that we have Special Agent Baker on the assignment, you use him for all of your initiatives. And it may be obvious, but from herein out, let's keep this all to ourselves. Also, there are these murders to consider, which may or may not have anything to do with what we have been discussing here today. But there are some strong odds that a connection could be found. I'm choosing not to go into that today, since there are others involved from another side of this building."

Mandy said, "This may be new information to you, but it may be four murders that are connected here. My sister was working a case involving two bodies that turned out to have been ex-Allzient employees. Actually, employees originally with Spruance Corporation."

Alan Frenche looked at Steve Baker and said, "Please take that into your work." With that he smiled, shook hands, and left.

Everyone headed out, but before Steve got away Mandy pulled him aside and had a short discussion with him. "OK, following orders now from Mr. Frenche, I need to fill you in on the work by Ray Hanson. He found out our senior vice president of strategy Emily Jenkins, is having an affair with Harold Menzies. I don't know if it goes beyond sex, but it is already a violation of our internal rules for keeping a safe distance between management and board members. He also happens to have a Washington, D.C., address, which we didn't know about before. I'll text it to you. Our guy's still watching what else might happen, but at least now you know what I know."

Reggie picked up Mandy late that afternoon and they drove back to her apartment in Quantico, where they had some dinner. Saturday started with an early run in Prince William Forest Park, then shopping at Potomac Mills Shopping Mall, and finally a visit to the U.S. Marine Corps National Museum. Along the way the sisters had a discussion about Minnesota.

Mandy said, "I've been thinking about that kayaking trip we did a couple of years ago in Minnesota."

"That was fun. From that little trickle of a stream leading out of Lake Itasca all the way down to Minneapolis/St. Paul on the Mississippi. Too bad we weren't up for portaging around dams back then. We've got a long way to go if we want to finish. You've still got the two-seater kayak, don't you?

Mandy said, "Sure do. In fact, it looks like having that kayak is responsible for meeting Patrick Carney."

"Am I sensing you've got a buzz going about him?"

"Oh, yeah."

On Sunday after a short run along the Potomac River, Reggie drove Mandy back to the airport for the flight back. While waiting to board her flight, Mandy stopped in the airport bookstore and picked up a copy of Patrick's *Blackhawk's Revenge.*

On Monday morning Mandy was on the phone with Special Agent Steve Baker learning what he had put into motion. He'd gathered the investigators he needed to pursue the backgrounds of Armand Moines and Harold Menzies. These should be easy enough for good FBI snoops to dig up, but Philip Ray was another matter. There had been nothing to work with like photos or a biography. The FBI artist had already sat with Booth while he was in Washington, D.C., and even though Booth had been skeptical, he could recall Ray's looks and he had produced something that could be useful.

His team was on high alert. A death by this means signaled a professional being involved, and pushed the Bureau intensity to its highest level. He wasn't going to have to jockey for assets; more likely than not, Baker might be having to restrain them while he tried to manage the process. He was very interested in learning the background of Erik Spenser, and what he learned made him anxious. The search of Erik Spenser's apartment and office had been conducted with search warrants. They came back with little in the way of useful data. There were no paper files to speak of. Nothing other than routine paperwork existed in his office. His phone was issued by the company, but he had a second phone which he used most of the time. That was discovered in a hiding place they found. There was a new SIM card in the phone, and a supply of SIM cards was found as well. These were signs of tradecraft. They had gotten the same information about Spenser that LaSalle had gotten from Allzient. They knew that he had come from Spruance Corporation, and they would need to follow up on that, but expected the same sort of information — that is, little. A fingerprint check left a gaping hole. He had no history. *What the hell?* The Bureau referred to this as a "ghost." There was no family to whom his death could be communicated. Allzient was taking responsibility to handle his remains, but for the moment, they would be kept by the lab and released when the case came to a close, unless someone turned up to claim them.

The next task was going to be a hard look at the two directors, Armand Moines and Harold Menzies. He had added Emily Jenkins to his list, based on the conversation Mandy had just had with him. Baker would give his team several days to get what they could on them. For now, he was interested in the story on the nerve agent the lab had identified. He reached out to Dan Aleri and was given a short course on the poison and on its antidote. The point about the antidote was that if this means of attack was being utilized, everyone should be conscious of how it behaved and what could be done about it. He analogized it to a stroke; if a person was having a stroke, the speed with which the person reached a medical facility and received the newest stroke drugs, could mean the difference between a full recovery and dramatic life-altering consequences or even death. Baker took the point.

His next step was to connect with the team dealing with the bribery violation at Allzient. He found the agents involved and learned that they were preparing to execute a search warrant at Allzient headquarters in New York, as well as arrest warrants for the two Allzient employees. He volunteered that if the need for materials from LaSalle arose, he would be happy to obtain them on a friendly basis. He knew that the company was already reeling from the engine theft ring arrest, and wanted to avoid further difficulties for them. He also learned that the Justice Department was preparing charges against Allzient and its employees, and would be filing them with the U.S. District Court for the Southern District of New York on Monday morning. Despite Allzient's robust internal investigation and decisive disciplinary action taken against its employees, the Justice Department was exercising its power.

Baker was satisfied that enough initiatives were underway. He called Alan Frenche and reviewed what had been started. Finally, he asked, "Can I ask what you will do about Philip Ray, since I don't really have that on my list?"

Frenche said, "I think we should wait and see what the artist's sketch leads us to. We really don't have a database with that name, much less one that has photos to let Booth go through. Even if we were to, let's say, have him look through all agency personnel photos, could we even get our hands on them to enable him to do that? I think the agency wouldn't cooperate with that. I may have to go up to the director on this one and get some guidance."

"OK, well if there's anything you want me to do on that, let me know. Otherwise, I have a lot to keep me occupied," Steve said.

First thing Monday morning, the U.S. Attorney's Office for the Southern District of New York filed a multicount indictment in Federal District Court against Allzient Corporation for violations of the anti-bribery provisions of Section 15 of the U.S. State Code. FBI agents simultaneously appeared at the New York Allzient office and served a search warrant, and as a result, seized thirteen boxes of records relating to the Allzient accounts in Spain, Italy, and Paris. Since Allzient was a private company, the accounting-related provisions of the law didn't really apply. Mandy considered the filing to be a huge favor to LaSalle. If the case had been filed after the acquisition was closed, the Justice Department and the SEC could then file charges against LaSalle for Allzient's actions. As a public company, the full range of charges and remedies could be sought.

The U.S. attorney for the southern district held a news conference to announce the action taken that morning by her office, describing the charges and the foreign governments who were implicated.

In Chicago, a meeting on the situation included Ed, Mandy, Rick, and Emily.

Emily spoke up first. "I see this prosecution as driving a silver stake through the heart of this deal, pure and simple. Nobody in management or on the board is going to want to touch Allzient now."

Stunned, Mandy replied, "I don't see it that way. In fact, I think we may be incredibly lucky. Nobody else is going to want to touch Allzient, if you're thinking about other acquirers. The government has done us a huge favor, as I was saying to Rick earlier, by striking before we acquired the company. Also, if the case results in millions in fines, which it surely will—think $100 million easy—that bill goes to Allzient, and it can translate into a purchase price reduction. We can still keep the deal alive and wait out the federal case, then we snap up all the intellectual property, at least. I'm only repeating what I've already heard you say, Emily."

Emily said nothing, but she was obviously uncomfortable. Right out in public, Emily had just been defanged by Mandy by going right to Emily's own conclusion that a price reduction could cure the problem. *That bitch!* Rosen recommended that he and Emily brief Jim Kerwin and stay poised to move in Mandy's direction. Rick and Mandy left the meeting. In Jim Kerwin's office, Rosen laid out the idea for Jim and he asked what Emily thought, sensing her displeasure.

Emily said, "It probably won't surprise you that I don't like it. No offense meant, but I think as soon as Mandy got her teeth into the bribery issue, this deal has been in a death spiral. I feel like I'm looking at our final strategic stroke getting a knife in the back. Look, I get it that Allzient has a major problem and they have to get it solved, but the idea that the Justice Department is doing us a big favor, strikes me as naive. They smell blood and are trying to kill Allzient and our deal by charging Allzient now. If we don't close this deal now, we'll give Allzient an opening to terminate, and there are plenty of other bidders who could emerge. I think we should negotiate with the Justice Department to get immunity from these events, even if we do close before their case has ended. We should proceed with Allzient, but restructure the deal to provide for a healthy price reduction, or to carve out the portion of the purchase price that could represent the fine, and set it aside in escrow to support the payment. We've worked a long time on this, and I don't want it to go up in smoke."

Jim said, "Look, I can see both sides of the argument. Let me discuss it with the chair and get his sense of what the board would favor. In the Executive Committee meeting last week, there was quite a lot of discomfort with the situation and the continuing drag on the stock price. I think they're afraid this will taint the company. What do you have to say to that, Ed?"

"Mandy's just doing her job. If you think her idea is so bad, or if you want to see if the Justice Department would give immunity, I can ask her to try for an immunity agreement. But I don't want to lose sight of the fact that there's not just bribery going on here. There's a murderer on the loose, and murky director and intelligence agency involvement. And we don't have an explanation. I could easily see board members saying we should back away from this until the smoke clears, because some things are going on that we can't explain or control."

"I would want to participate in that discussion with Justice," Emily said.

"Do that, and let me know what happens. I'll hold off calling the chairman until I hear back," Jim said.

CHAPTER 19

STEVE BAKER'S ACTIVITIES were heating up on a number of fronts. By midweek, he was getting the first set of results from his investigators and invited Mandy to participate in a conference call to hear the results.

Steve laid out the agenda for the meeting.

"First, on the persons known as Armand Moines and Harold Menzies. The photo analysis that the bureau did at Reggie's request has been formalized and concludes with 80 percent confidence that they were the same person. If they could come up with fingerprints and DNA samples, that would be decisive. But that was proving to be doubtful. For Armand Moines, not a trace exists. Last known address was found and checked, and proved to be a dead end. At one time, he apparently had a post office box, but not anymore. His biography was brief, and much like Menzies, it only refers to him as an international business consultant.

"Next, as to Harold Menzies, the result isn't much better. His address in Chicago was listed only as a PO box, and it too had been closed down. It was suspicious that he didn't have a street address. He had to live somewhere, didn't he? We looked for recent travel outside the country, and had found that his passport had been scanned in Seattle within the last week when he had boarded a flight to Hong Kong. Where he went, when he disembarked, was anybody's guess. His employment details revealed little, and his proxy statement disclosure referenced only his employment as an international trade consultant. The search for passports, driver's licenses, and Social Security numbers for both individuals had yielded neither current addresses nor other information that would help."

Mandy asked, "Is there anything we can do to help on the location issue?"

Steve said, "Can you see if there were any items in LaSalle's possession that might be helpful in identifying Menzies?"

Mandy said, "We could have some useful materials on Harold Menzies in our corporate secretary's department. Also, we just got a Washington address for him."

Mandy leaned in to Steve Baker and whispered, "Ray Hanson."

Steve also talked with Alan Frenche about getting photos of CIA personnel, and letting John Booth look at them on a computer screen. This would be a logical next step, except that he knew the agency wouldn't make photos of its personnel available outside the agency. It was either going to be the Booth sketch, or nothing.

Mandy listened to Steve's report. "On a more positive note, Alan Frenche has made some headway on the history of the call that Dan Aleri had made to the human resources management office to raise the names Ray, Moines, and Menzies. The person who had received the call had asked what the nature of the inquiry was, and had been told it was in connection with an FBI investigation, but no more than that. Frenche's office had placed a call to Sherman Haskins, his counterpart at the agency, but had been told he was unavailable and would call back. A callback had occurred later that same day by a deputy of Haskins."

They'd had a short discussion in which the deputy explained that the agency didn't release information about agents' or possible agents' names due to national security concerns. Frenche asked whether the deputy was confirming that the names were of agents, and he was told the deputy couldn't comment on that. That was a strikeout, leaving it for Frenche to decide if he wanted to try a face-to-face meeting with Haskins, or elevate this to a director-to-director level. The agency was clearly stonewalling. If that didn't yield anything, he would have to go up through the attorney general to the director of national intelligence. That was a big step to take, and he'd better be sure he had something solid.

The following day, the FBI artist came to see Steve Baker, who was now operating temporarily out of the Hoover Building. The artist showed him what Booth was able to generate from memory, but it was an "anyone" portrait and could probably be a million different male Caucasians. But he took the drawing and posted it on the Bureau's website, identifying it as a possible "Philip Ray," and asking for any information about such person in connection with various federal crimes. He sent a copy to Alan Frenche, who looked at it and thought it looked familiar, but he couldn't place it.

He wanted to meet with Dan Petri as well and discuss Novichok, so he drove to Quantico and met with Dan on the autopsy of Erik Spenser, and Dan asked if Regina Doucette could join them for the meeting. They waited until Reggie came. Steve was momentarily unable to speak when Dan introduced them.

Dan broke the spell by saying, "I know. That happened to me as well. Yes, Mandy and Reggie are identical twins. Also, they have the annoying habit of dressing identically to make it even harder."

Reggie said, "It will be better if you don't see us together. Just remember that I'm the more sociable and talkative sister, and Mandy's the more cynical and introverted."

"In my dealings with your sister, she has seemed to be neither cynical nor introverted, but I guess now I get to compare you with her," Steve said. "Tell me everything I need to know about Erik Spenser's death."

Dan was the examining pathologist, and went over the file in detail. "We discovered a pinhole injection site on the back of the neck. Cause of death from collapsed lungs and paralysis of the heart muscle. We really got lucky and were able to reclaim some soft tissue from the distinctive chemical signature of the nerve agent Novichok. He must have received a massive dose."

He noted the further details of the autopsy: "The absence of any other identifying marks on the body such as dental impressions, had yielded nothing, nor had fingerprints or DNA."

Steve Baker added, "He was supposed to have a top-secret security clearance due to Allzient's defense businesses in Europe, but the Personal Security Clearance he held through NATO, didn't yield any useful information. From the findings of interviews at Allzient New York, the consensus was that Spenser was a very secretive, uncommunicative person who traveled a great deal and kept to himself. Probably not an uncommon demeanor for a security officer. When training was necessary, he hired outside contractors. He handled things individually, and wasn't a team player."

Reggie said to no one in particular, "Sounds very similar to Mandy's Willis Traynor, of the engine theft mess she told me about. Both these guys were corporate security managers, correct?"

Steve said, "Pretty ironic."

Spenser's apartment had been another fruitless source for the agents doing the search. Other than clothes and a few kitchen and bathroom items, the apartment was barren. His computer and any work files he had, were missing. The entire apartment seemed to have been wiped clean, and the few samples of DNA material taken, were his, with none from other individuals. Nothing more would be learned from Erik Spenser, unless one wanted to draw inferences from the things that were seemingly missing. Only the hidden burner phone had been found.

After Dan and Reggie left, Baker called Mandy and gave her an update.

Steve said, "Why didn't you tell me Reggie was your identical twin? I about had a heart attack."

Mandy said, "We get tired of warning everyone so we just let happen whatever's going to happen. Sorry."

Steve said, "More on that later. Our results were decidedly skimpy, I have to admit. Have you had any luck in your corporate secretary area?"

"Yes, let me tell you what I learned from Susan Chambers. She's our assistant corporate secretary and manages all things involving the Board of Directors, whether it be information, materials, travel arrangements, or more. She told me that each director has his or her own iPad for meeting materials, which they take with them when they leave. All materials are delivered by a downloaded iPad board book, with only occasional exceptions. When Menzies cycled off the board, the company allowed him to keep his iPad, so it's gone. The company provided chargers for use in the board meeting rooms, but those were collected and stored along with other chargers. There was a director nameplate put out at every seat, and those were collected at the end of each session, but may not have been touched by him."

Then Mandy had one final thought. "I remembered that at the January meeting, there was a special presentation deck of materials for the Allzient acquisition that had been handed out and gone over by the investment bankers. We requested them to be handed back for destruction, but Susan still has them. They had directors' names on the covers, so I believe I can pull Mr. Menzies' book out of the *to be shredded* box for you," she said.

"Brilliant! Did anyone else handle them?" Steve said.

Mandy said, "Well, whoever made the presentation booklets at the banker's office, I guess, but once here, it was only by Susan. It may be evidence, right? Harold Menzies has disappeared, and he may have been involved in something. You're trying to track him down, right? You should send an evidence technician to take possession of that binder, so we won't touch it. We'll just keep it locked away exactly as it is right now."

Mandy called Susan Chambers and related all this. "The FBI will probably want to take our fingerprints and get DNA samples from us. Also, we'll have to track down the banker's people who may have touched the booklets, and get all their prints and DNA too. They'll want to be able to see if there is a match to anything they find on the materials," Mandy said.

Susan said, "You might want to collect some clothing from Emily Jenkins then."

"Why?"

"Well, if you're looking for Harold Menzies' DNA, it should be all over Emily's stuff."

Mandy said, "How would you know that?"

"There's very little that gets by me. Also, those kinds of people tend to think people like me are invisible, so they're uninhibited in showing things that might be dead giveaways. Oh, yeah, those two are a couple, if you know what I mean."

"I knew I liked you for a reason."

She left Susan and called Steve to get the process moving. By the next morning, the evidence technician had come to the office and got what was needed. The banker's office had also been visited, and the technician got what was needed there too. Rick and Mandy had a call with the banker to confidentially explain that this was an investigation that required their cooperation, and they were being asked to accommodate this need without asking any questions, though they were assured that no one in their organization was suspected of having done anything improper or was a target of the investigation.

A number of things were happening that were the direct result of the U.S. attorney's charges against Allzient, and the associated news conference over the case and over the death of Erik Spenser. The Allzient deal team was slow to respond on a long list of outstanding due diligence items that had been in play before the charges were filed, and this was an ominous sign to Emily Jenkins. There was some dialogue between Allzient and Rick Crawford, but it wasn't very productive. The two Allzient employees who had operated the bribery scheme had been individually charged with criminal violations and arrested, and their cases were processed through the usual steps involving a hearing for bail. Details had leaked out regarding the specifics of the Spanish, Italian, and French government contracts involved, and those customers had separately begun internal investigations in their own countries. Prosecutors in those countries had announced investigations into their respective parties to the Allzient contracts, and it looked like some indeterminate period of time was going to be involved for this painful interruption in their relationships.

On the LaSalle side, the local and national media were camping out in the lobby of the LaSalle building, and for the time being, the comings and goings of the senior executives was tricky while a paparazzi-like atmosphere ruled the scene. Luckily, the media had chosen not to blanket the Lower Michigan Avenue entrance, preferring to operate in the sunlight. The public relations staff was doing the best they could with what limited answers the company was prepared to give out, and soon, Jim Kerwin would step before the microphones to make a statement and to take questions. That would hopefully end the media siege and let them pursue fresher targets.

But before that could take place, LaSalle was on the verge of releasing its first-quarter 2009 earnings. This would take the form of a news release before the market opened, accompanied by a securities analyst conference call also taking place before the market opened. Rick had been working with the public relations and investor relations staffs to craft the acquisition-related parts of the messages to be accurate and as elegant as such statements could be under the circumstances. They had to walk a fine line between standing behind the company's strategic initiative and expressing righteous indignation over blatant illegal activity by its acquisition partner. They reserved the right to weigh the pros and cons of proceeding and keeping the deal alive in the meantime. From public relations and investor relations perspectives, in other words, this had to be a whirling dervish maneuver that, if successful, would earn a cocktail or six by day's end.

The only good features of the current LaSalle landscape were that the company had blown past street expectations in the first quarter, and it still retained control over whether the Allzient deal would proceed or not. When Jim Kerwin and his CFO opened the securities analysts conference call, the financial results were summarized as laid out in the release. Kerwin discussed the operating highlights, and then did a workman-like job addressing the Allzient situation. Upon opening the lines for questions, however, the tone was negative and completely preoccupied with the wisdom of proceeding with the acquisition. It was clear where the analysts stood, and represented a preview of what would be in the written reports issued soon after the call. If that hadn't been bad enough, one analyst also raised the first engine theft ring debacle that remained an open sore, and piled on with a flaming critique of the company's second theft ring in five years. The involvement of the company's own corporate security director hadn't gone unnoticed and was a big black eye.

Once over, Kerwin retreated to his office to lick his wounds and to watch the market open. The share price was down 3 percent on the open, despite the excellent operating results and financial optics. As analyst after analyst report was issued, and the investor relations department circulated them with highlights, the mood worsened throughout the day. At the close of the day, the price had bounced around but settled out at a depressing 5 percent decline. No celebratory cocktails would be hoisted that day.

Mandy took this all in and concluded, *who cares? That stuff doesn't matter right now. If we don't put this Allzient fire out right now, we're screwed.*

Mandy was less than enthusiastic about having the conversation Emily Jenkins had pushed. She went into her office and shut the door, stood back and looked out at the Chicago River at the Locks to Lake Michigan. It seemed to her that Emily Jenkins was feeding a compulsion to continue the Allzient process. The browbeating that Jim Kerwin had taken at the hands of the market was like a body blow, but she thought that was what Jim got paid to do. Emily wouldn't be satisfied until a door was shut in her face by someone other than a fellow staff member, especially by one of the sinister lawyers she clearly hated so much. She also wondered what exactly had been said among the directors at the recent Executive Committee meeting, since no staff officers had been invited, not even Ed Rosen as corporate secretary. Normally, if the board met in executive session, it meant that Ed would have to rely on whoever chaired the meeting to tell him what transpired, so that he could prepare minutes and be able to carry out *to-do* orders from the group. If the meeting were in executive session, then, it promoted secrecy rather than good corporate governance. Ed hadn't shared with anyone what he was told had transpired in the meeting. Maybe no one had told him.

Mandy had set up a call with Stewart Simons, who also brought along Deputy U.S. Attorney for the Southern District of New York Bryan O'Neill, who was handling the Allzient case. Rick, Mandy, and Emily were on the LaSalle end of the phone. After introductions, Stewart led off by explaining that while his section was still very much involved, as was the SEC, the control of the matter had now passed to the Southern District, and Brian specifically. If the call was to ask Justice for anything, it would have to go to Brian anyway and he might as well hear it directly. Rick responded to that by thanking him for the call.

"What can we do for you?" Brian said.

Mandy led off. "Thanks for giving us the time today. As you may know, we've been working on this acquisition for a long time, and this surprise hit us right between the eyes. We have a long-term strategy, and this was the last piece of the puzzle. We wanted to see if there was anything the Justice Department could or would do for us to keep this deal in place so all of our efforts are not in vain."

Brian said, "What exactly did you have in mind?"

Mandy continued. "Well, if we complete this deal, we could end up being in the unusual position of stepping into Allzient's shoes and in essence be their alter ego for this indictment. Unless I'm completely misreading the situation, we could be a public company paying for the sins of a private company, and have the kind of remedies inflicted on us that would not have affected a private company. That isn't something that would motivate us to complete the deal."

"And how could the federal government do something to alleviate that, even if it was willing to help in some way, which I'm not saying it is? As you know, we're not here to help deals get completed or to keep you motivated."

Rick said, "We were thinking that under the circumstances, the government might be willing to grant LaSalle limited immunity in favor of the directors and officers and of LaSalle itself as a corporation. If a financial penalty was levied, we could work that out between LaSalle and Allzient, under our purchase price. So, another thing to ask for would be protection from LaSalle or from Allzient business units being barred from entering into government contracts with the U.S. Department of Defense or other federal agencies. Defense contracts are a large part of our business. Emily or Mandy, is there anything else I'm missing?"

Emily added, "I think we would also want to be protected from any current LaSalle or Allzient federal contracts being terminated."

Brian said, "Well, I'm sympathetic to your issue and that this happened to you while you were just getting ready to close, but I don't know that the federal government can do something like that here. We're are not in place for the purposes of carving out remedies for anyone, especially at this early stage of the case. That being said, we do appreciate your cooperation with us so far, and hope it'll continue. We can have another conversation if you wish, at some point down the line. But for right now, the department needs to channel all of its energy into investigating and prosecuting these defendants. As to federal contracts, we don't have any jurisdiction over Defense Department contracting or the qualification of contractors, so that would be outside our scope."

There was nothing else to be said, so they said thanks and hung up. Mandy's immediate thought was that she cringed inside from having to embarrass LaSalle in front of her old colleagues at DOJ. That move of asking for immunity was clearly going to guarantee a big "NO." Mandy would not have made such a request were it her, knowing how the DOJ rolled.

"Well, that was a clear *NO,*" Emily said. "I thought

you did a good job of articulating what we wanted, so thanks for that." Emily went to Jim Kerwin's office and related the outcome of the call, and Jim planned to call the chairman to fill him in.

That night after work Mandy's phone buzzed with a text message from Patrick Carney: "Dinner this weekend?"

Why not, Mandy thought. She texted, "I can do Friday. Does that work?"

Patrick texted back. "You bet. I'll pick you up at 7:00 p.m."

Well, she thought, *this may become a thing.* With that, the tingle came back.

CHAPTER 20

JOHN BOOTH was a creature of habit. Every night on Siesta Key it was his routine to make sure his boat was secure before turning in for the night. This involved walking around the edges of the boat as he gripped the top for stability to make sure everything was secured and covered, snapping the tarp as he went. The night after he had spent several hours with an FBI artist doing the best he could to recall facial features of Philip Ray, and after his wife was asleep, he went out to his boat and looked at the stars before making the usual swing around the outside of the boat. As he rounded the boat one foot inexplicably slipped and he went into the water, striking his head on the edge of the boat as he went down. As he went under, only semiconscious because of the blow he'd taken, he thought how embarrassing this was, and that this had never happened to him before. Once in the water, trying to pull himself together, he realized something seemed to be holding him down below the surface. He couldn't overcome the downward pull, and a frantic fear overcame him. When his struggle ended and he was still, the hand that had been holding him surfaced and wiped the slippery compound off the edge of the boat, then silently swam away from the dock and disappeared into the dark. John Booth's wife found his floating body early the next morning, and was paralyzed with grief after dialing 911.

Mandy got a call from Steve Baker on Thursday morning. "Mandy, I'm calling to let you know that John Booth was found dead. The FBI is asserting jurisdiction over the death as suspicious and possibly connected to our investigation."

Mandy said, "Oh, my God. This is terrible. I feel so bad for getting him involved in this."

"I don't know what to tell you at this point. We're assuming it was murder and connected to the investigation of Philip Ray. The Sarasota County sheriff's office was happy to have the Bureau take control, and we've asked for a news blackout on its involvement, since we fear that the death isn't accidental. We don't want that revealed to the public."

Mandy made several calls in the minutes following the news from Steve Baker. The first was to her father, since he would want to know about what had happened to his old friend. He was shocked by the news and said immediately that he and her mother would want to travel down to John's funeral. Mandy said she would go as well. Next, she called Reggie and told her what had happened, and how badly she had felt for involving Booth. She asked Reggie to take extra care of her surroundings and to be alert for anything suspicious. Remembering the black SUVs that seemed to be swarming them, she asked if Reggie had seen any, but she hadn't. She also asked Reggie to warn Dan. Mandy suggested she might want to go away for a while, and that she was going to ask Steve Baker to provide protection for her and Dan, just in case. Finally, she called Beverly Barrow, Booth's former HR colleague at Spruance, and told her what had happened, but let her think it was probably just an unfortunate accident. Mandy made sure the rest of the LaSalle team knew what had happened.

In Alan Frenche's office at FBI Headquarters overlooking E Street, he and Steve Baker got Mandy on the phone and they mulled over what had transpired. They went over the timeline of Booth's involvement, and the Bureau artist's trip. They called the artist and asked him what his every action had been. When he got to the end of his day with Booth, he revealed that he'd had a thought, so he'd called Booth. He admitted to Booth that his rendering didn't look promising, and suggested that it might be helpful if he were to come up to Washington, D.C., again and look over photos they were collecting. Booth said he was happy to do so.

Baker said, "That's probably it. I'm betting Booth's phone was bugged."

"Let's list all of the people who had anything to do with the Philip Ray name, and see who's at risk. And get Booth's phone."

Mandy said, "At LaSalle it's me of course, and maybe one or two others I've dealt with there. Then there are two people in your lab at Quantico, one of whom is my sister. As a matter of fact, I'm wondering if you're going to provide protection for me. Then I suppose there are some at the agency."

Frenche said, "That reminds me. I never did speak to Sherman Haskins at the agency. He fobbed me off to a deputy who stonewalled me. I think I need to have another go at him. I don't like being snubbed by a spy."

Frenche asked what had been learned about John Booth's death, and Baker told him that there was nothing to suggest foul play, but it wasn't a satisfying explanation because John Booth had been a good swimmer. He had a blow on the forehead that was most likely from his head hitting the side of the boat if he'd slipped off. There had also been no natural causes like heart attack, stroke, or anything else that would explain the death. He had water in his lungs and drowning was deemed to be the cause of death.

After they finished their meeting, Alan Frenche again called Sherman Haskins' office and asked his assistant for a date to have lunch. He got a date at the end of the week to meet at the Hoover Building cafeteria. She asked if there was a subject and he told her interagency relations.

Bob Doucette used the company plane to make the trip to Sarasota with his wife and his daughter for the funeral of John Booth. The three left Chicago Executive Airport in Wheeling, had dinner in Sarasota, and went to the wake. They paid their respects to John's widow and met John's children, and then went to the Ritz-Carlton for the night. The funeral home had been filled with people, as there was another wake besides John's that night. Mandy knew no one there, but one person there had recognized her. It was the same person who had pulled on John Booth's pant leg in the water. Mandy had arranged to catch a flight up to Washington, D.C., to see Steve Baker and to catch up with Reggie after the funeral service the next morning. She had emailed her flight details to Reggie, and told her she'd get a cab to Quantico.

When she got to Washington, Mandy wasn't aware of the interest another passenger had in her, or that she had been followed out of the terminal and then down to Quantico by a silver SUV that had been waiting to pick up the other passenger in the prepaid ride line. Once the cab ride ended and she disappeared into Reggie's building, it was a simple matter to enter the lobby and to spot the apartment number labeled "Doucette." They would return when they could be pretty certain the lawyer would be out of her apartment. They needed an empty apartment for what they were planning.

Mandy spent a quiet night with Reggie and they discussed everything that was taking place. In the morning, Mandy headed out by cab to the Franconia Springfield metro station and at the end of her ride, exited two blocks from the Hoover Building. She walked over, trying to be vigilant about anyone following or parked in a black SUV, but saw nothing. Probably overly paranoid, she thought. She caught up with Steve after he had finished meeting with his team, and they went over the results of the Harold Menzies materials. He said they had good prints on front and back plastic covers of the Allzient banker's report, and by carefully going through the booklet, were able to get some stray brown hairs, which they felt pretty certain would be his. For the prints, by process of elimination, they thought they had his. All but one set of prints had been matched to Susan Chambers and to the bank staff who had prepared the reports, so they were relying on those to be Menzies' prints. The fingerprints had been run through the FBI fingerprint database and hadn't been returned with any match. She shrugged her shoulders and asked, "Is that a problem?"

Steve said, "Well, LaSalle's a sizable defense contractor, right? As I understood it, Menzies worked as a consultant in government defense contracting. We kicked that around here and discussed it with one of our sister agencies, the Defense Counterintelligence Security Agency. They ran his name through the system and came up empty. They also said that someone in that line of work probably would have been given a security clearance and would have been fingerprinted. But there were no prints, and no security clearance issued, no record of his name in their system. Nada." The FBI and other intelligence agencies were required to advise if issues arose concerning the security of a defense contractor, so the information on Harold Menzies had been handed over.

It had been determined initially by the now-deceased John Booth that Menzies and Moines had been the same person, neither of whom could really be identified in detail. And Armand Moines, at least, had been very interested in accommodating the CIA in finding homes for exfiltrated U.S. undercover assets, and then in arranging for Spruance Corporation to be acquired by Allzient. Allzient would have been consolidated into LaSalle if it was acquired. It also had very sensitive information on next-generation electric batteries and fusion research. It seems that several of those exfiltrated agents had been employed, and one of them, Eric Spenser, had been murdered using a nerve agent. Harold Menzies, alias Armand Moines, had also been interested in the acquisition of Allzient by LaSalle up until his final meeting as a board member.

Since LaSalle's involvement in electronic countermeasures, composite carbon materials, silicon chips, and electronic sensors were all subject to security classification, the Defense Department was concerned that someone at the highest level in the contractor had no background information.

Mandy was now putting this all together in her head. She asked about the status of the calls between the CIA and the FBI. Steve told her that Alan Frenche was scheduled to meet with his counterpart at the agency Sherman Haskins, this coming Friday. Steve didn't have high expectations for that meeting, but wanted it to take place to see if it would yield anything. There were now five in the body count in this matter—James Whitney, Erik Spenser, John Booth, and the two ex-Allzient bodies buried together—with maybe more to come.

As tempting as it was to pursue the intelligence agency angle to this, Mandy still had an obligation to see the bribery matter through. She knew that the investigation involving the bribery of the Spanish, Italian, and French government officials by Allzient was ongoing. The individuals involved had agreed to be interviewed with their counsels present, and Mandy was hopeful that some useful information would be forthcoming. The ex-employees proved to be very open about their actions on the contracts, but were adamant that they had nothing to do with the murder of Erik Spenser or the others, nor with any transfer of classified information that their company might possess. They also claimed not to know any employees who may have come into Allzient from Spruance Corporation. Steve couldn't be precise with Mandy about the details of the investigation or what the status was, but he did say that he believed the individual defendants would probably plead guilty. The bigger catch for Justice would be the conviction of Allzient and a sizable fine in the neighborhood of $200 million for the corrupt practices. Allzient's foreign subsidiaries had also been charged in separate proceedings by the three countries' prosecutors, and similar convictions and fines were expected. The three countries involved would probably seek extradition of the two Allzient employees for prosecution under their laws. Allzient was just a house on fire, with nobody manning the fire hoses.

Mandy was staying in Washington, at Steve Baker's request. She'd had a call with Greg Carlucci that was unsettling. He was shaken by what she told him about the Justice Department not cutting LaSalle any slack, but he was ready to meet with Defense as soon as they wanted to do so. He'd alert LaSalle's senior management, who would want to be represented at any meeting. This was LaSalle's golden goose and nothing could be allowed to undermine its strength. It was also destined to be the home of the Allzient division, if and when it came into the company. Greg would carry forward the message and be prepared to respond in the morning. Rick was stunned and worried about where this would lead, and would have to think hard about whether this was a rupture in the code of conduct compliance fabric of the company. If so, what could Mandy do about it? Rick was coming around to Mandy's views and was shaken by Harold Menzies' presence in the company. It would be very easy for the government to bring down LaSalle, given what was happening under its very nose.

The next morning, Mandy spoke to Greg Carlucci again. He had briefed the Defense Systems Division management head, and they had committed to be as responsive to Defense as possible. Mandy and Greg called Steve Baker, who promised to get a contact person to call them and to set a time for early afternoon. Rick came in and said that their internal control programs on security and classified documents were being examined, and would give her conclusions by the next day. Ed, shaken by everything, had briefed Jim Kerwin, who wanted to call a special board meeting to update them on the situation. Ed was now setting that up.

Wednesday afternoon, Mandy received an email from Stewart Simons saying he was sorry but the U.S. attorney had declined to provide the immunity requested. Mandy called Emily Jenkins to let her know the outcome, and Emily said, "Actually, I'm not disappointed. Yes, I'd wanted some clear path to move forward, but if they reach a conclusion and we can handle that with a purchase price adjustment, maybe we can move forward. Am I missing anything?"

Mandy said, "There's more to it than that, as we discussed before. If they get a huge fine, which they will, we can deal with that. I'd expect them to have to enter into a consent decree where they have to meet a lot of conditions going forward. Maybe all things that people would expect, like training, improved compliance programs, government reporting, third-party audits, and so on. Maybe that's all OK. Remember, though, that there are still the foreign actions pending against them. Also, if you recall, he disavowed completely any ability to address government contracts."

"Well, I'm still encouraged. I'm going to tell Jim so he can let the board know, once something is announced. Thanks, Mandy."

After hanging up, Mandy said out loud to herself, "Wow, a rare, happy Wretched Witch."

Once off the phone on her end, though, Emily made a beeline out of the building. Scurrying across Pioneer Court and halfway across the Michigan Avenue bridge over the Chicago River, she punched in Harold Menzies' number. "Well, you would have been very proud of me just now. I was all Ms. Optimism and didn't give a hint of unhappiness with Raggedy Ann and her band of deal killers. You need to weigh in here when you have a chance. Those hard asses at the Justice Department just flat out refused to give us immunity. Can you do something?"

Harold said, "Let me see what I can do. Leave it with me. Miss you."

She made a kissing sound and said, "You too. Sorry for all of the background noise. I'm paranoid now, so I came down to the street to call you. Love you."

When the call ended, Harold thought to himself, *Emily, you have no idea what a hopeless case you are right now.*

That night, to blow off some steam and to get her head out of the LaSalle mess, Mandy pulled up the Grandma's Marathon course map and identified the start and finish lines. She also looked at the elevation chart, a perpetual evil in marathoning. As a Chicagoan, there was nothing in racing as challenging as elevation, unless it was elevation at altitude. Fortunately, she found that elevation was nothing to be feared in the grandma's course; if anything, it was a gentle downhill course. Next, she looked at lodging options and found that every hotel room within a sixty-mile radius of Duluth had been booked solid. Such was the popularity of this race, or the lack of sufficient hotels. That left only one option, and a miserable one at that, for she and Reggie would have to share a dorm room at the University of Minnesota at Duluth, a whole five-mile distance uphill from the finish line. At least school would be out of session. On a happier note, for entertainment purposes, she found a long-running play with seats available, written by Howard Mohr, based upon Garrison Keillor's *A Prairie Home Companion*, called *How to Talk Minnesotan*. She thought that would be a great distraction for her and Reggie after the race. That done, she bagged it for the night.

On Friday, the directors of the counterintelligence sections of the FBI and CIA met at the Hoover Building cafeteria and had a table off on their own, well away from earshot of others. A discrete distance away, Steve Baker and Mandy were pretending to have lunch in the same room some distance away from them. The two directors sat down with trays and some FBI delicacies for lunch. Sherman Haskins had known Alan Frenche for a number of years, and they saw each other at the occasional meetings of the U.S. intelligence community's counterintelligence sections. These meetings of the highly secretive individuals occurred occasionally so as to share information of general import. Alan Frenche thought that they were really competitions of who could share the least.

"Thanks for coming, Sherman. Hope you're staying busy these days," Alan started off.

"I am, and I assume the same for you. I see we have an outstanding *interagency relations* issue between us that you want to discuss?"

They both started to eat. Across the room, Mandy stared hard at the two men at the table.

Steve said, "And that's Sherman Haskins, Alan's counterpart at the CIA."

Mandy said, "If I didn't know any better, I would swear that's Harold Menzies."

As inconspicuously as possible, Steve stared over at the table like Mandy was doing.

"Are you sure?"

"I'm positive. I have a pretty good sense of these things. I'd be willing to make a bet on it."

Alan said to Sherman Haskins, "I assume your deputy passed along our request for assistance on recognizing a person possibly from your agency who was contacting U.S. companies?"

"What makes you think this person was from the agency?"

"Because he said so, and he had a reference from a company's director who confirmed the fact. We have some persons who were also possibly involved," Alan answered.

"Look, you know as well as I, that we can't go identifying agents or providing information that might get in the wrong hands. We're talking about national security concerns here. You're worried about the same things every day."

Haskins was just about done with his meal and was in a hurry to end the conversation. Alan Frenche realized he had just worked out the funny feeling of familiarity he was having with Haskins — it was the face on the FBI sketch from the John Booth session.

"Fair enough," Alan answered. "I would be happy to have a confidentiality agreement that our director would sign, and we would want to request employee photos as well for review."

"To be reviewed by whom?" Haskins asked.

"By witnesses who believe they can recognize a subject. And by our team, who's trying to complete an investigation that might involve national security."

"You're asking me to give you a set of employee photos and to put names through our system to identify them?" Haskins said. "I don't see that idea getting past first base, Alan. Sorry, but the answer's no. I've got to run. Good seeing you." With that, he was off abruptly, picking up his tray and walking it to the return belt and right through the door to the elevator.

Alan watched him moving and tried to keep his temper in check. His mind was troubled by something in Haskins' look.

As Haskins dropped his tray and left, Frenche then

noticed Mandy Doucette racing across the room to the return tray belt and she lifted the Haskins' tray off the rollers before it started moving.

Steve Baker quickly popped out of his seat and made his way to Mandy's side and asked her what she was doing.

Mandy said, "We need to get the DNA off this tray. I can't let this go. Can you get it tested?"

Alan Frenche joined them at the return belt. "I don't know what you two are doing, but I just had the impression that Sherman Haskins bore a striking resemblance to the drawing our artist did of Philip Ray based on the input from John Booth."

Steve said, "Mandy recognized Haskins as a knockoff of Harold Menzies, the LaSalle director."

Alan pulled out his cell phone and called his office, asking his secretary to stop by the supply room and to pick up a pair of rubber gloves and an evidence bag and to meet him in the cafeteria. Within fifteen minutes, they had the unexpected gift of silverware bearing Sherman Haskins' prints and his DNA sample on a Gatorade bottle, all secured in a plastic bag. Frenche thought to himself, *And that son of a bitch had been way too anxious to get away from me.* He only regretted that he didn't have a still-living John Booth to look at Hoover Building surveillance photos of Haskins coming into the building to see if he recognized him. Pieces were falling into place in this puzzle, though.

Alan said, "I guess we had the same idea. Let's see what Sherman Haskins' DNA tells us. Steve, did you get anything from John Booth's cell phone?"

"It was loaded up with spyware from a remote location."

"Damn."

CHAPTER 21

FINALLY, back in Chicago, the weekend was a welcome relief for Mandy, as she had to decompress from the intense week she'd had. She needed to gear up mentally and physically for Grandma's Marathon, about three months away. Take away three weeks for tapering before race day, and that left her with nine weeks to train up to the long distance she needed. She didn't have to start this weekend, but she needed to chip away at the stress of the week.

But first, she was having dinner Friday night with Patrick. He picked her up at 7:00 p.m., as planned and he hugged her and opened the door to his BMW and she got settled. She was dressed in a simple black dress with a pearl necklace, with her red hair down. He was in a dark grey tweed sport coat and black pants.

Patrick said, "Wow, you look beautiful."

"Thank you. And you look like a successful author."

Off they went to Lincoln Park and he pulled into the parking garage of a high-rise building on N. Lakeview Avenue. On the way they talked about their weeks, with Patrick doing most of the talking about the new book he was writing. He had been spending lots of time in the Chicago History Museum's *City on Fire: Chicago 1871* exhibit and records, doing research for the book. She told him she had an interesting week but would wait until dinner to fill him in.

Mandy said, "Where are we going?"

"This is my building. I'll just park and we can walk across the street to the restaurant. One of my favorites, the North Pond. Have you ever been there?"

"No, but I've heard it's good."

They walked through the park over to the restaurant and got seated and continued the discussion. They ordered some white wine and he had the duck and Mandy the salmon. Mandy took him through the drama of the week and he was very intensely interested.

"Wow. You're leading a pretty interesting life at LaSalle, aren't you?"

"More interesting than I want it to be. I didn't sign up for murders. Maybe you can write a book about it when it's all done. By the way, I picked up a copy of *Blackhawk's Revenge* when I was at the airport."

"Great. I need to autograph it for you. And it's clear I have to see more of you so I can stay abreast. Actually, I want to see more of you anyway. Is that OK with you?"

Patrick was making no efforts to conceal his interest in her, which pleased her.

"I think I'd like that. Maybe you'd like to come up to my apartment to autograph the book tonight."

They left the restaurant and before heading back to her apartment, he invited her upstairs to see the view. His condo was on the thirty-eighth floor looking out east over the lake. She loved his unit, decorated with expensive artwork and with three bedrooms, one of which he used for his writing spot. On one wall Mandy spotted a framed genealogy chart and stared at it for a minute.

She said, "I love this. My sister and I are the family genealogists, and I think we need to do something like this for our family."

"You should. It's a great thing to have your family laid out like that."

Mandy said, "I'm thrilled to hear we have a common interest in genealogy. I'd like to hear a lot more about you, actually."

He stopped at her building and let her out, hugging her. She hugged back and when she pulled away, he leaned in and kissed her. She pulled back and leaned in and kissed him a second time.

He said, "Thank you for tonight."

She said, "I had a great time. Maybe you can come up and sign that book for me?"

Saturday morning, after Patrick left, she ran along the lake to Bryn Mawr Avenue and back. Just for kicks, as she passed Diversey Avenue she slowed and stopped to look west, imagining that she could see Patrick Carney on his balcony on the thirty-eighth floor of his building. Back on the run south, she thought it would be helpful to get some laughs and to catch up with some of the "Lowers"—the term she and Reggie used for the younger siblings in the clan, the elders being the "Uppers." She called numbers eight and ten, Will and Prudence, and suggested dinner at Portillos, followed by lounging at her apartment. Will was a twenty-three-year-old financial analyst at the Chicago Mercantile Exchange, and Prudence was a twenty-year-old junior at DePaul University where she was an English major. She was also the baby of the Doucette clan, but would give you a slit-eyed death look if you called her that.

The threesome had beef sandwiches dipped in the gravy at Portillos, and talked about everything going on in their lives in and the rest of their siblings' lives. Later, back in her apartment and hanging out on the balcony, the three surveyed the skyline.

Mandy said, "Will, how are the commodities doing these days?"

"Great. Need some pork belly futures or corn options?"

"Are you kidding me, all you do is push computer buttons and get rays from your terminal all day. Am I right?

Will said, "Yeah, it's a little boring. But at least there are some great women there. What about you, how are you getting along without Reg?"

"We've seen quite a lot of each other lately, though some of it's been for bad reasons."

Prudence said, "What kind of bad?"

"I had some bodies turn up on a deal I'm working on, and the FBI got involved. Voilà! Reggie at your service."

Prudence said, "Sounds a lot more interesting than Ralph Waldo Emerson or Shakespeare."

Will said, "Wait. I thought dead bodies popped up in Shakespeare all the time?"

"Yeah, but nothing like the real thing."

Mandy said, "Are you still planning to apply to law school?'

Prudence replied, "I am, and I'm signing up to take the LSATs next fall."

"Dad and I will be very proud."

Prudence said, "I just read Scott Turow's book *One L,* and that didn't make me too enthused about law school. It sounds like three years of hell. Enough about me. What's your big deal with all the bodies about?"

Mandy said, "We're in the midst of buying a company. Just as we announced it, they get a whistleblower letter about a big bribery scheme. Then all of a sudden people start dying. So far there are five dead guys."

Will said, "Jesus, I think I'll stick to sow bellies. Are you in any danger?"

"Not so far, though I almost got run over by a car on a run the other day and then swamped in my kayak by a speedboat. Fingers crossed."

Prudence said, "That sounds very Shakespearean. What about Reg?"

"She works for the FBI, remember. I think she would be the best protected out of all of us involved."

Will said, "Any men in the picture yet? Nobody has swept your feet, have they?"

"Is that all you Lowers think about? Sex?"

Another of Grandma Francesca's Italian superstitions was that if a broom touched an unmarried girl's feet, it was an omen that she would never marry. Grandma always wagged her finger at the unmarried Doucette girls and warned them about it, saying, "No old maids here! Keep away from the broom."

On their way out, Will saw the Patrick Carney book

on the coffee table and said, "*Blackhawk's Revenge,* what's that about, the hockey team or the Blackhawk Down story?"

"Neither. It's about the Blackhawk War in the 1800s, and it's written by a friend of mine." Fortunately, he didn't open the book and see the amorous inscription from Patrick.

The sibs said their goodbyes and headed off in their own directions, and Mandy was happy to note that she was feeling no lactic acid after her ten-mile run that morning.

On Sunday morning, Reggie went for a run and was spotted by watchers in the waiting silver SUV. They had gotten a call Friday with instructions to strike at the lawyer with as much finesse as they could muster, but with certain results. This was deemed necessary due to the clumsy handling of Erik Spenser and the other two, whose bodies had been found in no time at all, not to mention the bungled attempts on the lawyer on her run. Once Reggie disappeared down the street, the watcher slipped out and made his way into the building and up to the apartment. After knocking and getting no response, he picked the lock and entered, quickly looking for an appropriate place to empty his syringe. He had lots of choices. One was to cover the door handle, but he had been trained that anything that would rely on absorption through the hand wasn't preferred. Hands were frequently washed, and besides that, the toughness of the palms wasn't conducive to absorption, compared to other skin sites. Food was another choice, of course, but it wasn't certain that wherever he placed the syringe full of poison, it would be consumed. He finally settled on a half-empty spray perfume bottle. He drained the vial into it, and made a quick exit, keeping his hoodie up and his face away from security cameras. From entry to pulling away in the SUV, it took no more than fifteen minutes.

Monday morning, Mandy read an email from Greg Carlucci saying that the Defense Department was requesting a conference call with LaSalle on a matter of some urgency. Mandy showed up in the Law Department conference room, in which Greg Carlucci and Arthur Ross were already waiting. Arthur was the president of the Defense Systems Division and had responsibility for over $12 billion in LaSalle's annual sales. After an introduction, Greg explained that the meeting had been set up after the government was alerted to the situation by Steve Baker of the FBI.

Greg dialed into the call, and they found themselves with four staff members of the security agency, led by Rhonda Graves, the senior agent of the four. She introduced the others, and briefly referenced her conversation with Steve Baker, and summarized what had been conveyed by him. Agent Graves said they didn't want to get ahead of where things were in terms of any consequences on Lasalle, but first they wanted to understand the issue and what was being done about it. Their interest was in understanding the exact situation with the director who had left the company. LaSalle would be expected to identify everything it could about Harold Menzies, what his involvement was with the Defense

Systems Division, whether he had any access to classified documents, and other questions that would try to compartmentalize Harold Menzies' access to defense secrets. At first it would be responding to written questions and then probably followed up by in-person interviews. In the meantime, LaSalle shouldn't expect to see anything different about its status as an acceptable defense contractor or its ability to bid on future contracts. Greg was designated by Arthur for coordination and to receive paperwork to start off the process. Arthur thanked them and said that LaSalle apologized for them having to deal with this.

"Not what we needed," Arthur said, and slipped out the door.

Just then, Rick stepped into the room and said they had to see what was happening on CNN. Rick turned on the TV and pulled up CNN to see a news conference underway at the U.S. attorney's offices in New York. The U.S. Attorney herself was speaking. Running across the bottom of the screen was the crawler reading *"Federal prosecutors charge Allzient and its employees with bribery of foreign officials. Allzient agrees to guilty plea, consent decree, and $230 million fine."* The story continued from the U.S. Attorney, now talking about the charges filed against the individual defendants, as well as the expectation that foreign governments were preparing to bring charges against Allzient and its employees and to seek extradition. They watched for a while as the media posed some questions, then turned off the TV and ran out of the room to tend to their next steps.

Mandy's cell phone was on her desk, ringing away.

She quickly grabbed and answered it. She was confused about why she was getting a call from Dan Aleri.

"Mandy, it's Dan Aleri. I've got some bad news. We just had to rush Reggie to the hospital here. I wanted to get to you before I follow her over. She's on her way to the Naval Health Clinic here at the base."

Mandy started shaking uncontrollably and fell into her chair. "What is it? What happened to her?"

"She was at her desk near me. She started to act disoriented and wheezing and was having difficulty breathing. Then she collapsed. That's all I know right now. I may know more later, but I wanted to alert you right away. I'm going to head over there. If this is something serious, we might have to fly her up to Walter Reed, where they've got the best trauma facilities."

"I'm coming out there. Text me with updates. If you know where she will be taken, let me know right away. Dan, did you notice any SUVs hanging around there today?"

Dan said, "No. What does that have to do with it?"

"I was almost run over by one on a run not too long ago and it felt intentional. Reggie also noticed one lurking on a run in Chicago while I was out of town. Then I felt like I was being followed in Washington, a while back, and warned Reggie to watch out. Do those symptoms sound like that Novichok stuff used on Spenser? You've got that antidote there, right?

Dan said, "Yeah, it could be. I didn't connect the dots on that, but you may be right. We've got the atropine mixture here. I'll make sure it goes with me. And no, I didn't see any SUVs."

"Get going. You told me speed was essential in dealing with this."

Mandy hung up and called home, getting her mom out of the garden. She told her mother what was happening, and that they had to get the company jet and get to Washington, D.C., fast. Her mother said she would get Bob, and Mandy should rush out to Chicago Executive Airport. Josie had raised ten kids and was pretty good with staying calm during emergencies. Mandy grabbed a cab and shot out to Wheeling, where her parents were ready to board the plane. On the way she had called Steve Baker. He promised to order guards for Reggie, and a swat team sent to the apartment in Quantico. She also called Rick and told him what was going on, and asked him to alert Ed Rosen and to be a clearinghouse for info going either way within the company. She had nothing that wasn't manageable by delegation or delay on her desk right now, thank God, and wanted only to be able to focus on her sister, the most cherished person in her world.

Walter Reed National Military Medical Center was in Bethesda, Maryland. While Mandy and her parents were en route to Wheeling, Steve Baker texted her to have the flight go to Joint Base Andrews in southwestern District of Columbia, and Steve would have an FBI helicopter waiting to take them across town to Walter Reed. Meanwhile, Steve had the evidence techs and a team of agents swarming Reggie's apartment, and he'd spoken to Dan to get his guidance on what to look for. Dan told him to take anything that could be ingested, sprayed, applied topically to the skin, or applied in any other way. They were also told to test all surfaces, starting with the doorknobs, for any powder residue that could have been touched. Mandy and her parents made it to Andrews in less than two hours, then it was fifteen minutes to setting down on the Walter Reed helipad. They were rushed up to the intensive care unit and met Dan and the doctors. They were taken outside Reggie's room and could see her hooked up to machines through the room window. But so far, she wasn't on a ventilator, and hopefully she wouldn't need one.

The doctors gave a quick status report on her condition, explaining that atropine and pralidoxime chloride had been administered in Quantico before she was even airlifted to Walter Reed. She had that going in her favor. But the diagnosis was still waiting to be confirmed that it was Novichok, versus Sarin, or any number of other nerve agents. Reggie had been unconscious and wheezing, with a greatly constricted air passage. Her lungs were laboring to provide oxygen to her organs, but they were still doing the work on their own. Reggie's heart had been under much stress, but the antidote was holding its own. Her entire body had been scrubbed thoroughly with a reactive skin decontamination lotion so as to prevent any remaining substance to continue entering the body, if that was the method of attack. The doctors explained that the military antidote would be effective against at least five lethal doses of the agent, but they couldn't determine how many doses she'd received. Her symptoms had included disorientation, constriction of the pupils, wheezing, difficulty in breathing, and a racing heartbeat. The good news for Reggie was that she hadn't vomited or experienced any seizures, at least so far. The doctors were hopeful that the combination of a low dosage of the poison and the quick treatment of atropine would prevent Reggie from going into asphyxiation or into cardiac arrest. One of the doctors pointed out that the sixteenth-century alchemist Paracelsus had identified one of the fundamental principles of the use of poisons by coining the statement that *the dose makes the poison*. The final thing they said was that Reggie appeared to be in great shape in terms of her lungs and heart, no doubt from her long-distance running and triathlon training, and that could aid in her war against the poison.

By midafternoon Monday, Mandy had had a chance to hug Dan and to properly introduce him to her parents, as well as to call Patrick and to let him know what was happening. Steve Baker had joined them and got a room to talk close to the ICU. Steve informed them that the Bureau was treating this as attempted murder of a federal agent and was giving it the Bureau's highest priority. What they weren't sure of, however, was whether Reggie was really the intended victim. When his team worked through all of the trail of contacts and appearances, and who could be a threat, it was hard to see Reggie as the target. It was Mandy, Steve thought, who was the real target. The fact that Mandy had been to Reggie's apartment a couple times recently, and that they were identical twins, had led his team to conclude as they had. It was Mandy who might have a chance to recognize someone, not Reggie. Reggie was just in the wrong place at the wrong time and was a dead ringer for the real target.

"We're going to assign a protection team not only to Reggie, our employee, but to you too, Mandy," Steve said. "We have had five deaths so far, two indisputably by the Novichok nerve agent, two probables, and one by drowning. We're considering John Booth's drowning as a probable murder, not an accident. The attack on Reggie, especially if it turns out to be Novichok, has put us into full-blown crisis mode. An attack on an FBI employee will concentrate all our resources. You have my word on that."

"Thank you. What can you tell us about the time it will take to confirm what was used on my daughter?" Josie Doucette said.

Steve said, "The agents have finished collecting the possible sources from the apartment, and they're being tested at the FBI lab as we speak. We have also gotten the images from the apartment security system and from the street cameras for the forty-eight hours before Reggie experienced symptoms, and we're searching for any suspicious people. I expect to have those preliminary results within the hour."

With that, they broke up. Mandy and Dan stayed with Reggie, while her parents went to get some food. Their parents were a mess, understandably. When they returned, Mandy and Dan would get something to eat. Meanwhile, two FBI agents were brought over by Steve and introduced, and they would be joined by others later, some to stay close to Reggie and the others to stay with Mandy. In less than an hour, Dan got a call from the lab, telling him that it was indeed Novichok, and had been found in Reggie's spray perfume bottle. They had also determined that a single spray would deliver about one lethal dose, so depending upon how liberally she had applied it, they could be looking at a manageable job for the antidote. Once off the phone, Dan asked Mandy how much perfume Reggie would typically use. She said one spray on a wrist, and then she'd rub the wrists together. She didn't use much in Mandy's opinion. Dan left to report this to the doctors. All things considered, a pretty good report, they thought. Maybe it was only a slight aerosol contact, or none if the spray was away from the nose. If it was only one spray, maybe it was only one lethal dose.

Baker returned with some other agents a little while after dinner, so there was now a full team to guard both of the sisters. He also reported that the cameras had revealed a hooded male figure in Reggie's apartment lobby who had picked the entry lock early Sunday morning, and left after ten minutes. Probably enough time to place the Novichok and to get out without being confronted.

As he thought about it, he said, "I think it would be worthwhile comparing the hooded figure here to those various videos — the apartment entryway, the speedboat, the Bahá'í Temple, and Union Station — to see if we have a match."

The street cameras had identified a silver SUV with Virginia plates that had been there at the time, but left when the hooded figure got in the vehicle and pulled away. The Virginia plates turned out to have been stolen from a Volvo. The agents reviewing the street camera watched the film over and over again. They slowed it to show the hooded figure running from the apartment to the SUV, reaching out and grabbing a sign pole and using it to swing out into the street to jump into the passenger seat. A team had been sent back to dust the pole for prints. There was nothing in the FBI's National Crime Information Center database to match the prints, and they were now waiting for a match. Other teams had been sent to John Booth's house and to Erik Spenser's apartment to conduct another sweep for fingerprints. But now there was no question, this poison used on Reggie was the same nerve agent used on Erik Spenser, the two bodies in Pennsylvania, and on James Whitney, and there was a murder team on the loose. Mandy elected to sleep in the chair in the room with Reggie, while her parents were taken to the Bethesda Marriott for the night.

Tuesday morning, while Reggie was continuing her treatment with the antidote, Mandy and her parents had an update with the doctors. They were upbeat by what they'd learned and what they'd been observing with Reggie. The fact that her dosage was low was a very helpful sign, when combined with the military-grade antidote. Not that they were minimizing the situation, because one lethal dose was nothing to treat lightly. But if the antidote could counteract at least five lethal doses, and Reggie had received one to two doses, the doctors liked those odds. Right now, they were keeping Reggie asleep while the magic was working and her system was recovering, but they thought she could be brought back to consciousness by the afternoon, if the signs continued to improve.

Mandy called Rick to update him, and afterward she learned what else was going on in Chicago. Rick filled her in on the Executive Committee meeting scheduled for that afternoon. He told her that Ed had requested that he and Rick be allowed to sit in, so they could be available to give the latest information. Jim Kerwin had approved that request, but Rick had noted that Emily Jenkins hadn't been invited to participate. Mandy recommended that Rick get briefed by Greg Carlucci on the Defense Department call. She also said that when she got back, which would be when she felt Reggie could be deemed safe and secure, she would have an FBI protection detail with her. That would make for an interesting dynamic in the office, she thought. If people were scared of her before because of her role as a compliance cop, what were they going to think now?

Her parents said they had taken the evening to speak individually to all of the siblings to let them know what was happening. Everyone was in shock and worried not only for Reggie, but for Mandy as well. Shortly thereafter, flower arrangements started arriving in Reggie's room.

Walter Reed received a call from *The New York Times* requesting confirmation that a patient had been transferred there from Quantico, who was being treated for a nerve agent attack. The reporter was referred to the FBI. When the reporter followed up with the FBI, he learned that an FBI employee from the Quantico lab had become ill by poisoning, and was now being treated. The reporter asked if this was linked with the recent incidents involving deaths of two New York residents, one whose body had been found slumped in an Amtrak seat, and the other dumped in the New Jersey woods. So far, no connection was made with the Pennsylvania bodies or with John Booth. The FBI declined to answer, based upon the incident being involved in an ongoing criminal investigation. The following morning, an article appeared in *The New York Times* describing the two incidents and attempting to link them and raised the possibility that there was a series of attacks by deadly nerve agents in an ongoing criminal activity.

By midafternoon on Tuesday, Mandy was able to call in to Rick and get updated on what the Executive Committee had decided. After its deliberations over what had been presented to them, they agreed that while the Allzient transaction was attractive, it should be considered to be on life support for now. If the looming legal outcome of the government actions beyond the $230 million fine left it a viable company, they would reassess. No news announcement would be made, because no sooner did a position come out, than the circumstances changed and it spun off into a new dark corner. The company didn't have the resources to investigate a rogue director, if that was what Harold Menzies was, so that should be left to the FBI. But a real soul-searching had to be done on director candidate background work, and before any new candidates were proposed, the Nominating Committee would have to take charge of the process and review it, strengthen it, and manage the process directly. As to any risk to the company's Defense Systems Division, they would have to await the Defense Department process, and then address it accordingly. Finally, as to any threats to Mandy and to her family, the greatest amount of support and attention needed to be paid there, and Jim and Ed would manage that. With that, the meeting was adjourned.

Late Thursday afternoon, Reggie was brought out of her induced coma. Her numbers had been steadily improving, and the doctors felt that she would be better off being conscious. They didn't like induced comas to last for any longer than was necessary.

As she opened her eyes and looked around the room, she saw a sea of faces. She whispered, "What's going on here? Where am I?"

The Walter Reed doctor spoke first. "You're in the Walter Reed Military Medical Center in Bethesda, Dr. Doucette. I'm Dr. David Simpson. You were poisoned. Your friends and family took care of you right away by getting you the medicine and treatment you needed and got you to us. You're going to recover, but we're going to have to keep you here for a while, OK? I'm going to let your family talk to you now, and when you feel like it, I can describe everything more fully, including what will happen next. Tell me how you feel."

"I think I feel OK physically, but I'm weak and groggy. I need to understand how I got poisoned, and everything that's going on."

Dr. Simpson left Reggie with Mandy and with her parents, Dan, and Steve Baker. The detachment of FBI agents was outside the closed door. Her family took turns hugging her and saying they loved her, and just gave her some time to get her head clear. Then Steve and Dan took her through the things they'd learned from the cameras. Dan explained the treatment with the antidote that they'd used, based on her symptoms. Reggie thanked them all and asked if she could have some alone time with Mandy, and the two were left alone in the room.

Reggie then said, "So where do things stand? Just give me the Cliffs Notes version."

"You're one tough twin, Reg. OK, here goes. Allzient was charged by the feds and decided to surrender on the spot. They pled guilty and are paying a $230 million fine. Charges are pending in Spain, Italy, and France too. I'm thinking our deal with them is on life support right now. The search for the CIA agent is still a mystery, but seems to be more important now. Speaking of mysteries, our former director Harold Menzies has disappeared, but we've managed to get his prints and DNA for matching. I was with Steve at FBI Headquarters and I thought I recognized a CIA agent as a Harold Menzies look-alike, so I was able to get his DNA to test. I suspected, and now I've confirmed, that Emily Jenkins was shacking up with Harold Menzies and may be mixed up in some of what has been going on. Is that enough for now?"

"What do you mean, *I was able to get his DNA?*"

"I just went right up to him and demanded a cheek swab; what do you think?"

"You didn't."

Mandy said, "OK, maybe I got his food tray with a bunch of DNA on it."

"That's better. How did you nail Emily Jenkins?"

"The investigation, the one that got approved."

"Doesn't that get you in trouble?"

"The investigation? No, the company authorized it. I told you that. You're too groggy from Novichok to keep up."

"How has Dan been handling this?" Reggie said.

"He's been great. Really swung into action to get you help. It's interesting that you're worried about him."

"Why would they have poisoned me?" she said.

"Steve Baker thinks they mistook you for me, and maybe they don't even realize we're twin sisters."

"Change of subject. What are you doing about our next race?"

"Those are pretty bodacious words coming from a girl who can't even walk to the bathroom. But just to humor you, we have a room, some entertainment lined up, and, if you're ambulatory by that time, maybe you'll be a halfway decent spectator."

"Call Mom and Dad back in here, please. And I'm not ready for spectatorhood just yet."

Mandy bent down and gave Reggie a big hug, saying, "You're not ready for anything yet, but thank God you're conscious and talking."

CHAPTER 22

STEVE BAKER AND MANDY went back to the Hoover Building while Reggie continued her treatment and visits with her parents and Dan. Reggie's attack caused him to pull his team together and to double down on their tasks. Harold Menzies' tracks had led them to Hong Kong, which was now in Chinese control. The relaxed handling of the island community after the handover from the British in 1997 had hardened considerably, and the ability to operate as freely as they once had, turned to the opposite. The British still had resources, though, which the FBI called on now with a sense of urgency. British intelligence still had a significant presence in the form of Hong Kongers loyal to, if not in the employ of, Her Majesty's government. The resources of Britain's MI6 were tapped to help identify and to track

Menzies, with the aid of passport control and airport cameras, to which they surprisingly had access. It only took a little time to spot Harold Menzies and to follow his tracks to a Shanghai-bound flight, from which he disembarked and disappeared into the Shanghai airport throng. Shouldn't be too hard to find him; there were only 25 million residents in Shanghai.

While that was going on, the cousins at MI6 had been able to get their hands on an Air China passenger list for the flight to Shanghai. No person on the passenger list by the name of Harold Menzies appeared. The team asked if a copy of the full passenger list could be scrutinized with passport photos, to see if Menzies was traveling under an alias.

Steve's team met with them to discuss progress on identifying Reggie's assailant. The camera shots from her building had proven to be unhelpful due to the subject's skill in avoiding visibility to the lens, but Steve made a point of looking at all of the separate hoodie photos. The first hoodie photo was in Washington, D.C.'s Union Station location of James Whitney and his backpack. The second was at the Bahá'í Temple when Mandy's family home was being photographed. The next was the pilot of the speedboat. Finally, the figure at Reggie's apartment. As far as Steve and his team were concerned, this was the same person and they tied all of the events together as evidence of a concerted effort to harm Mandy with no connection to the bribery event. Steve thought, *If it wasn't about the bribery, what was it about then?*

The agents turned their attention to the silver SUV. The plate number had been visible. It was registered to an address in Cherry Hill, Virginia, just off I-95 between

Washington and Quantico. It turned out that the plates had been reported missing as well, and agents were sent to the apartment complex address of the owner. They came away with a time range to use in trying to spot a silver SUV, assuming it was the SUV that was used for the plate search. If not, it would make it much more difficult. The agents were able to use the time frame, as they had hoped, and a search of traffic cameras was used to spot the SUV before the plates were stolen, and after. This took some hours, but it yielded results. The SUV was picked up sporting the stolen Virginia plates near the owner's location approximately two hours before the break-in at Reggie's apartment. Further searching found another camera nearby with the SUV heading toward the apartment complex. This vehicle was carrying a Maryland plate, which was tracked to an Enterprise rental car location at the Baltimore airport. Agents paid the rental car company a visit, and with their assistance, they came up with the car and with the person who picked it up. They got a Maryland driver's license and picture. The car had not been rerented since that day, and while it had been washed and cleaned, there was still the possibility that some identification could be located. The vehicle was impounded and taken to an FBI location, where evidence technicians could examine it. Any slim possibility of matching fingerprints or DNA that could have been collected in Erik Spenser's or Reggie Doucette's apartments, would be a prize.

The search for the driver using the Maryland driver's license quickly determined the license to be fake. The photo was run through the FBI facial recognition system. No match was produced, so the agents decided to try the State Department's passport database, and there it was: a match to a person from a passport application in the name of Mark Joseph. The passport number, though, told something by itself. The State Department identified it by its numbering as belonging to a group of passports specifically provided for special assistance to a sister agency within the U.S. government—the Central Intelligence Agency.

Mandy interrupted to ask, "Does that mean that the CIA arranged for new passports for the people being pulled out of Russia?"

Steve answered, "It sure looks like it."

Mandy said, "Then if we have all of the names of the people Spruance took in, can we see if there are any 'special' passport numbers, and you can round them all up?"

Steve said, "Sounds like your old DOJ instincts are kicking in."

Friday morning in Washington, a call was scheduled with their colleagues at MI6 in London. Alan Frenche and Steve Baker were in the room with others on the team, including Mandy. Commander Clive Culbertson of MI6 was the spokesman on the British side of the call.

"Gentlemen, good morning. I trust that you're prepared to hear some good news?"

Alan said. "Please, Commander, we'd love for you to start our day out with something positive."

"Very good, indeed. We've used the photo you supplied us and checked the passenger record for Air China Flight 112. We've matched the photo for a person named Edward Fennstrom. Does that name mean anything to you?"

Looking around the room and seeing unanimous head shakes, Alan said, "No, should it?"

"Well maybe not, but it does to us. You see, as old China hands for decades, we take an intense interest in anything approaching threats to Her Majesty's government. This name Fennstrom is of interest to us because Professor Lawrence Fennstrom, an American ex-pat, became something of an apologist for the Chinese and pulled no punches in his critique of the West, especially the United Kingdom and the United States, from his lectern at Shanghai University. He had two sons, Edward and Winston, until now apparently missing in action. We were also able to find that the two brothers each own a luxury condo on the eighty-ninth floor of the Jin Mao Tower. Not too shabby. Anyway, Director, that's all we have at this point, and I'll have our chaps send on the full file to you forthwith. Now we have a sharing arrangement and an understanding with your brethren at the agency. Any objection to us following through with that?"

Alan looked around the room. A lot of raised eyebrows returned his gaze, so he said, "Would you be at liberty to share with us with whom you communicate?"

"Well, it's usually to the director of counterintelligence in your sister agency, since the usefulness of the information usually goes to the purpose of protecting any U.S. assets outside your country."

"May I ask that you take a couple of days to share this information?"

The commander replied, "Well it's 17:00 here, and our weekend is beginning. I don't see any problem with sending the information Monday morning, though I'll have to get it to our chief today. Have yourselves a good weekend."

Alan said, "Thank you so much, Commander, for all of this information and for the accommodation. I think it'll be invaluable to us. Just one other thing please. Do you have photos of the Fennstrom brothers you could share with us?"

"Let me check on that and if we do, we'll send them along to you."

They hung up. Frenche looked around the room and said, "Where the fuck are those DNA test results?"

Mandy added, "That was the last puzzle piece to fall into place. This is a Chinese spy network. That's what this whole thing has been about — not bribery, or not *just* bribery, I should say. Sherman Haskins was Philip Ray, but in fact he's Winston Fennstrom. Armand Moines and Harold Menzies were the same man, who's really Edward Fennstrom. The two are brothers and Chinese spies. Jesus H. Christ!"

No one tried to talk her out of it.

Mandy called Rick Crawford on Friday afternoon.

Rick asked, "How's Reggie?"

"For a person who isn't on the firing line like the rest of her FBI buddies, and wasn't trained to take these risks, I think she has taken a massive hit that she didn't get paid to take, but she's doing very well under the circumstances. This is just not in her job description. And I'm feeling a massive amount of guilt, because Steve Baker believes I was the intended target. I walk around with a protection detail, and Reggie will have agents posted outside her room for the duration, or until we get to the bottom of this. But please tell me what's going on around there."

"Well, before I do that, what exactly happened to her?"

"She got poisoned. With the same nerve agent that killed Erik Spenser and those other guys. Thank God they had the antidote at the lab and they were able to get it into her before ever airlifting her up to Walter Reed."

"That's fantastic. What's her prognosis?

"Don't know yet. All they know right now is that she has the best chance at recovery. They brought her out of the coma and she's thinking and talking clearly, though, so those are great signs. Fill me in."

Rick said, "Since the Justice Department announced the Allzient case and the resolution all in one news conference, we've regained some optimism that a deal may work. We're going to make sure that the remaining diligence steps get taken, both here and in Europe. Our investment banker's coming up with a revised purchase price that factors in the fines. If some of the current purchase price has to be allocated to settling the fines, we can deal with that. If there's any amount that exceeds the estimate and beyond the amount set aside out of the purchase price, the sellers will have to pay that excess. They're a wealthy family, but we might have to lien some asset class of theirs to secure a payment."

"How's Wretched Witch doing with all of this?"

"I think she's getting over the initial shock and is starting to adjust her expectations. If she can still realize her strategic vision, she may back off from her attitude. She's keeping a low profile right now, though."

Mandy said, "What about our defense systems guys?"

"We think they're sweating bullets. We haven't heard back from the government yet, but expect to next week. Fingers crossed. If the defense business takes any kind of hit, we're in trouble."

"And what about the big guys?"

Rick said, "The chair wants biweekly reports submitted to the Executive Committee. Ed has asked me to prepare the first for Monday, so I'm trying to gather everything we know. I think Ed's feeling pretty shaky about the whole Menzies thing, even though Jim has taken responsibility for it. Ed believes that even if someone is foisted on us by an unimpeachable source, like Jim, he has the overarching responsibility to make sure there are no surprises coming. He's right about that. Think about it like this—if a director candidate was recommended by another director, wouldn't we, as lawyers, still be expected to research the other boards they served on, to make sure that there wouldn't be any conflict of interest? We couldn't very well expect a fellow director to think through that kind of obscure thing and to rule it out. That would be a classic anti-trust violation, and it's pure lawyer stuff. No CEO should have to be thinking about all of that, even if he was a practicing lawyer at some point. I think that's where Ed's coming from."

"I get it. Are you OK if I stay here close to Reggie until she's out of the woods?"

Rick said, "Of course. Reggie wouldn't be in the hospital fighting for her life without us in the first place. All of our thoughts are with her, and with you. Just stay in touch so we can make the updates we're supposed to do. We need to know everything that occurs on a real-time basis. Go take care of your sister now."

By midafternoon, the FBI lab had delivered the fingerprint and DNA test results from Sherman Haskins' utensils and Gatorade bottle to Alan Frenche. Baker was called up to Alan's office immediately and was asked to bring Mandy with him. She was retrieved from the hospital and they walked into the conference room, where Alan and two others were huddled over the results with smiles on their faces.

"Mandy, we wanted you here for this since it was your quick thinking that enabled us to make this check. We got a match!" Alan said. "You're not going to believe this. Haskins' DNA is a match for Harold Menzies."

Baker asked, "You mean that's for sure? No doubt?"

"Right. The lab guys say that there's over 60 percent sharing of DNA between Menzies and Haskins. That's the high end of the range in full siblings. Now, if they'd been identical twins, like you Doucette sisters, that would be a perfect match, but this is pretty solid. Based on what Commander Culbertson told us, I think we have Edward and Winston Fennstrom on our hands."

Baker said, "That makes another piece of the puzzle make sense. Mandy has a private investigator watching Emily Jenkins with Harold Menzies, and one of the things he found was an address for Menzies here in Washington. That address was checked out but seemed empty, with no association with Menzies."

"I'm going to have to push this up to the top. Let me get started on that. Do you have anything else going on that I may need to know?"

Baker said, "A couple things. I've collected fingerprints at the Quantico scene that we think are from the assailant. We're sweeping again on the other two crime scenes to see if we have anything to match against, so that might yield something. Also, we had a comparison of the nerve agents used, and they all have the same chemical signature. I think we can conclude that from the first deaths, which I guess would be the two bodies in Pennsylvania, to James Whitney to Erik Spenser, and finally to Reggie, it was the same source. This has been about a whole other subject than Allzient's bribery from the beginning, I think."

Alan Frenche said, "I think Mandy called it right. This is a Chinese spy ring, and that's what this is all about. The bribery popped up and interfered with the whole operation. We have to move fast here. Commander Culbertson is sending his file to Haskins on Monday morning. That could cause the dam to burst for Haskins. We don't know what he'll do, or what he's capable of doing. Mandy, are you staying in Washington, for a while?"

Mandy said, "I'm staying put until my sister is out of the woods. Why?"

"I have an idea, but let's get moving on lining up things upstairs first."

Alan Frenche's position as director, Counterintelligence Division, sat within the National Security Branch of the FBI, which was headed by an associate executive assistant director and by an executive assistant director, who in turn reported up to the deputy director and to the director of the FBI. The director of the FBI reported to the Attorney General of the United States. If what Alan Frenche had in mind was to get any traction, he had to go through all of those layers. He picked up the phone and called to get in to see the next two layers above him for the first step.

By the end of the day, he had finished his story and his idea, and was waiting for a reaction. The executive assistant director placed a call and asked the person on the other end of the line for an emergency meeting with him and with the director on a matter of national security. By 5:00 p.m., Alan Frenche was sitting in the director's conference room surrounded by six other people, two of whom were Mandy Doucette and Steve Baker. After explaining why a civilian was in the room, he took them through the entire story from beginning to end. He summed it up by saying that a corporate acquisition had triggered a bribery investigation. It had come in the midst of a due diligence undertaking by a large Fortune 500 corporation, that had led to five murders and to an attempted murder. Nerve gas was used, probably coming from foreign government sources. He also described the revelation of two Chinese spies, one of whom was believed to be running the CIA's counterintelligence division, and the possible infiltration of defense contractors possessing massive amounts of highly classified secrets and technology.

The director said, "Jesus Christ! What's your level of confidence in all of this?"

Frenche said, "Most of it is 100 percent."

The director looked at Baker and said: "You?"

Baker said, "Same."

The director then turned to Mandy. "Same question?"

Mandy said, "I'm absolutely convinced."

The director then said to Frenche, "I'm assuming you have a plan?"

He answered, "Yes, sir."

"Tell me, and then we're going to the attorney general." He stepped out and asked his assistant to make a call and then came back in and heard Frenche out.

Early Friday morning, two FBI evidence teams had descended upon the former apartment building of Erik Spenser and the home of John Booth. At Booth's house, his widow had been very willing to cooperate in any way, and at the agents' request she allowed them to dust for prints over the entire surface of the boat and dock for several hours. It was a long-shot chance that any prints had survived any rain since the night of the murder, but one worth taking. They also took her fingerprints and collected prints from John Booth's personal articles so they could rule out any prints they pulled and narrow down the others found to be potential suspects. The New York team expanded the search for prints inside and outside the apartment, knowing that they would harvest a vast amount. This would present the needle and haystack challenge, but that was what computers were for.

By Friday night, the evidence teams had concluded their analysis of all of the prints found at the four sites: the Booth boat and dock, the Erik Spenser apartment, the pole outside Reggie Doucette's apartment, and the silver SUV rental. The result was that one set of fingerprints, some full and some partials, at all four locations had matched. There was still no identification, but it could now be inferred for certain that the same person had participated in the three attacks. Now all they had to do was arrest a suspect.

CHAPTER 23

SHERMAN HASKINS hadn't gone into the office on Friday, choosing instead to turn the weekend into a three-day holiday. He had lots of work to do. His plans had steadily been falling apart, and if he couldn't dispose of Mandy Doucette, it was probably time to put his backup plan into effect. There would have to be a way to effectively use his remaining assets who had so spectacularly fucked up by attacking the twin sister of the real target, the only possible remaining person who he thought could recognize him. He had dealt with Booth, but that still left the redheaded lawyer. She had to be the only one who could identify him; and, that might have occurred. This was his conclusion over the brief but abortive lunch he'd had with Alan Frenche.

He was now practically a man on the run, he thought,

even if his pursuers had not really caught on yet. Mistakes were piling up, and he had no one to blame but himself. Putting nerve agents into the hands of clumsy henchmen was obviously a mistake, because they could not succeed in disposing of a body while the Novichok was still detectable, and because they could not distinguish between the two sisters and attack the right one. Even if the poisoning of the lawyer had taken place and poison had been credited as the cause, her death would have at least eliminated a key witness who might be able to identify him. When they did make someone disappear, it didn't take long for the bodies to be discovered. Fortunately, they could pull off an *accidental* drowning without leaving a trace. He had seen *The New York Times* article on a series of linked nerve agent attacks. If his boys were going to be put to effective use again, some other less-subtle means would have to be introduced. Finesse was the preference, of course, but for effectiveness, they may have to just shoot the bitch.

He thought back on the long haul it had been, and what he'd been through. He and his brother had been thoroughly persuaded that the U.S. government was evil, from years of indoctrination by their father while growing up in Shanghai. The father, Lawrence Fennstrom, had been a professor in Western history at Shanghai University for years, after spending time in Rangoon in a similar capacity. He befriended Carleton Ames, a former academic who ended up working for the U.S. government. Their friendship had taken the form of long drinking bouts that had eventually ruined Ames' foreign career. He'd been recalled to Washington, to run out his remaining career in an undistinguished, dead-end job, at what their father had come to find out was the CIA. Enough bitterness and cynicism toward the West had been injected into Lawrence Fennstrom that, after his friendship and association with Carleton Ames had been abruptly ended, he had begun passing his jaundiced mindset along to his two sons Edward and Winston. The sons had been educated in the Shanghai secondary school system, and became fluent in the Mandarin and Hu dialects, as well as in Russian. Their father had nurtured their hatred for the West as an extension of his own, leaving them ripe for recruitment by the Chinese intelligence services.

Edward and Winston had been born in the United States, and as American citizens they were easily able to attend college stateside and to remain in the country. That was exactly what they did. Lawrence and their mother had passed away after the sons had relocated to the States, and as time rolled on, it seemed natural that their loyalties lay with the Chinese, who took such a dedicated interest in their careers and well-being. Stipends were provided and career counseling accompanied the tuition payments that were made for the best schools in the Northeast and in Washington. D.C. This was in return for their grooming as agents, with the attendant schooling in tradecraft. Winston was eventually introduced to contacts that provided job opportunities in the intelligence services, and he'd joined the intelligence arm of the CIA and worked his way up in the organization. Edward had been routed differently, being encouraged to obtain business degrees at the bachelor's and master's levels, and from there being invited to join consulting firms. Before their higher education began, though, they had been given different identities to inhabit: Edward as Armand Moines and Winston as Sherman Haskins. Each had an additional identification, if necessary, and their counselor made it clear to them that the time of switching, if at all, would be determined for them.

For now, it was enough that they pursue their internal advancement at their respective organizations and make periodic reports as requested. Sherman, née Winston Fennstrom, was counseled to pursue associations with U.S. agents operating in the Soviet Union or its satellites, and to build a network of agents to whom he would be owed loyalty. Armand, née Edward Fennstrom, was coached to make associations with business leaders at specific firms, to ingratiate himself with them, and, if offered, to take advantage of board memberships. In an odd twist of fate, the efforts of Sherman Haskins in his work caused him to cross paths with Aldrich Ames. The history of Ames, who had become a Soviet asset and was identifying U.S. intelligence assets in the Soviet sphere, was that of a long and disgraceful disaster doing maximum damage to the CIA, leaving an unenviable trail of indiscretions and misconduct, as well as blatant recklessness. Despite the collapse of the Soviet Union, Ames continued on as a Russian asset, betraying his country and causing U.S. assets to be revealed and swept up by Russian intelligence, never to be heard from again. Though Sherman had some recollection of his father's strong friendship with Carleton Ames, Aldrich's father, there was no love lost between Sherman and the disaster that was Aldrich Ames. In part because he was seeking to protect his own network in the now-Russian arena, and further because he sensed an opportunity. Sherman was invited to join an elite group seeking to unearth the mole that turned out to be Aldrich Ames. Ames' flamboyance with the use of his Russian funds eventually led to his arrest in 1994, as he was preparing to attend a conference in Moscow. Sherman Haskins played a very prominent role in that group, and he was rewarded with a senior post in the counterintelligence arm of the agency. From that perch, he had great success in carrying out his long-term plan, as provided to him by their Chinese handler. The plan was to use former U.S. intelligence assets to be employed in U.S. defense contractor organizations. From those assets, or Humint, as they were known, whose financial stability would be assured, valuable technical and commercial information would be obtained and transferred to their handler. One of his more successful appearances, but not his only one, had been to a Chicago company using his identification as Philip Ray, a foray into placement which had netted a half-dozen or so positions in the late 1990s, with Spruance Corporation. Many more were to come, but after some time as the information started to flow and Haskins had climbed the ranks, he was told to stand down from recruitment and to nurse the stable of sources he had created. The emphasis was now to be turned toward the maneuvering of organizations that housed the individuals so that they became more productive. This was a task that had been laid out for Armand.

Edward Fennstrom, the younger of the two brothers, had an aptitude for numbers, a skill that enabled him to cruise through his business education and to achieve the degrees he had collected—*ticket punching,* as it had come to be called in Corporate America. As Armand

Moines, he had gained entry to prestigious consulting firms and wormed his way into the rarified air of defense industry consulting. Over time, he had acquired a pedigree in the inner workings of U.S. military contractors, and from there onto technical start-ups and research and development operations. It was from this position that his prowess grew from spotting technical advances and prime candidates for corporate successes and on to strategic combinations and wealth-generating mergers that could produce so much opportunity.

Edward learned to be a corporate director from his many assignments in the consultancies. He also found that associating with high-level attendees at the right conferences was an exceptionally productive way to be known to the people whose circles he wished to enter. The goal was to be invited to join boards. From a board position, he could influence corporate strategy and push for corporate alliances. He wouldn't only lay out paths for organizational growth, with companies whose employment ranks had been packed with "referrals" from Philip Ray, but his personal wealth would mushroom with the incredible growth of the equity holdings he'd acquired over the years from his director positions, supplementing his board retainer fees and his funding from his uncle-cum-handler. His handler had encouraged him to utilize his other identification of Harold Menzies on a parallel basis just as insurance from being too easily spotted in coincidental locations in mergers and in acquisitions trails. This he did in the cases of Spruance Corporation and LaSalle Enterprises, with whom he had pulled off some impressive corporate architecture, if you asked him. It had been explained to him, though, that there would come a time when his sun would set, and he could collect his trophies and enjoy his fortunes. That time had finally come at the end of his term with the LaSalle Enterprises Board of Directors.

He'd always prided himself on long-term planning. It was one of his goals to secure a safe haven in the city of his history, Shanghai. As he was keeping his eye out for a spot, he came across an opportunity, and in the early part of the millennium he'd secured two side-by-side condominiums on the eighty-ninth floor of the Jin Mao Tower, located in the Pudong area east of the Huangpu River, before its confluence with the Yangtze River and their rush to empty into the East China Sea. From the western view of the condos, off to the northwest, he could just about see Shanghai University, the site of his father's professorship. Immediately below him, and just on the other side of the Huangpu, lay The Bund. It was ironic that he could literally look down upon the former Western district of the European masters of China, while figuratively he was gloating over the Fennstrom brothers' mastery of the U.S. defense industry treasure chest. Soon, Edward hoped, it would be China as master. Now the clock was running until Winston could join him and take up residence in his companion condo. But first Winston had to make his exit.

Sitting in his Jin Mao condo, Edward checked his cell phone and saw that it had numerous texts and voicemails from the pathetic disciple of his — Emily Jenkins. He had only kept the phone to be able to keep track of what she was up to. Checking up on her latest desperate messages, he read one that put him into a panic. Emily had texted that she was concerned about him and would be coming out to his Washington, D.C., home to try to check up on him. She missed him desperately, she'd added. He had, in a weak moment, provided her with his Washington, address. She had kept pressing him to know where he lived. He'd concluded that he had to build her trust. It would be difficult to do that if he wouldn't even let her know where he lived. His own personal calculus was that she would not want to blatantly advertise their relationship by showing up at his home, though she might want to mail him. He concluded that she had to have the correct address. But now it seemed that was exactly what she was planning to do — travel there. He thought about get a warning out to his brother, but he had avoided having direct contact with his brother if it was possible to do so. Winston had told him not to contact him. Edward would have to wait for his brother to contact him. This was the protocol they had to live with.

CHAPTER 24

ON FRIDAY EVENING, Alan Frenche, Steve Baker, Mandy Doucette, and the director of the FBI, entered the fifth-floor office of the Attorney General of the United States in the Department of Justice Building, a two-minute walk from the Hoover Building. There, the story unfolded just as it had in the previous meeting, but with a much higher sense of urgency, because the discussion was now about treason and espionage at one of the highest levels of government. There was also the possibility that untold amounts of top-secret materials had already been taken, and numbers of foreign agents had been placed in positions of active continuing access.

The director took the attorney general through the story as best he could, relying on Alan Frenche to correct and to add as he went along. He had known some of what had happened since a good portion of it had been in the news, and he'd gotten reports through the Justice Department channels as well. When the presentation was done, he pointed out that this was pure dynamite being set off, and there had better be no doubt about the situation. When he was assured that it was solid, he asked the others to step out into the anteroom for a minute. He picked up the phone and dialed, and when it was answered he said, "This is the attorney general. I'd like to speak to the president, please."

Dr. Simpson came in to check on Reggie that evening. He took her vitals and had a nurse take another blood draw to check on the progress of the nerve agent leaving the system. Reggie asked him about the dosage level and how the antidotes were working. Once at Walter Reed, they had administered a second antidote of pralidoxime chloride. That, along with the continued use of atropine, were considered the best defense against the Novichok attack on the body. Dr. Simpson talked about her steps that day.

"How did you apply the perfume that morning?"

Reggie said, "I was running late, so I caught a quick spray on the wrist before running out of the apartment and rubbing my wrists together going down the hall to get the elevator." That confirmed what Mandy had thought.

"Could you have inhaled any of the spray? If not, that's a helpful indicator that the dosage was low and the method of entering the body was pretty much limited to skin absorption through the pores. You've had three doses of the two antidotes, and I think that's sufficient to block the acetylcholine receptors in the brain from welcoming the nerve agent into the nervous system. Your nervous system has the best chance to recover and to allow the irritation of the lungs and heart tissue to diminish."

"I can't remember something like that."

The luckiest thing for Reggie had been the application of atropine as soon as it was seen that she was under attack, and this was Dan Aleri's doing, pushed by Mandy's observation. Since she had a minimal dosage applied, the chances were excellent that she would be back in action soon. As Dr. Simpson was wrapping up his conclusion, her phone buzzed with a call from Mandy.

"Hi. I hope we didn't interrupt your meeting with the doc. I've got Steve here with me."

Reggie gave a thumbs up to Dr. Simpson, who ducked out of the room, and she said, "Thanks. I was in with Dr. Simpson, but we're all done. What's up?"

Steve said, "More importantly, how does the doctor say you're doing?"

"He says I'm bouncing back pretty well. Still have some labored breathing and they gave me more of the antidotes, but that's probably all I need now. I'm really improved. Our parents have gone back, since Mandy will be sticking close to me."

"Well, we may have to borrow Mandy for a little while, but she won't be far away from you," Steve said.

"Borrow her for what? What's going on?" Reggie said.

"I can't say. We're going up to Camp David early tomorrow with Alan and the director. I need to bring Mandy for that visit. Whatever happens there will decide what we do. I just need you to stay accessible, and for God's sake stay in the cocoon we've created for you," Steve said.

"Isn't that the presidential retreat?"

"Yes, but I can't say more."

Mandy said, "OK. You're being pretty mysterious, but I'm happy to go as long as Reggie is protected," Mandy said.

The helicopter ride from the roof of the Hoover Building to Camp David in Catoctin Mountain Park in Maryland, took thirty minutes. The passengers had little to say on the way out, other than to make it clear who would lead the discussion for the group. It was to be the director first, then turning to Alan Frenche to provide the details. The attorney general had not shared with them who else would be in the meeting. Mandy was in a state of awe. Steve Baker felt like he had just been yanked from a single-A minor league team all the way to the majors. But he was freshly invigorated by the fingerprint discoveries he'd learned of late last night; in turn he had called Alan Frenche to share this information.

When the FBI chopper landed at the helipad, golf carts were waiting to shuttle them to the cabin complex just two minutes away. They were met by Marine guards and passed through metal detectors, then all were ushered into the cabin containing a large conference table. The president's chief of staff was waiting for them, and invited them to sit and to wait for the others to arrive. Shortly after their arrival, a car pulled up outside the cabin and two other individuals exited and entered through the same door as they had. The director of national intelligence and her direct report, the CIA director, came in and shook hands.

Mandy witnessed, within minutes of all participants arriving, the chief of staff leaving through a connecting door to another cabin, and soon returning accompanied by the president. Everyone stood and greeted the president. He asked everyone to take a seat and thanked them for coming on a Saturday. All were dressed casually for the occasion, although the occasion was anything but casual.

The president turned to Mandy and asked, "Ms. Doucette, how's your sister doing?"

Of course he already knew, but Mandy was charmed that he would start out with a touching question to her. She said, "She's making a comeback thanks to some quick thinking. Thanks for your concern, Mr. President."

The president said, "Please give her my regards and my thanks."

The president then said that some important information had been brought to him yesterday by the attorney general and that it involved serious national security issues. He invited the attorney general to lay out what had been found.

The attorney general laid out in broad brushstrokes what had been uncovered through a series of connected incidents which had in part been very public and involved announced legal prosecutions taken by the Department of Justice and five murders and one attempted murder of a federal employee. The involvement of MI6 had helped a large part of the puzzle fall into place. He then turned the discussion over to Alan Frenche, and asked him to take them through the entire story step-by-step, if the president had the time to sit through all of that. The president nodded, and with that Frenche laid out the whole story in detail. He added in the confirmed fingerprint information tying in the same individual to the murders and attempted murder. He ended his part by saying, "Mr. President, all of this has come to light because of the dogged determination of Ms. Doucette, and we're in her debt for her persistent work. We wanted her in this meeting in case you had any questions she could answer."

When Alan was done, the president turned to the director of national intelligence and simply raised his eyebrows.

She said, "These are very strong assertions you're making today, and I would like to ask our CIA director to respond."

The CIA director said, "I'm taken aback by this, to say the least. Sherman Haskins has had an exemplary record, and was one of the team that uncovered the Aldrich Ames debacle years ago. I need some time to digest all of this and to do my own vetting of these pieces."

The FBI director spoke up. "You will remember what happened with Aldrich Ames, I assume? When we fully understood what had happened with him, it was decided to strike before he could disappear into the Russian wilderness and we might lose all hope of seizing him and discovering all of his betrayals. And that is exactly what we believed Ames was doing, heading to Moscow for some conference. If we'd hesitated in acting, he may have disappeared into Russia and been beyond our reach forever. Unless we do something to get it delayed, we're looking at a Monday morning delivery to Haskins of information from MI6 that might send him into immediate flight. That's what I'd do if I were in his shoes and realized my world was collapsing in around me — make an immediate run for it. Assuming he is what we think he is, he must have an emergency extraction plan. To let him get away would be more embarrassment than we could take, after the national security disaster it looks like he's inflicted already. We have a plan to move against him, and I would like to lay that out."

The CIA director then asked if he could have the chance to investigate this rupture in his own agency. The FBI director immediately quashed that idea, saying that enough was already known for making a move, and anything taking place within his own agency could arouse Haskins to believe he needed to flee, and they might just lose him. No, he said, he had to be taken unawares.

The president then interrupted. "Let me leave you to this. I believe this is a huge intelligence disaster we'll have on our hands, not to mention a foreign relations setback with China. I want to get hold of the secretary of state and to discuss the bigger picture of the fallout with China and where this could lead. But let me add that as I have listened to this discussion, I'm in total agreement that the CIA must do absolutely nothing to push this traitor into flight. I'm looking at all of you and saying that the time for doing double checks is over. I'm persuaded that we have a national security code blue on our hands and I want it acted upon immediately. Are we clear?"

He then turned to the DNI and to the CIA director. Pointing to them he said, "If you can visualize CNN's pictures of the man who nabbed Aldrich Ames disembarking into God-knows-where China and escaping a net we hesitated to throw, you'll appreciate that I don't want that to come to pass. I don't care how much embarrassment this is going to lead to, it would be unforgivable if we let him slip away. And to you and your team," he said, turning to the attorney general, "a job well done, and you have my eternal thanks. Especially to you, Ms. Doucette. Now, let's catch the bastard. We may not be able to nail Osama bin Laden twelve thousand miles away, but we sure as hell ought to be able to catch a known traitor right here in our midst."

With that, the president and the chief of staff left the meeting. Two hours later, when all of the handwringing by the CIA director was over, the president was advised that the CIA would verify, in the most confidential of discussions but only hand in hand with the FBI, the information that had been proffered by MI6. Assuming there was no change in its import, the FBI would undertake an operation on U.S. soil to apprehend the suspects of both the murders and attempted murder, as well as the U.S. traitor.

Mandy thought to herself, *Wow. What have I gotten myself into?*

Steve said, "Mandy, if it hadn't been for you and your determination on this, we might have gone on living with a large cell of foreign agents living right alongside us for a lot longer."

CHAPTER 25

SATURDAY AFTERNOON, the directors of National Intelligence, CIA, and FBI dialed a call over an encrypted line to the chief of MI6. The director of national intelligence said, "Good evening, Chief. Thank you so much for interrupting your Saturday evening to take our call. I believe you know my colleagues on the line?"

"Yes, I most certainly do, and I don't mind the occasion to have a chat with you. I believe you wish to discuss the information that will be coming from our Commander Culbertson this Monday morning. I received it late yesterday, and have been over it. How can I help?"

"Chief, we're most interested in whether you can confirm the information from Commander Culbertson about this Professor Fennstrom he identifies, as well as that of his sons."

The chief of MI6 said, "Yes, I think it's right on the mark and consistent with our knowledge for years now. I'm surprised a little, though, that you're even asking."

"Why is that?" she said.

"Well, it has been in reports to you chaps over the years, and should come as no surprise."

The DNI said, "Well then, I guess we'll have to go back and look more carefully at what we've got in house. I'm so sorry to have disturbed you for something that we may already have. But just to give us a little time for homework on our end, could we ask that you send me the report immediately, but then hold off on sending the report through the channel the commander would normally use until Wednesday, another two business days? And if there have been years of reports on this family, could we trouble you to gather those as well, and to send them along to me?"

"Happy to, and enjoy the rest of your weekend. By the way, we found photos of the brothers you wanted and those will be sent to you immediately."

They signed off on the call. The CIA director said, "I'm beginning to think that our own Mr. Haskins has been directly receiving these reports about his true identity. All he had to do was suppress them. He was the fox, to whom MI6 was directly feeding the hens. It's pretty damning for him. But shame on us too."

The DNI said, nodding, "Director, put your plan together. Be prepared to put it into action Wednesday. In the meantime, we will keep our mouths shut, as we've been told."

Steve Baker was put in charge of preparing the three-part operational plan to take the actions necessary. Sunday morning, he kicked it into high gear, with Mandy in attendance. Part one was a plan to lure the assassin or assassins out into the open and apprehend them. Part two was a separate initiative to place Winston Fennstrom, alias Sherman Haskins, under surveillance and conduct an arrest when it was considered the best time. The surveillance was intended to allow Fennstrom to demonstrate his likely true nature. Part three was going to be riskier, but involved the assistance of MI6 in breaching the enclave of Edward Fennstrom and extracting his information. Steve was relieved that the additional days were provided, and he got to work. He had been feeling out of his element the last day or so, especially at Camp David, but now he was in his comfort zone. The director had gathered his assistant directors and ordered that a formidable team be made available to carry out the plan Steve was putting together with Alan Frenche.

Steve immediately instructed a surveillance team to provide round-the-clock observation on Haskins. Next, two arrest teams were being gathered, and plans were being made to take in both targets. They anticipated Haskins' attempt at flight out of the country, possibly using an alias. Photos of Haskins had been harvested out of the Hoover Building monitors when he visited Alan Frenche, and were prepared to go into the hands of the Transportation Security Administration agents within a three-hundred-mile radius of Washington D.C. Once Steve got all of this going, he took Mandy aside and suggested they go to Reggie's room. Before heading out,

Steve received an envelope containing the photos from MI6 of the Fennstrom brothers. One of the photos was of a much younger, but clearly identical image of the Sherman Haskins photo just recovered from the FBI monitor. He shared them with Mandy and watched her eyes get bigger.

They headed over to Walter Reed and made their way up to Reggie's room. He brought flowers for Reggie. When he got to the room, the guards outside said nothing suspicious had happened. He entered and came to a dead halt when he got through the door. Mandy and Reggie were decked out in identical hospital scrubs. Steve thrust out the bouquet and held it to one side then the other and said, "Oh, c'mon."

Reggie held up her hand and said, "I'm Reggie. Sorry, we like it better this way." She took the flowers and they all laughed. Both had their red hair pulled back into ponytails and had painted each other's nails in matching red polish.

"But we didn't put perfume on!" They laughed again.

"I can see you're feeling a lot better, Reggie," he said.

"Well, I doubt I could walk all the way down the hall, but at least I can get out of bed and go to the bathroom. No more bedpans for me."

He made them sit down and he briefed them on what was happening.

"Let me plug in this phone first. It's been going dead on me really fast."

They were pretty excited about the Camp David story, the fingerprints, and the phone call with the chief of MI6. Steve went through what they were trying to accomplish.

Mandy asked, "How are you going to lure these assassins out into the open?"

Steve said, "That's where you come in."

Reggie popped up out of bed and yelled, "NO WAY! You're not using my sister for bait."

Steve held up both his hands, palms out, and said, "Hold on. She may already be bait. And we'll make sure she's not at risk."

Then to Mandy, he said, "Let me see your phone."

She handed him the phone and explained that it had been losing its charge more rapidly than normal and had to be recharged regularly.

Steve held the phone and asked her, "Is it always this hot?"

"No, I think the battery is going bad on me," she said.

"Do you have auto-correct turned on for your keyboard?"

"Yeah, but that's screwing up too."

"This is perfect," he said. "Your phone's been infected with spyware. Please power it down, and let me pull the SIM card out of it."

She did that and he explained himself. He was no digital expert, but had access to them and would get one over to the hospital. He took a moment to poke his head out the door and ask one of his colleagues for a favor. Steve asked if someone could remotely install spyware, including something called a keylogger, on your phone. The software would be undetectable and would let the installer know where you were, what messages or texts you were receiving or sending, to or from whom, and what the messages said. All the while, you would be clueless.

If a phone was so afflicted, it would be behaving just like Mandy's—losing power quickly, feeling hot, dropping in processing speed, having a surge in data use, and most telling, the auto-correction function malfunctioning.

"Can you get it off my phone?" Mandy said.

"Yeah, but we're not going to," Steve said. "Have you been running?"

Confused by the change in direction of the discussion, she said, "No. Why?"

"Do you have your running stuff?" he asked.

"Always, but I'm not too interested in running with my sister suffering here."

"You don't want to sit here and get fat, do you?"

"Hey!"

"If you look out that window, you see I-495 over there. There's a little road called Cedar Lane that goes under that expressway and drops you off at Rock Creek, which runs for miles either way with a greenway and woods. You're gonna go for a run. Actually, several runs."

After he had explained to them what he had in mind, and Mandy was about finished asking her questions, a knock on the door came and he let a young colleague of his in and introduced him as Todd.

"Todd is my digital guy. Please hand him your phone, and he'll study it a bit and let us know what you've got." Todd took the phone with the SIM card, and went out in the hallway for a while.

Reggie was back in bed and showing some signs of exhaustion. She picked up *The New York Times* from a few days back that had been brought into her room by a nurse so she could see the article about the nerve agent attacks. She asked what the Bureau was doing about the news reports, and Steve told her that they were trying to give out as little information as possible so as not to tip off the people they were after. He speculated that they were either going to strike more decisively, or just fold up their operation and try to disappear. The Bureau, though, was trying to flush them out and to force an encounter. They didn't want anyone to get hurt, but they also didn't want to let them just fade into the background and elude the Bureau's grasp. This was already a massive security breach as it was. The director didn't want it to be one without nailing the instigator, and he certainly didn't want the targets to just melt away.

Todd brought the phone back in and confirmed Steve's assumptions. The spyware would allow tracking if the phone was on, as well as full visibility of emails and texting, with the capture of phone numbers. He said that the software had been there for weeks. Mandy said, "That would be around the time I was at Allzient and met with Erik Spenser. That means someone has known everything I've been doing, including the meeting with John Booth in Washington, with the Bureau, and my trips to Reggie in Quantico. Are you telling me that if your phone has this software, it gives you a window into all that is happening with the phone's owner?"

Todd said, "That's right. We found the same spyware on John Booth's phone."

Mandy looked at Steve and said, "Are you able to remotely install this software on someone's phone?"

Steve said, "Yes, we are. What are you getting at?"

Mandy said, "I'm going to give you a cell phone number, and I want you to install the spyware on it. I can guarantee you that it will be very revealing."

"OK. I can do that if you can assure me there's a reasonable evidentiary basis. I've got to get a federal judge to approve it."

"You've got my assurance."

Mandy handed him a slip of paper with the phone number and the name Emily Jenkins written on it.

Steve looked at it and back at Mandy and raised his eyebrows. Then he took an envelope out of his briefcase and took a photo out and handed it to Mandy.

"Can you recognize this person?"

"Sure, it's a younger Harold Menzies."

Steve said, "That's Edward Fennstrom. Another piece of the puzzle has just fallen into place. There's something else I want to say to you. I know this whole bribery situation has been the precipitating event that thrust you, and all of us really, into the thing we're now in. But you must know by now that that was just the warm-up act to the main event."

Mandy said, "And that is?"

"You may have, through your dogged detective work on the bribery, led us into uncovering and apprehending the largest foreign espionage network this country has ever seen. It has penetrated with a vast array of foreign agents into our military-industrial defense system and into the very inner circle of our intelligence system, and may have done unimaginable damage to our national security. Think about that."

Mandy looked at Reggie, and they both looked at Steve and said together, "Yeah, we will."

Monday morning, Mandy headed out early with her two FBI escorts for a run up the route Steve had instructed her to use. She carried her powered-up phone, still behaving oddly, wore her red hair in a ponytail and had on sunglasses and a lightweight Patagonia vest. These were also Steve's instructions. Her escorts hung back a bit, as she went up the Rock Creek route for a mile and made the turnaround. This was repeated Tuesday and Wednesday. Steve had explained to her that her movements were being tracked, and the game plan was to establish a daily routine that her phone trackers would rely on.

"Rely on for what?" Mandy asked.

"We want them to count on you continuing that route so we can take them out, but don't worry," he said.

"We are anticipating that you will be targeted again as soon as MI6's report is received. That will be Wednesday, so you will run the same route you have for three days prior. They'll know that route since they've been tracking you all along."

Wednesday morning in Chicago, a call took place with the Defense Department and Greg Carlucci and Arthur Ross as a follow-up to their earlier call. Mandy phoned into the conference call. Rhonda Graves led the discussion from the government side. Greg had told Arthur that the purpose of the call was to pose follow-up questions. When the call began, Graves had a very abrupt formal manner, and proceeded to advise the LaSalle group that this was a courtesy call to let them know that LaSalle would be receiving a letter from the Defense Contract Management Agency, the contract administration unit that managed all Defense Department procurement contracts. That letter would put LaSalle on notice that its status as a *responsible contractor* was being suspended for purposes of pending defense contract bids, but that existing contracts would be allowed to complete. A full security review by the Department of Defense would be initiated without delay, and LaSalle would be expected to cooperate fully with that review.

Ross indicated his shock at this, and his disappointment that the agency had acted so aggressively. Especially since the last call had ended with the expectation that a process had to take place. Graves said the agency regretted that this step needed to be taken, but the concerns over the Harold Menzies matter had escalated. Her agency had strong concerns that Defense Department classified documents and secrets may have been compromised, and could continue to be compromised. That had led them to act decisively. The call ended and then Greg Carlucci rushed up to Ed Rosen's office to advise him while Ross headed to Jim Kerwin's office to do the same. It was clear that once the formal letter was received, that would start a four-day period running within which the company would have to file a disclosure form with the Securities and Exchange Commission, with notice of the loss of contracting power with the federal government. They assumed that a sharp negative market reaction would drive the stock price down even further than what the Allzient hiccup had created. Jim Kerwin had wondered what kind of developments the update going to the Executive Committee would yield, and now he knew the answer. This was a gut punch. Mandy sat quietly after the call and remembered the dire warnings from Arthur Ross of so long ago.

Wednesday morning also saw the delayed delivery of the update message from MI6 to Sherman Haskins. He took the translation of the encrypted message out of the inter-office envelope and read the exchange with horror. Not only was his family name jumping off the page at him, but it detailed the tracking of Edward's identification and itinerary to the safe harbor of the Jin Mao Tower. His own internal calculus was roaring. The Chicago lawyer had burned him. It was now of the utmost importance that Mandy Doucette be taken down, but he probably still needed to prepare his escape. This report was going into his briefcase, then directly into oblivion. But that was tonight. Now he needed to visit a downtown park and to make a burner phone call to the boys with instructions. He canceled meetings he'd scheduled and headed out of the building to his car carrying his briefcase, too anxiety-ridden to notice two vehicles starting to move from the parking lot as he did. In the next few minutes, Sherman Haskins unknowingly led a caravan of followers on a ride down George Washington Memorial Parkway along the Potomac River and into Arlington National Cemetery. The Bureau's agents were well prepared with parabolic microphones that could pick up conversations from almost three hundred feet way. Haskins' conversation, at least his end of it, was recorded. The call he made lasted less than two minutes. The FBI also picked up the burner phone number Haskins was speaking with. He hopped in his car and left, this time without the caravan. There was no need to follow now, since the GPS tracker on his car allowed the followers to arrive at Haskins' home unhurried and unseen. The one-sided content of the call he had made was not of the highest fidelity, but sufficient for Steve Baker to put his plan into effect.

Haskins drove directly to Fashion Center at Pentagon City, parked his car, and entered the mall. Once inside the mall he threw the MI6 package in a trash receptacle and went down to the Pentagon City Metro station. He boarded a Blue Line train, changed to a Green Line train at L'Enfant Plaza, exited at the Navy Yard, and hurried to his backup apartment on M Street SE.

Meanwhile, Steve Baker had some checking done now that he had the burner phone number of Haskins' colleagues, and the number clicked. It matched the phone used to send the threatening text message sent to Mandy last month. Just more confirmation that this had been a consistent and continuous plan of attack on Mandy.

Steve decided it was time to check in with his watchers at Haskins' Maryland home, who reported that he had not yet shown up, a full hour after his rendezvous at the cemetery. A quick check with his tracker revealed that Haskins' car was parked at the Fashion Center Mall. Fear gripped Steve that Haskins had slipped the trackers, and an hour later his team reached a consensus that Haskins was gone. There was a frantic and furious effort to find him, and finally the various cameras disclosed his trip down into the Metro. Much work would be needed to find him.

CHAPTER 26

THURSDAY MORNING at 6:30 a.m., Haskins' boys were in position in the woods around Rock Creek. The call they received from their controller Sherman Haskins, the day before had triggered their mission on the running route they'd been tracking for days. Having listened in on their call with Haskins the previous day, the FBI also knew today was the day. One of the boys was near a copse of trees two hundred yards north of the point where Cedar Lane crossed under I-495. He had a Ruger Precision Rimfire .22 caliber rifle fitted with a suppressor and scope. His partner was in the black Range Rover around a bend on Beach Drive. A runner coming up the trail along the creek wouldn't be able to see it, and yet it was within only one hundred feet of the spot where the shooter was waiting. Once the runner came off Cedar Lane and entered the path, she would be presenting a flank target to the shooter and too far away for his comfort anyway. He had to wait until she came down toward the creek and turn in a mostly northern facing direction, so as to present a full-frontal target.

Minutes later, right on schedule given the pattern of the last couple days, his phone spyware tracker showed the target pinging up Cedar Lane and moving under I-495 toward Beach Drive. At the intersection of Cedar and Beach, the pinging showed the redheaded runner turning to the left onto the running path. He could see a thin figure between trees, making the turn toward him to where she neared the creek, then diverging from it directly toward him and about 150 yards away. He fingered the trigger and squared the runner up in his sights and fired two rounds in quick succession—tap, tap. A split-second later the runner with the sunglasses and swinging red ponytail went down backward and fell flat on the trail. The shooter folded up his stock, picked up his brass shell casings, and prepared to run to the Range Rover. Just as he was making his move, two figures following the girl came around the curve and broke into a sprint toward her.

The two FBI agents sprinting up the path reached the downed runner, now flat on her back and not moving, the red wig blown off her head and lying to the side. One agent spoke a command into his shoulder: "Take 'em alive." At the Range Rover, as the shooter reached the door, silenced shots rang out from his right, flattening the right-side front and rear tires. Three SUVs roared down Beach Drive from the north, and three agents with automatic rifles came in from the right flank and yelled for the two to get face down on the ground. They did as they were told, and were cuffed around the back, loaded into the SUVs, then driven away.

The female agent lying on the ground said, "God, that hurts. No bikini for me for a while." They unzipped the Kevlar-lined Patagonia vest to make sure there were no punctures.

Two miles away in an FBI safe house in a suburban street in Silver Spring, Maryland, the Doucette sisters were drinking coffee when their security detail got a phone call with the action report, and that the faux-Mandy was OK. As he was talking to Steve on the other end of the line, he flashed a thumbs-up to the sisters. Mandy said to him, "Tell Steve I need my phone and that Todd guy."

The two men captured on Beach Drive were brought to the Federal Central Detention Facility on D Street in the Southeast District of Columbia and kept there for interrogation. Steve had secured the cell phone they had in the Range Rover and following the instructions they had noted in the overheard call from Arlington National Cemetery the day before, texted back to Haskins: *Done. Going underground for two days.* They were also able to see that the burner phone they had in hand had the same number used in the exchange with Sherman Haskins the day before.

After the keylogger software had been remotely installed on Emily Jenkins' cell phone, the FBI was able to view a huge cache of text communications between her and Harold Menzies, as well as quite a few that had gone from Emily that remained unanswered by Menzies. Todd had breathed easy when he found that Emily Jenkins hadn't installed antivirus software on her cell phone. It had allowed the data collection they now had, as well as the ability to track Emily's whereabouts. She was now tracked to O'Hare Airport. Emily was on the move. She would later pop up at Dulles International Airport, and from there she was tracked to a Washington, D.C., location on M Street, the address Harold Menzies had given her. By that time, of course, she had company a safe distance behind her.

Sherman Haskins heard his phone ping, saw the message from the boys, and gave a fist pump. He went back to preparing for a long trip. If the lawyer was finished off, and the MI6 report was gone, he might just have dodged the bullet, but he wasn't taking any chances. He would bolt, and if it was an overreaction, he could slip back in. He had nothing to regret after a ten-year-plus success record.

Steve left the shooting detail and headed over to the safe house with Mandy's phone. They were in one of the bedrooms, and after letting Steve in, they returned to the bedroom. Steve took off his hat and was throwing it on the bed when the sisters simultaneously dove for the hat and knocked it onto the floor.

Mandy, getting back up off the bed and smoothing her dress, said "Phew! That was close."

Steve said, "Jesus, that was pretty dramatic. What was that all about?"

Reggie said, "Where we come from, putting a hat on a bed spells bad luck for whoever sleeps in that bed. We just couldn't let that happen, especially given our recent string of bad luck. Our grandmother would have a heart attack."

After that everyone high-fived. Mandy and Reggie both had on jeans, black Hoka running shoes, and Paris Marathon T-shirts. Their hair was down and they had on matching ruby earrings. Steve held out a phone in front of him and said, "Whichever one of you is Mandy, here's your phone. Todd's on the way."

Mandy said, "How's my stand-in?"

"She's got two big bruises on her sternum that will hurt for a couple of days, then she'll be back to normal. Thanks for asking. Now, I want you to call your parents and to warn them that we're planting a story that you've been shot outside Walter Reed, so they don't freak out if they see a CNN report or something. By the way, thanks for the Jenkins' cell phone idea. We got lots of useful stuff from it. Also, she's coming to Washington. D.C., we think. She's going down, and she'll be a classic case of aiding and abetting."

Mandy said, "So she was dirty. Why am I not surprised? What about Menzies?"

Steve said, "Being handled."

Within two hours, a report surfaced that a Chicago lawyer identified as Amanda Doucette had been shot in an early morning run and had been taken to Johns Hopkins Medicine-Suburban Hospital on Old Georgetown Road in Bethesda, Maryland, where she was pronounced dead. Bethesda police were actively looking for suspects, but there had been no witnesses. Anyone having information that might help law enforcement was encouraged to call, then a number was shown.

Sherman Haskins had the TV on CNN and heard the report. Other than stopping for a minute to see the story, he did a fist pump and kept on packing.

At 9:00 a.m., Thursday, the attorney general entered the Oval Office. "Good morning, Mr. President. I can report to you that our team has apprehended two men near Walter Reed who attempted the murder of the sister of our poisoned FBI pathologist, and our agents were unharmed. We have planted a report with the media that the sister was shot dead, but that is to help bring in Sherman Haskins, so it will be corrected soon as being in error. As soon as we apprehend him, that is."

"Any of our agents hurt?"

"One agent from some serious bruises from a bullet hitting a Kevlar vest, sir. But she's fine."

"The sister was not harmed?"

"No, sir."

"And what's the status of the FBI pathologist?"

"She's making a strong recovery. I think the speed with which she was treated and the low dose she sustained combined to set her up for a good bounce-back," said the attorney general. He went on to say that the Justice Department was preparing multiple federal murder and attempted murder charges against the men apprehended. They were being questioned and if the men invoked their rights to an attorney, they would have to provide public defenders unless the men had their own counsels. Once all of the defense stuff was sorted out, the plan would be to start reconstructing the whole network so they could neutralize it. Until they got Haskins, the effort couldn't be thorough.

The president asked him to get the secretary of state up to speed, and to get a game plan started on the fallout with China that would ensue. Meanwhile, he would ask the chief of staff to call a cabinet meeting together, to have a completely coordinated administration approach to the incident.

Mandy and Reggie were watching the CNN report about Mandy's death. She said, "Oh, shit!" She picked up her cell phone and punched in Rick's number. When he saw who was calling, he answered hesitantly and said, "Hello?"

"Rick, it's me, Mandy," she said.

Rick said, "Thank God! CNN is reporting that you've been killed! I'm not talking to a ghost, am I?"

"No, I'm still alive and fine, but everyone needs to think I'm dead right now. Something big is going on, but I can't say I'm alive. It's because of an FBI operation. But I wanted you to know. Can you just keep it to yourself?"

"How long?"

"Not for long, a couple of days" she said.

"So now I have to act like I'm grieving when I don't have to? Fine. Well, I'm glad you're OK. By the way, watch for an 8-K filing today. Bad news on the Menzies fallout."

"I know. I was on the call with Greg. Sounds like Arthur Ross's predictions coming true."

"Yeah, Greg's a basket case. How's Reggie?"

"She's amazing. Really bouncing back. Speaking of

Menzies, I have some other news you should be prepared for. Wretched Witch is finished and will probably be arrested and charged with espionage. And Menzies turns out to be a guy named Edward Fennstrom, and is a spy for the Chinese."

Rick said, "What?"

"Yeah, I didn't tell you this before, but the FBI put some spyware on Emily's phone and it turns out she's been right by his side all the way in his activities. They don't know if she was aware of what she was involved in, but it's too late for her. She's getting swept up soon and will have cuffs on. LaSalle's going to have some heavy-duty public relations work on its hands here."

Rick said, "How did the FBI know to bug her phone?"

Mandy said, "Uh, you know how I always hate when some manager says *it's better not to ask permission, just ask for forgiveness?*"

"Oh no, don't tell me."

"Yeah, so will you forgive me? I had that investigator also watch Emily, and damned if he didn't catch her meeting Menzies in his hotel room for a little sack time. That was enough for me to go to Def Con One on her. I asked the FBI to tap her phone, and voilà, she's implicated herself in a big espionage case. Bribery's just minor league, it turns out."

Rick said, "I guess you're forgiven, as long as it all pans out the way you say it is. But how are we going to get prepared to handle that?"

Mandy said, "I don't know yet. I'm just a newbie in big spy cases. OK, gotta go. Thanks."

Mandy next made a phone call to Patrick Carney, who picked up on the first ring. "Hello? Is that you, Mandy?"

"You're not watching CNN, are you?"

Patrick said, "I am, and either it's got really bad sources, or I'm talking to a ghost."

"Neither of the above. I just went through the same conversation with Rick Crawford. I'm alright, and I'll explain it all to you soon. Keep this quiet for a couple of days and all will be made clear."

"Hey, I'm just relieved you're OK. I already had enough for a book. Don't scare me anymore. Do I need to be worried about someone named Rick Crawford, who gets a call before I do?"

"Gotta go. Miss you."

She hung up and thought to herself, *Did I detect a little jealousy there just now?*

That afternoon Mandy pulled up the Securities and Exchange Commission website and punched in the company's ticker symbol. It yielded the Form 8-K which had been filed, advising of a "material event" regarding the Defense Department's suspension of LaSalle's federal contracting rights. This report that the registrant, LaSalle, had to file publicly just because it was a public company, cited the dollar amount of the federal procurement contracts pending, but said it couldn't yet be determined what the effect would be on the company's revenues. It stated that the company was in the process of repairing its status and resuming that part of the business. By the close of the market, LaSalle stock was down another 2 percent—an ugly end to the week.

Rick hadn't had a chance to update Mandy on the status of the Allzient deal. Allzient had made significant strides with prosecutors in Spain, Italy, and France to settle charges with those countries over bribery of their officials. As it had done with Justice, Allzient was in the process of negotiating fines that would, while being substantial, allow it to get beyond the crisis and to rescue the deal. The next step was to get a price reduction, which would probably fall to him to manage.

Sherman Haskins had prepared his departure from his backup location as a precaution in case he had been uncovered, and he was in place with another car parked nearby. As Steve saw it, once Haskins was found, the dilemma was whether to pick him up, or let him go for a while and see what he did. Maybe he would lead them to something they would not otherwise find. They just had to find him and to make sure they could track him again.

About an hour before he was ready to leave, his doorbell rang. He went to the door in stocking feet to keep his steps quiet and looked through the peephole. An attractive, middle-aged woman was outside, unknown to him. He turned on the outside light and opened the door and said, "Yes, can I help you?"

The woman said, "Hi, I'm Emily Jenkins. I was hoping to see Harold, if he's home."

"I'm sorry, Harold isn't here right now. In fact, he's traveling. Can I let him know you were here so he can get back to you?"

"No, that's alright. I should have made sure he was here before I came. I haven't been able to get in touch with him. Are you a friend of his?"

"We live together here. Sorry you went to the trouble. I'll let him know you came by."

"Thanks," she said. She left the house, thinking that Harold bore a strong resemblance to that guy. *Who was that guy?* She got in her parked rental car and pulled away, bewildered by what was happening and wondering what had happened to Harold. Three blocks away she suddenly saw blue flashing lights in a police cruiser pulling her over. A black SUV pulled in front of her car, blocking her way. When she lowered the window, a uniformed officer asked her to step out of the car, but didn't bother asking for her license and registration first.

Another man wearing an FBI jacket produced a badge and ID card and said, "You're under arrest. Please turn around and put your hands on the roof of the vehicle."

Emily said, "What's going on here? I haven't done anything wrong. Under arrest for what?"

She was cuffed behind her back, read her Miranda warning rights, and placed in the rear of the cruiser, then taken to the federal detention center. She was questioned for over an hour and placed into a cell, after her phone was confiscated and after she refused to answer any further questions without a lawyer present. Her cell phone was examined and found to still contain many calls and texts to the cell phone of Harold Menzies. Emily Jenkins was about to be charged with aiding and abetting a violation of U.S. espionage laws, as well as multiple charges of aiding and abetting murder and attempted murder.

The remainder of the FBI team trailing Emily had installed themselves watching the building she had visited. They were poised to acquire Haskins once he left.

The decision was made to let Haskins run, knowing they could sweep him up any time they wished. Sure enough, he made a run for his alternate car after 10:00 p.m. and then headed up I-495 to 1-95 for a while, stopping somewhere close to Philadelphia for some shuteye. A massive caravan, including multiple helicopters, had been organized to accompany him on his journey, wherever it was headed. The FBI wanted to see if he would reveal any other secrets before they grabbed him.

Once Haskins was in for the night, FBI agents attached tracking devices to his alternate car, though it was probably belt and suspenders at this point. Once Haskins had given them the slip, eyes would be on him permanently until he was in custody. Emily Jenkins had provided a valuable service to the government, albeit unknowingly.

Early Saturday morning, the journey began again with what would turn out to be a five-hundred-mile journey through Pennsylvania, New York, and to Ontario. Once Haskins headed up I-476 north out of Philadelphia and connected to I-81 north, they decided that Toronto was a likely destination. The director called his counterpart, the director of the Canadian Security Intelligence Service, and requested assistance to apprehend a major crime suspect involving national security. They agreed on arrangements to allow Haskins to pass through the border and to track him to his destination. Meanwhile, airline flight manifests were checked in a number of directions with a handful of aliases Haskins might be using. After the long journey with a border crossing and one hundred agents involved, Sherman Haskins, traveling on a Chinese passport in the name of

Winston Fennstrom, was arrested without incident in a parking garage at Toronto Pearson International Airport by agents of the Canadian Security Intelligence Service along with members of the Royal Canadian Mounted Police and the U.S. FBI. Canadian intelligence and law enforcement had to take the lead on Canadian soil, of course, but their relationship with the FBI was tight. After the arrest, they were pleased to hand him off to U.S. authorities. Haskins was immediately packed off into a waiting FBI jet. Overnight the traitor was placed in a cell at Thule Air Force Base on the western shore of Greenland.

The Canadian authorities had been reluctant to have any foreign intelligence activities, including interrogation, taking place on its soil, so the alternative was to use the nearby U.S. base that would involve permissible FBI operating jurisdiction and to avoid the Canadian hesitancy.

An FBI interrogation team confronted Haskins upon his arrival at Thule and began to question him about his activities. His first statement was that he wanted a lawyer. The interrogation team was prepared for this, and led him through his activities in a thorough listing of his betrayal and crime spree. He was told that under the federal crimes he had committed, he would be eligible for the death penalty or life imprisonment. Absent any cooperation on his part, the government intended to seek the death penalty. When he continued to resist cooperating, he was told that his brother was also in custody and providing information. This caused him to reconsider and ask if he cooperated, would he be guaranteed that no death penalty would be sought in his prosecution. The team told him that while it couldn't assure that a judge would be bound by promises made by government prosecutors, they could assure him that if he cooperated, the government wouldn't ask for the death penalty. There was one condition, which was that any information he gave would be compared to that provided by his brother. If his information proved to be deficient or inconsistent with that from his brother, the promise not to seek the death penalty would be voided. Haskins thought to himself, *I can manage this. Get to be a guest of the U.S. government until a prisoner swap could be arranged, and I should be able to get through it.*

Once an agreement was reached, the interrogation team began a week-long series of sessions with Haskins that included the identities of all of the individuals who had been pulled through the various companies in Europe and in the United States over the years since he had been running his operation, which began shortly after assuming his role in the apprehension of Aldrich Ames. Over a dozen agents had been carefully placed in foreign companies operating in countries allied to the United States, including Allzient, as well as U.S. companies operating in such countries, regardless of their products or services. Once there, then the brothers would seek to influence the movement of the agents in those companies as well as the acquisition of their host companies by critical defense contractors. The goal was to put as many agents as possible in places where they could then be used to extract information useful to the Chinese government. The individuals weren't aware of the end destination for the information they provided. It was only an income-generating activity on their parts, and if there was political bias that could be used as an enhancement to their cooperation, that was encouraged.

Haskins wasn't the end of the system. Once he and Moines were done with their stocking of individuals and nursing corporate aggregations, from there others would take over and manage the active accumulation of information. There would be another extensive investigation of individuals rolled up in the sweep that the Bureau intended to undertake.

CHAPTER 27

AS THE HOUR APPROACHED midnight in Shanghai, a special team of agents, who were already in position in Hyatt Grand Hotel rooms in the floors below Menzies' eighty-ninth floor condominium, prepared for their visit. MI6 had been most helpful in securing the condominium layouts to the Moines' unit, as well as getting security cards for entrance to the residential elevators that would take them to the eighty-ninth floor. Early in the morning, the team made its way into the corridor of Menzies' floor and to his door. Reasonably sure that he would be asleep from the lack of activity on the cameras that had been placed in his unit and the sounds of a sleeping person, they prepared to enter. Out of an abundance of caution, no move would be made until the brother had been taken into custody and interrogated in a secure facility.

The team entered the condo, with the lead agent wielding a dart gun loaded with tranquilizer. Shortly thereafter, three of the team members quietly entered the bedroom and fired the dart into Menzies. It usually took several minutes to let the drug take full effect. Using too much for more immediate effect would risk the target's death. Once he was hit with the dart, two team members secured the surprised and thrashing man, bagging his head while the tranquilizer worked its magic. Then he was carried to the adjoining empty unit through a connecting door. This was the unit owned by his now-detained brother Winston Fennstrom, a.k.a. Sherman Haskins. He was being prepared to have a series of drugs administered that would open him up to provide a history of activities in the past ten years.

While he was undergoing his chemical adjustments, the team members found his cell phone and arranged to transfer all of the cell phone contents onto their device. The cell phone data would later evidence a history of phone calls between himself and Emily Jenkins that was highly indicative of suspicious contacts with a LaSalle officer beyond what would be expected for a board member. This cemented the connection Emily Jenkins unwittingly had with the espionage and with other crimes.

Once he was conscious, and they administered sodium pentothal, his information began to flow. This wasn't going to be an interrogation like that of his brother. There was no interest in trying to extract a Chinese citizen out of the country. He would serve no ongoing purpose that could negatively affect U.S. interests, but his information was critical to vetting received from his brother. Once the man was drained of his information, he would be drugged again and left to sleep it off as if nothing had ever happened. He was extremely chatty after his injection, happy to describe his activities from Spruance Corporation, as Armand Moines, to LaSalle Enterprises, as Harold Menzies. His detailed listing of all of the individuals brought into companies to which he had access would be matched to what was being extracted from his brother Winston. His affair with Emily Jenkins was generously detailed in the discussion as well. There was more than enough to lay a foundation for his grooming of her to advance the plans for the acquisition of Allzient. Finally, his long, carefully cultivated activity with Sherman Haskins and a multitude of figures inserted into a variety of American companies came pouring out, including their plans to occupy their luxury condos and to enjoy their views of the magnificent Shanghai skyline. His "visitors" would depart and eliminate any evidence of their presence, slipping out of the country and back to their bases. Of course, he would be named eventually as a foreign agent, but would remain forever outside the United States. The Justice Department had used its power to block any trading of his equity accounts based on national security, depriving him of any wealth he had failed to transfer into safe accounts beyond the reach of the U.S. government.

The two attackers who were apprehended after the faux-Mandy had gone down on the Rock Creek path had been undergoing interrogation for days. Eventually, they yielded valuable details from their original locations in Russian cities, then their posts in Spruance, followed by Allzient, and eventually as the exclusive tools of Haskins. The puzzle that was being completed through their interrogation as well as the interrogations of Haskins and Menzies provided a broad picture of an intelligence operation that had, and was to have, far-reaching effects on the national security interests of the United States.

The collective information from the interrogations of the Fennstrom brothers had served two purposes. The Bureau felt reasonably comfortable that what had been learned from Menzies had corroborated what was coming from Haskins. In addition, the expansive network of individuals and their employers laid out a roadmap for the FBI to arrange a series of raids that were being staged to take place in the next two days across the country. It was shaping up to be the largest breakup of an espionage ring ever in the country's history. Haskins was being brought from Thule to Washington, D.C., where he would be in federal custody and able to have his attorney for the upcoming prosecution.

Mandy and Reggie had spent most of the days following the attack calling their parents and each of the siblings, no quick task when that amounted to so many calls. None of them could be quick calls, since both sisters were on each call and there were two stories that had to be told. A wave of relief spread across the family members as each of the siblings was told the whole story, though no one could yet be told the underlying cause.

By the following Friday morning, the sisters were still living in the care of the FBI at the Silver Spring safe house, watching CNN with the various reports of the nerve agent deaths and Mandy's shooting death, when Steve Baker showed up. He told them the story from Haskins' dash out the back door, to the attempt to board an airplane in Toronto. He told them nothing of what happened after that.

He asked them if they would like to go for a ride. They were excited to get out of the house, and wanted to get dressed up a bit. During the week they had been going out and working themselves up from walking to running, to then running some mileage. Reggie was getting back to some semblance of herself and feeling good. Steve said they had to get moving, but was evasive when asked where they were headed. They were used to that by now. They scrambled and showed up in a few minutes in matching black pants suits and with their hair in ponytails, and they were out the door. They were both wearing red chili pepper earrings. A driver in a black Suburban shuttled them down Georgia Avenue NW for twenty minutes, followed by some turns on streets that eventually led them across Pennsylvania Avenue and into the White House grounds to pull up to the West Wing entrance. Mandy and Reggie looked at each other and wordlessly mouthed, "Oh shit." Steve Baker opened the doors and they were met at the entrance by the chief of staff, who led them through the West Wing and into the

Oval Office. Waiting for them were the attorney general, the FBI director, Alan Frenche, and the president, who shook hands with each of them, saying, "Special Agent Baker and ladies. Amanda and Regina?"

They each identified themselves and the president said, "Thank you for making that clear. We wanted to let you know that the drama that has been unfolding so painfully for you has come to an end, at least for you. In Toronto, Winston Fennstrom, alias Sherman Haskins and Philip Ray, was arrested attempting to board a flight that would have taken him to China. This entire week he has been in the process of cooperating with U.S. authorities, and has provided a treasure trove of useful information about his activities over the years. He's on his way back to face the music and to receive justice, in large part as a result of the ordeal he has put you through. Mr. Attorney General, could you please list the charges that Fennstrom will face"?

The attorney general said, "Fennstrom will be charged with multiple violations of the Espionage Act, federal murder charges, and attempted murder, including attempted murder of federal agents, including you, Dr. Doucette. He'll be arraigned upon his arrival. All of those charges will also be lodged against his two accomplices who made your lives so miserable. In addition, Amanda, your colleague Emily Jenkins was apprehended after appearing at Fennstrom's residence, and she'll be charged with aiding and abetting espionage as well as the other crimes, all resulting from her association with Edward Fennstrom, a.k.a. Armand Moines and Harold Menzies."

The president said, "We're deeply in your debt for protecting this country the way you have, and I wanted to express it to you first, in person, before the arrests are announced. To you, Dr. Doucette, I sincerely hope that your recovery is swift and complete. And to you, Amanda, I regret that your safety was endangered, but appreciate the part you played in creating the trap that snared Fennstrom's two murderous accomplices and the complicit LaSalle officer. And as I understand it, it was because of your excellent pursuit of the truth in the course of your business deal that this whole situation came to light in the first place. It seems like we should all be grateful that a bribery whistleblower stumbled into something much bigger, although we all do grieve his murder. And I guess I would have to compliment you for doing some impressive due diligence work! You served in our Justice Department, I understand. I would like to see you back there at some point. I'm keeping my eye on you."

Both sisters thanked the president, and Mandy said, "Mr. President, can we know whatever happened with Harold Menzies? I'm afraid my company may be suffering due to his involvement, and whatever schemes he was mixed up in. I'm hoping that we can get back into the good graces of the Defense Department."

The president turned to the attorney general, who said, "We have found a way to get value out of Mr. Menzies, who is no longer on American soil. As to his activities with LaSalle Enterprises, I would be happy to intercede with the Department of Defense to see how the impact Harold Menzies had on its business can be minimized. We're truly in your debt, as the president said."

The sisters were given a tour of the West Wing and eventually taken back to Silver Spring, where they decompressed and drank coffee, waiting to watch the CNN coverage of the unfolding events that day. Wolf Blitzer broke into the morning talking heads show with breaking news to announce the arrest of a high-ranking CIA official during an attempt to flee, and his ensuing return to Washington, D.C., in custody. The charges signaled the most dramatic espionage case that had occurred in fifteen years, the last being the Aldrich Ames arrest. Also revealed were the charges leveled against him and two accomplices for multiple murder and attempted murder charges. Film footage of Fennstrom being led from an airline parking garage and of the other two being placed in lockups were shown on a loop. Finally, he reported that an officer of LaSalle Enterprises had been arrested in connection with the espionage ring. He said that at 1:00 p.m., the attorney general would be holding a news conference at the Department of Justice to brief the nation. Finally, he reported that the previous news story of a fatal shooting of a Chicago attorney was being retracted and was explained as part of the federal efforts to capture the suspects.

The attorney general stepped up to a podium in the media room at the Justice Department headquarters, and flanked by the FBI director, Counterintelligence Section Director Alan Frenche, and Special Agent Steve Baker, held the biggest news conference of his career. He announced that the federal government had uncovered an extensive espionage network that had been operating in the United States for over a decade. The network had involved the infiltration not only of six defense contractors, but also at a high level in the Central Intelligence Agency. The defense contractors were named, and video feeds of arrests taking place simultaneously across the country were shown on the networks' screens as the attorney general spoke. Seventeen individuals were arrested and would be charged with violations of the espionage act on behalf of China. The arrests of the CIA official and those charged with the murders and attempted murders were described as well. A photo of an attractive woman was displayed on the screen and she was identified as Emily Jenkins, a senior executive at LaSalle Enterprises in Chicago, who had been charged as well in the espionage ring. The espionage and treasonous activities were described in broad outlines, with statements of significant damage to national security and theft of secrets involving military and scientific information. He thanked the FBI for its efforts and also those of identical twin sisters, Dr. Regina and Amanda Doucette. The former was poisoned and the latter put at risk of a shooting attempt. He also explained that the federal government would make a detailed damage assessment of the activities of the network that had been apprehended, while simultaneously pursuing the cases against the defendants.

Several days later, the State Department announced the expulsion of two dozen suspected intelligence operatives from the Chinese embassy and consular offices, including U.S.-based police offices of the Chinese secret police, which were used to spy upon and to harass Chinese nationals residing in the United States. The U.S. government also reduced its staff at its Beijing embassy and the numbers of staffers at its consular offices in China, and recalled its ambassador for consultations. A number of joint U.S.-China cooperation projects were put on hold. It would be a number of years before there was a thaw in relations between the two countries.

Back in the safe house, Reggie and Mandy discussed what had happened.

Mandy said, "You better slap me. I just dreamed we were in the Oval Office."

"That was no dream, Sister. You better get used to some bright lights and media interviews. I think you're a celebrity now."

"Look who's talking," Mandy said. "Right now, I'm a little curious what will happen with the Allzient deal, and whether LaSalle can salvage its status as a defense contractor."

Reggie said, "That's not your responsibility, is it?"

"No, and I guess the bigger picture is how much damage the Fennstrom brothers have done to our country."

"Thank God you're not responsible for that either. Somebody has a big problem on their hands."

Mandy said, "There are going to be a lot of ripples through these companies where the spies were placed. There will be some of that if we complete the Allzient deal. That could become my problem because of the compliance program stuff. By the way, if I haven't said it before, this is the kind of thing you have on your hands from lying, cheating, and stealing."

Reggie said, "Oh, yeah. You've said it before."

Because no acquisition of Allzient had taken place, Mandy felt that no LaSalle secrets could have been at risk yet. That wasn't true for Allzient secrets, though. Eric Spenser had been absorbed into Allzient through Spruance Corporation, so there was a lot of investigative work to be done there by the FBI. And it had been made clear that through the efforts of the Fennstrom brothers, other U.S. corporations had been infected with agents whose thefts of industrial, commercial, and military secrets had undoubtedly resulted in a pipeline of information getting into the hands of the Chinese.

Reggie said, "You know, now that I think about it, this could be a big assist in the romance department."

"Who are you talking about? You or me?"

"Both."

Mandy said, "Well, I'm sure Patrick is working up a plot for his next book right now. And your *colleague with benefits* Dan wants to get you back in his orbit."

Reggie said, "Both good points, but working up a plot isn't romance."

"Maybe he's working up a romance plot?"

CHAPTER 28

THE DOUCETTE SISTERS returned to Chicago in Bob Doucette's company plane and Mandy's apartment in the week after all of the news hit, which still dominated the national news media outlets. Their now-frequent appearances in the media made them easily recognizable, especially if they were together. It was good to get back, and Reggie looked forward to the extended recovery the Bureau had insisted on. She was approaching normal and was game for some light running, just not ramping up for Grandma's Marathon.

The night before she returned to the office, Mandy got a call from Patrick Carney. "May I please speak to the national celebrity?"

Mandy said, "Hello, Patrick. What's happening?"

"Are you going to invite me in?"

"Where are you?"

"I'm in your lobby, but your concierge says you have to let me in."

She buzzed him up and a minute later he showed up at the door with a big bouquet of flowers. The door opened and there she was, looking beautiful and smiling from ear to ear.

"Are those for me?"

Patrick said, "My heroine! And maybe my protagonist!" And handed her the flowers, then hugged her.

"I'm so glad you're safe."

Mandy said, "Come in. There's someone I want you to meet."

Patrick came in and immediately saw the carbon copy of Mandy.

"This is my sister, Reggie."

"Hi, Patrick."

"Hello. Of course, you were the one who got poisoned. I guess I had a surprise coming, didn't I?"

"That's me. Please have a seat while Mandy puts those in water."

Patrick sat and the three of them talked for three hours, ordering in pizza and drinking wine, until Patrick had the full story. When he finally said goodnight and promised Mandy a call to get together, it was nearly ten o'clock.

After he left, Reggie said, "I like him, a lot."

Mandy said, "You can't have him, though. You've got your own."

"I know. I mean I like him for you."

Mandy's return to the office was a celebration with all of her colleagues, and then catching up with Rick and Greg on what had happened to the Allzient deal and the spanking they'd gotten from the Defense Department. Rick advised her that the Allzient deal had been saved, and that the fines, which by that time had been largely quantified, were accounted for in a reduced purchase price. The customer relationships Allzient had burned were slowly coming around to being willing to work with LaSalle. As to the defense contracting mess, the attorney general had been a man of his word and interceded with the secretary of defense to get the company back into business and off the dunce's stool. CEO Jim Kerwin held a reception for all involved in the recovery effort and praised the work that had been done.

Kerwin asked Mandy, in front of the assembled group, "Mandy, we all know now that you were able to zero in what was going on here and bring it to a conclusion, but what I think we would all like to know from you is, what gave it all away to you to allow you to figure it out?"

Mandy answered, "Jim, I think you get yourself in a mindset of observation, and the closer you look at things, the more will become clear if you keep picking at things that don't make sense. It also helps to have people who are no good at lying, cheating, and stealing."

Not a word was said about Wretched Witch. But the common sense about her was that she was a stain on the reputation of the company. The Allzient deal was scheduled to close in July—not a bad setback at all, considering the challenges.

At 6:00 a.m., in late June in Duluth, Minnesota, the temperature was an ideal sixty degrees. The starting time of Grandma's Marathon was 7:00 a.m., on county road Route 61, probably close to the western shoreline of Lake Superior, where the Doucette ancestor had pulled his birch bark canoe out of the water en route to the Mississippi River. Mandy was in the starting chute and Reggie was spectating (doctor's orders). The race director blared Bob Dylan's song *Highway 61 Revisited* just before the starting gun went off. The lyrics made the sisters think that they had been through their own private test with everything they'd been through, just like the test given to Abraham by God.

But now there was more immediate business to tend to. Mandy had to run like hell, but pace herself at the same time. Reggie had to be in various places to cheer her sister on, if she was going to do a respectable job as spectator. The route was an undulating straight line south along the lakeshore road with the occasional sighting and cheering from Reggie, who made five-mile advances to be able to spectate at intervals. Reggie was at the finish line when Mandy came across in 3:45, an improvement over the more crowded Paris race crowd. The finale was on the last stretch of Canal Park Drive, which dead-ended at Grandma's Saloon & Grill, the race sponsor. That done, the sisters retired to the dorm room they were sharing for some downtime. After dinner, they attended the performance of *How to Talk Minnesotan.* To finish off their day, Mandy had taken a call from Patrick and Reggie from Dan.

EPILOGUE

IN THE YEAR THAT FOLLOWED, charges brought against almost twenty individuals rounded up in the arrests of June 2009, resulted in convictions in all of the cases, with Winston Fennstrom being sentenced to life in prison without chance of parole. His murderous accomplices were convicted and similarly sentenced. The various foreign agents were sentenced to a minimum of twenty years. Emily Jenkins was charged with aiding and abetting the espionage conducted by the group, but was cleared in the murder and attempted murder charges, and in return for a guilty plea and cooperation and testimony, she was sentenced to five years in federal prison. Needless to say, she was terminated for cause at LaSalle and stripped of all of her incentive arrangements, including any restricted stock awards and stock options. Mandy was willing to bet she wouldn't be looking like Wretched Witch where she was now residing. Edward Wennstrom was never heard from again, though MI6 kept a close eye out for him. Some in the highest of circles speculated that he had met with an *unexpected accident* that might not have originated outside of China.

Alan Frenche and Steve Baker had huge promotions, and were being deservedly celebrated at the Bureau. A new CIA director was chosen, with the predecessor being retired as a direct result of the festering rot that had taken place under his nose.

The Allzient transaction had closed and no unexpected harm had come from the events of the spring and summer of 2009. LaSalle regained its status as a responsible bidder, and continued to build its defense businesses. Emily Jenkins' successor was on the prowl for the next acquisition. As a result of James Whitney's whistleblowing efforts, his estate was determined to be entitled to a bounty for his efforts. Based upon the $230 million penalty that was levied upon Allzient in its consent decree with the Justice Department, under the law the whistleblower was in a position to reap a bounty in the amount of 10 percent to 30 percent of the fine. In his case, Whitney's estate was awarded a 25 percent amount, or a cool $57.5 million. Were Whitney still alive, he would not need to work on spreadsheets after that. Jim Kerwin was chastised by the Board for the presence of Harold Menzies, but hewing to the wisdom that the general counsel and corporate secretary was supposed to be on watch for director issues, Ed Rosen was to pay the price. He was gently sent into retirement, and replaced by Rick Crawford. He would need to find someone else to manage transactions. Rick was still admiring his occasional cartoons found inside his office door, and was still in pursuit of the artist. Mandy and Reggie had given him three pairs of shoes in different colors, and importantly, different styles.

The shock of Emily Jenkins' affair with Harold Menzies and the even further strain it put on Jim Kerwin's relationship with the board did not come home to roost on Kerwin's doormat. He had enough on his plate to answer for and the board needed him to repair the wounds.

The dynamic duo that was Amanda and Regina Doucette was thriving. Mandy had been promoted to assistant general counsel and would continue in her role of chief compliance officer, with a big bump in salary and a generous grant of restricted stock in recognition of her efforts. Reggie was still finding the causes of death of corpses found in hastily dug graves, and whatever else came out of her bizarre profession. But now her work was being done as chief pathologist in the Chicago office of the FBI, a new satellite lab the Bureau had decided was worth testing to serve the Midwest region. They were sharing the River North apartment and doing some kayaking on the Chicago River.

In March of 2010, the sisters were invited to the White House along with a half-dozen other celebrated Americans. They were allowed to invite their families and friends, and the twins included their parents and siblings. Two other friends were present as well, Dan Aleri and Patrick Carney. The family was choked up witnessing Mandy and Reggie receiving the Presidential Citizens Medal, honoring them for exemplary deeds of service to their country.

When the ceremony was over, Reggie said to Mandy, "Glad that's over. Now we can get back to training."

Mandy said, "I second the motion."

A full three years after the events of 2009, a mass prisoner swap occurred between the United States and China. On the U.S. side, ten prisoners who had been involved in the Fennstrom affair were involved in the swap. Notably, Sherman Haskins, a.k.a. Philip Ray and Winston Fennstrom, was not among the group swapped. He was going nowhere in the foreseeable future.

THE END

ACKNOWLEDGMENTS

I wish to express my gratitude for my beta readers for their loving critique and insights: Elizabeth Roehlk, John King, and Mike Poteshman. I especially appreciated the insights of my technical expert, Dr. Orlando Gonzalez, on pathology matters. Also indispensable was the editing done by Leslie Wells. Finally, this book would not have come to fruition without the expertise of Meryl Moss and her staff at Meridian Editions LLC, especially Jim Parry.

THOMAS ROEHLK is a retired corporate attorney from St. Charles, Illinois. He worked at a variety of major international corporations, including companies in the defense sector, and businesses in consumer products, transportation equipment and financial services. He spent more than 20 years as a general counsel of a public company, and as a chief compliance officer.

Roehlk is a graduate of the University of Wisconsin and John Marshall Law School, and received a Master in Management degree from Northwestern University. A devoted long-distance athlete, Roehlk has completed more than 100 marathons and ultramarathons around the world, including marathons in every U.S. state and Canadian province. In addition, he has completed ten Ironman triathlons. After 46 years in the Chicago metropolitan area, Thomas and his wife now split their time between Florida and New York.

Red Deuce is his first book.

www.ingramcontent.com/pod-product-compliance
Lightning Source LLC
Chambersburg PA
CBHW020257030826
48979CB00026B/1376/J

* 9 7 8 1 9 5 9 1 7 0 1 0 5 *